Praise for Jordanna Kay's *The Price of Discovery*

4 1/2 Lips! "Jordanna Kay delivers a fascinating story certain to impel the reader straight through to the ending, with numerous pauses along the way to reread her steamy sensuality scenes! …I for one can't wait to see further stories from Jordanna Kay; I'm sure they will be equally as intriguing as The Price of Discovery" ~ *Two Lips Reviews*

4.5! "I always like a book that grabs my attention on the first couple of sentences. I instantly wanted to know what was going on. I reckon that's the mark of a good book. And the sudden ending of The Price of Discovery made me want to read more about the characters. I hope there is a sequel." ~ *Janet Davies,Once Upon a Romance*

"Secondary characters, particularly Drakor's family -- among whom baby sister Sitora is my favorite and Erin's brother...who falls in love with Drakor's sister Ankra -- play a huge role in the story, adding to the suspense. Everyone has a hidden agenda, including Erin's nemesis Rita, and it's a race to see who will win." ~ *Romance Reviews Today*

The Price of Discovery

Jordanna Kay

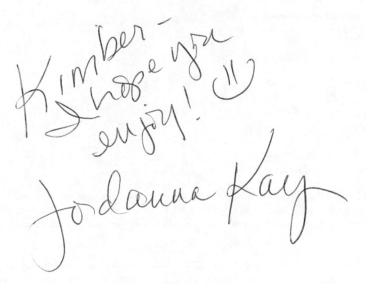

Kimber —
I hope you
enjoy! :)

Jordanna Kay

A Samhain Publishing, Ltd. publication.

Samhain Publishing, Ltd.
2932 Ross Clark Circle, #384
Dothan, AL 36301
www.samhainpublishing.com

The Price of Discovery
Copyright © 2006 by Jordanna Kay
Print ISBN: 1-59998-288-9
Digital ISBN: 1-59998-080-0

Editing by Jess Bimbery
Cover by Scott Carpenter

First Samhain Publishing, Ltd. electronic publication: August 2006
First Samhain Publishing, Ltd. print publication: November 2006

Dedication

I would like to dedicate this book to my family, who put up with my time on the computer; my pals at Writers At Play, who always encourage me; and to Jessica at Samhain for giving me the chance.

Chapter One

One dead male.

He was the key to saving Erin Price's career. It may be an odd lead, but she had nothing more to lose.

And if this story, given to her by an old friend at the police station, turned up zilch she'd have to find another. Erin had lived with this gnawing sense of failure and shame for long enough.

Damn, it was hot in the backwoods of Virginia. Erin glanced up at the intense sun. Vibrant and round like a dandelion in bloom and just as annoying. Her skin sizzled under the sun's fiery licks. June shouldn't be this hot. Nor should she be standing at the doorway of a perfectly recreated Victorian house.

Instead of the burned down little cottage she expected to find, Erin stood facing a Victorian, bedecked like a lady in all her finest jewelry.

Tucking her hair behind her ears, Erin shifted the bag on her shoulder. She had come to poke around for clues on the dead male. He died a few months ago from unknown causes, with an odd disorder in his bone marrow. The trail on who he was and what had happened to him had run cold.

She knocked on the colorful lady's door to get her answers.

Erin waited, the voices behind the door hushed like the gentle rustling of treetops. She tucked her notepad in the bag and waited.

The voices quieted and then the door swung open. Oh God.

The dark hunk in the doorway was at least six feet tall, powerful shoulders stretched the white polo-style shirt from one side of the door to the other. Black hair flowed wild and careless to his shoulders. He could be a god, recreated from a Greek statue, but he certainly didn't belong here.

Her stomach fluttered, her mouth dried. No way was this guy from around here. Exotic. Mesmerizing. Sexy. This creature seemed as out of his element in a renovated Victorian as a mighty lion would in a gilded cage.

Her gaze lifted from his full sensual lips to a pair of piercing black eyes. His stare spoke of predatory skill, as if he could eat her alive without ever touching her.

Erin tried to swallow, but her mouth was too dry. Heat pooled deep between her legs. Those three years of celibacy suddenly seemed like three decades.

He leaned against the doorjamb and crossed his arms, tendons rippling. "Not interested."

The smooth timbre of his voice sent an unexpected shiver over Erin's skin and her nipples pebbled in response. Even the unique accent coloring his words tickled that aching spot in her groin.

She licked her parched lips. Sweat collected under her breasts. "Your house," she managed to squeak. "I was driving by and wondered—"

His stare didn't waver. "No, thank you."

Erin wasn't giving up that easy. She had a story to investigate. Though she wouldn't mention John Doe, she had to make up something...like doing research on restoring old homes. Besides, she couldn't leave now. Not when those eyes held her to the spot.

"It's so beautiful...the house. I wanted to ask some questions—"

"I do not wish to be disturbed." He swallowed, his Adam's apple bobbing under swarthy stubble. A blink and a catch of breath and, for the first time since he opened the door, Erin noticed a crack in his armor. It seemed he had something to hide. Unfortunately for him, his secrecy was her personal invitation to stay.

"Have a pleasant day." He began to shut the door.

"Excuse me, sir!" Damned if she was letting him get off that easily.

He opened the door again, but those sexy lips were now set in a grim line. Damn it, she felt the urge to feather her mouth over his, nibble the bitter into sweet.

She had to stop fantasizing and get inside to check the place out. "Before I go," Erin said in her most pleasant voice possible. "May I have some water to drink?"

He looked at her blankly.

She prompted, "Water? From your kitchen?"

"No."

This man was infuriating. And yet, she noticed a tic leaping on the shadow of his hard-planed jaw.

"No?" More refusals lured her like a shark to blood in the water. She had to get in there now. Next time, he may not open the door. "Please, sir," she fanned her face with her hand, "it's extraordinarily hot out here today."

Finally, after another hard glare, he stepped back.

Erin moved in past him to the dim interior, the air suddenly cool, almost crisp. His clean, masculine scent sparked fire along her skin. Sexual awareness enveloped her, weakening her knees. She glanced at him, almost expecting to see flames shooting from his gaze, but instead he looked pained.

For a moment, Erin felt the urge to reach out and trace his lips with her fingertip. Instead, she quickly looked away and focused on the interior furnishings.

Beyond the foyer, an oak staircase rose to the second story. Past that, a parlor. Burgundy-striped wallpaper lined the walls. Heavy blue curtains at the stained glass window. Hell, there was even a painted fire screen in front of the carved fireplace. Chairs galore, a piano in the corner, and gas-looking lamps helped to make this parlor something straight from a book.

It was all so prim, so precise, so unlived-in. What secrets did the perfection hide?

"I'm Erin Price, by the way."

"Dracula."

What? Did she hear him right? "Dracula?"

His eyebrows knitted and he shook his head. "Drakor."

Ah, it was close. But he sure had the untamed dark hair and olive skin to match the legend. Her neck tingled with the anticipation of his bite.

Before Erin could ask if he had a last name, he pointed down a dark hallway. "Please be swift. The kitchen you seek is that way."

She was nuts.

Here in this house in the middle of nowhere, in an unlit hallway, next to a stranger who could have her sliced into bits within minutes. But his scent enticed her to run her tongue along the curve of his neck, his firmly sculpted shoulders begged to be caressed. Best of all, his odd behavior snagged her investigative intuition with a glaring red flag.

She'd nail this piece, she'd get that front page, and she'd prove she hadn't lost her edge. As long as she could keep her panties on.

More than ever, Erin needed water.

But instead of Drakor taking her in the room and getting her refreshment, he practically shoved her against the swinging door.

The touch of his fingers on her back sent a tempest of heat scorching through her veins. Water. Oh God, she needed water.

Erin stalked to the kitchen cabinets. The room looked barely used. The tile counter tops were barren, nothing was in the sink, not even dishwashing soap on the corner. She opened an oak cabinet. Empty. Opened another. Empty. Opened all cabinets in the room. All empty.

Nothing. No food, no plates, no cups, no spices. Not even a box of crackers. Everyone had crackers in their cabinets. This situation grew more strange by the minute.

But her throat was still dry, her blood still burned. She wanted water.

Maybe they hadn't unpacked everything. But if that were the case, where were the boxes? And why could they set up each little individual useless

Victorian knick-knack in the parlor, but not have time to get out the cups and silverware? Did they go out to eat for every meal?

She could turn on the faucet and just drink from her hands. But somehow she didn't quite trust the water in this house. Better to choke on the dirt in her throat than to drink unused, rusty water.

Erin swallowed her spit and pushed the swinging door. Whispering on the stairway stopped her. Drakor's deep growl was easy to discern, but who was the woman?

Erin cleared her throat to announce her presence and the voices stopped instantly. Drakor met her before she reached the foyer. She could barely see his face in the dark, but his dangerous eyes pinned her, seized her. Erin bit back her whimper.

"You're satisfied?" he asked, his voice low.

God, no. She wouldn't be satisfied unless his tongue was licking its way up her thigh or her hands were buried deep in that flowing mane.

He meant the water, of course. "No." But she was satisfied with the curious emptiness of the kitchen. Its oddness fueled her brain, stirring more questions. "You have no glasses in there. You have nothing in there."

His expression didn't change. "You'll be going now."

He ushered her to the front door. Footsteps clattered behind them down the oak stairs. Erin looked beyond Drakor to see a beautiful woman approach with long hair, a voluptuous figure, and exotic features.

Without warning, jealousy slammed through Erin's gut. Oh God. Had he just been up there with this gorgeous woman?

Erin heard Drakor groan beside her but didn't look over at him. Instead, she stood enthralled as the woman approached.

"I am Ankra," she said, her smile dazzling.

Erin hesitated, but then put out her hand. "How do you do? I'm Erin Price."

Ankra glanced down at her hand, thought for a moment, and then gently shook it. "Joyful to meet you, Erinprice."

Joyful? And why did she include the last name? Maybe odd word choices went along with the unique accent.

"I am Drakor's sister."

Sister. Jealousy trickled away leaving an unsettling sense of relief in its place. Yes, Drakor was sexy, but that meant danger in Erin's book.

At least this sister spoke sentences and didn't utter two-word commands. "You and I could chat sometime. I'd love to ask about this exquisite house."

Ankra nodded, but that must have been too much for Drakor's requirement for secrecy. He snatched Erin's elbow and he pulled her outside into the hot summer air.

Ferocity lurked in his eyes as he slammed the door closed behind them. But now it only made her grin. She could handle ferocity. It was the animalism she couldn't manage, the beast in heat that robbed her of breath.

Besides, Drakor was definitely hiding something. And she frightened him. Hell, he even took a step or two away from her. How could she, at almost half his weight, scare him?

He wiped the sheen from his forehead, then jammed his hands in his jeans. She glanced at the rounding apex of his legs. Was it just the lift from his full pockets or had he felt the pulsing awareness too? She gulped. It had been far too long since she'd gotten laid.

A cramp tightened in her chest, making it hard to breathe. She had to get out of here. A sexy man had gotten her into far too much trouble once and Erin swore she'd never let lustful yearnings sway her from her purpose again.

A man was dead, his life and death a mystery.

Another man lived in a house upon the same spot.

Somehow the two must be connected. It was up to her to find out how.

"Have a good afternoon," she called, trotting down the wooden steps to her car. She slid into the driver's side, where the blistering vinyl seat immediately stuck to her back and thighs.

Drakor stood on the porch, his strong arms folded across that come-bury-yourself-against-me chest, his bewitching eyes watching her.

"You don't mind if I come back on Saturday morning, do you?" she called and gave a small wave out the window. Then, without waiting for his refusal, she started the car and left him to choke in its dust.

Yeah, she might be nuts. But desperation did crazy things to people.

⁎

Why the *helta* was he on this planet? Drakor just wanted to retrieve Alaziri's body and return home.

But instead of finding his best friend, Drakor stood on the brightly painted wooden porch watching the small blue vehicle disappear behind a line of tall trees. Brown clouds of dust billowed behind it like an oncoming storm of Elliac's sand dunes. His blood pulsed hot, an erection throbbed behind his zipper.

Drakor gripped the porch railing, clenching his jaw. That girl. That Erinprice. *I'll be back on Saturday morning.*

He couldn't chance her seeing them again. *Helta*, he couldn't risk being close to her again.

Drakor swallowed, remembering the way her knees poked out beneath her short blue pants. He'd wanted to trace his tongue along the jewelry surrounding her smooth white throat. Small, firm breasts begged for his stroke, especially when their two points emerged for his pleasurable viewing. His arousal pulsed.

A warm breeze lifted his hair but did not cool the inferno in his veins. He shouldn't feel this way. Not on Earth, not with a human. No one but his *Mharai*, his lifemate, should make his heart accelerate, his willpower weaken.

But then why did his fingers itch to caress that sand-colored hair, his palms crave to yank her thin body against him? Her scent, something fruity, had enveloped him like the aroma of sexual awakening.

Drakor slammed his fist on the railing. "No!"

He had to make it disappear. Despite learning the techniques during his Crossing, no amount of mind control or even breaths could calm his raging bloodstream. His inward focus, thoughts of Elliac's windswept hills, did not take away the alluring images of that human female. Erinprice.

The door creaked open. "Drakor?"

He turned at the sound of his sister's voice and shoved his hands in his pockets. "You should not come out here."

"Is she gone?"

"Yes. But she said she would be back."

Ankra's eyes lit up. "Ah, good."

Drakor's chest tightened. "It is *not* good."

She tilted her head. "You are perspiring."

He cleared his throat. When the *helta* would his body recover? "It is warm."

"It is much warmer than this at home. You have said so yourself."

Drakor wiped his damp forehead with his arm. "Let us go inside to discuss this recent incident."

Ankra nodded and held the door open for him. They stepped into the dim house.

"Drakor!" It was the voice of his father.

They skirted the stairwell to the front room. Their reference book said this room was called a parlor. Drakor insisted that so many useless items created chaos, but no one wanted to listen to what he had to say. And they would not listen to him now.

Drakor stared at the ticking timepiece on the mantel and waited for his family to settle in behind him. He knew their patterns, their unbending need to keep to habit. Ankra would sit on the striped chair and take his littlest sister Sitora in her lap. His brother Brundor would stand by the side window, fiddling with something breakable. His parents would sit together on the flowered couch.

"Tell us," his father said at last, "what should we make of this stranger?"

Drakor turned to look at them. They all were positioned as he predicted. "We should be concerned."

"She caused no harm," Ankra threw in.

Drakor glared at her. "*You* should not have come down."

"I—" She glanced over at their father, whose face was pale, even in this darkened room. He didn't return the glance. "She caused no harm," she said again.

"But she will!" Drakor would have pounded his fist on the mantel but there was no room. If nothing else, his tormenting erection had dissipated. Anger easily cured that.

"You worry too much."

"No, Father, you worry not enough. You know what happened before."

"Drakor, we know Alaziri was your friend, but we cannot give up this mission because of one failure."

One failure. His friend was missing, presumed dead, alone on a foreign planet without the proper burial ceremony. Yet, his father spoke of failures. "We should find his body and then abort this mission."

"Absolutely not." His father sprang up from the couch, but then groaned. He rubbed his back, inhaling several deep breaths. Everyone in the room became motionless until he could continue. "This…this mission is high-priority and critical."

Drakor took a step toward him. "Earth is too risky." He was lucky to stare directly into his father's eyes. With almost every generation Elliacians grew shorter. Bone deformities and slow growth became more common on Elliac despite intense research. While the rest of the family escaped harm due to a dominant gene in their DNA, his father's health declined each year.

A breeze blew in from an open window, bringing with it the scent of approaching rain. For some reason it made him think of the water Erinprice wanted from them. What else would she want from them?

"We are in danger at all times of being discovered. Alaziri is missing, presumed dead. You see that we were found today."

His father sighed. "Our mission is vital to Elliac's survival. These humans will save us."

Drakor sucked in a breath, flexed his fingers, but could not calm his galloping pulse. He paced the floor before the fireplace. Great Sun, he must find a way to get off this planet. Once he found Alaziri's body, he'd find a way back to Elliac. He didn't belong here on Earth. He belonged at home, searching for his *Mharai*.

"I miss my friends."

They all looked over at little Sitora, who played with a cloth doll. Her dark hair cascaded over her small shoulders and her round eyes blinked up at them.

"Make new friends." Father patted her shoulder.

"You won't let me out of the house," she whined.

"We need to learn more about these humans first." He turned back to Drakor. "You and Ankra have a job to do. You must integrate with them, discover who they really are. What makes them different than us and how are we the same?"

Images of Erinprice flashed through Drakor's mind. She looked similar enough to them, despite the light hair and sky-colored eyes. Her frame was thinner than the females on Elliac, but he could still relish the weight of her breast in his hand, the feel of her white thighs under his tongue.

Drakor shifted as his groin once again hardened.

Father's gaze lifted with hope. "Tell us about the one who came here today."

"Find someone else." Someone who would not torment his body, confuse everything he ever learned.

"She seemed very nice," Ankra pushed Sitora off her lap. "Drakor is angry because he did not have control of the situation."

"I had control." But did he? The moment his gaze landed on her at the doorstop, Drakor felt his strength dissolve into a pool of lava. Every cell, every hair, every sensation came alert, pulsated. How the *helta* could he spend more time with her?

His father rubbed his back. "You will have two assignments on this mission, Drakor. To find any useful inventions for our home world and to seek out ways the humans keep their bones strong."

"This is suicide. Just like Alaziri, we will—"

"You will do it." Father reached for Mother and helped her to stand. "I have spoken, my son. It will be done."

Drakor bit his tongue to hold back his argument, but his pulse thundered in his skull. No, they wouldn't listen to him. Alaziri disappeared on his mission to Earth and he had kept minimal contact with the humans. Not only must Drakor integrate himself with these people, he now had to spend time with the painfully tempting Erinprice.

Drakor's gut clenched. His erection poked uncomfortably at the zipper. He stormed from the room and raced up the stairs, taking two at a time. Didn't they realize he didn't have time for these foolish endeavors? The anniversary of his birth was only a few weeks away. He'd be thirty sun-cycles and still without a *Mharai*.

Because of that Erinprice's nosiness today, he could end up an *Unmhar*. And be alone forever.

Chapter Two

"I'm telling you, Greg, something was really strange about these people."

Erin's brother lifted the remote from the armrest of his leather recliner and changed the channel. "Journalists are always looking for a story. You'll invent one if necessary."

"Are you saying you don't believe me?"

"All I'm saying, Erin, is that you've been searching for a big break for years. You'd believe the moon was made out of cheese if it could be your exclusive."

She rolled her eyes and glanced around the impersonal décor of his family room. Decorated by an interior designer, the art and furniture matched perfectly and yet said nothing about who her brother really was.

Erin tucked her hair behind her ear. "Sure, it's easy for you to say. You have your own company, your own house." She stood up from the couch. "I need a huge story, more than you realize…"

He looked over at her. "Oh, I realize how much you're pushing to prove yourself. Just because—"

"Don't go there." Past regrets swirled like sour milk in her gut.

Greg shrugged. "Whatever, but you know I've offered you a job many times. You're too damned stubborn to take it."

"I don't know anything about designing software and I'll be damned if I'm going to be my brother's secretary."

Besides, she went to school for journalism. Searching for facts, uncovering human interest stories, telling compelling tales was in her blood. Ever since she could ride a two-wheeler, Erin had been riding up and down the street looking for stories. A lost cat, a scratched up car, a missing toy—nothing could get by her.

He flipped off the television and stood. "You could learn a lot, you know, and maybe enjoy something other than snooping around."

Erin growled. This was not working out as planned. She wanted to bounce some thoughts off of him, to see if he thought that house and family were odd. But all he did was argue with her. As if it was his job to look out for her.

She was surprised he wasn't freaked about her going inside the Victorian alone. Of course, Greg didn't know about her immediate attraction to Drakor.

Her breasts tingled as she remembered the sculpted planes of his chest. Strong hands like his could cup her bottom with a swift ease as his sensual lips nibbled their way down to her navel. Oh God, the dreams she had last night. It had been a long time since an orgasm had woken her up like that.

Erin guzzled her soda, but it didn't do much to cool her down. "Well," she wiped her damp palms on her shorts, "don't you think it's strange that they don't have anything in their kitchen?"

"It's not like they didn't have one."

Erin rolled her eyes and headed into the cooler air of his kitchen. She sat on one of his metal barstools and tapped her fingers on the tile countertop. "You have an answer for everything. It's really annoying."

Greg followed her. "That's why I'm your brother. I can tell you how crazy you sound."

She shook her head. "They're the ones that sounded crazy. I'm telling you, I have an intuition about this one."

He raised an eyebrow and opened the fridge. "Want a bologna sandwich?"

"Sure." She took another swallow of soda.

"Didn't you say something about the guy's sister?"

Erin grinned. "Yeah. She's gorgeous. Beautiful dark eyes and black hair that goes all the way down her back."

"Oh? Hot, huh?" He turned from spreading the mayonnaise and stared at her.

"Very shapely. Soft-spoken." She sighed. "Just the kind of girl worth marrying. Oh, but I forgot, you'll never make a commitment. Not when there are so many fish in the sea."

Greg shoved the sandwich in front of her. "I can make a commitment when the right person comes along. And, at least I enjoy the fishing."

He leveled his eyes on her. "You haven't had a boyfriend, in what…three years? Not since that Evan guy—"

"Lay off, Greg." She suddenly lost her appetite.

"It's been a really long time, Erin. Give yourself a break."

A break from what? From her failures? She'd lost more than just her heart with Evan.

Erin pushed the rest of her sandwich away and reached for her keys. "I'm outta here."

"Wait." Greg put a hand on her shoulder. "Sorry I pissed you off. Am I going to meet these strange people?"

"Perhaps." She shrugged him off and went outside into the mass of sticky air. She slid her sunglasses on and stared up at Greg's end-unit brick townhouse.

Someday she'd have a house like that—or better. She nearly lost her job once due to idiotic, overzealous ideals and one worthless guy. Mixing business with pleasure had been the biggest mistake of her life. She was damn lucky to have this job in spite of it. But she could do bigger things, she could escape the blunders of her past. All she needed was one huge story.

Erin wiped her forehead with the back of her arm and started the car.

Something bizarre was going on in that majestic Victorian in the woods. She'd spend the next two days digging deeper into her John Doe and his burned down cottage, but then, come this Saturday, she was going back to investigate.

ॐ

Boredom added to their torture. It wasn't enough that they were a million miles from home, or that they were faced with a possibly hostile population, or that Drakor was only weeks away from losing the chance at a *Mharai*, or that a human female tempted him even in his dreams. No, they also had hours—days—of boredom.

On the bed opposite Drakor, Brundor tossed a ball of paper into the air and caught it. The house was still, the air motionless. A beam of sunlight sliced the room in half.

Outside the window, birds twittered in the trees.

Abruptly Brundor sat up. "I hear something." He moved to the window. "That small vehicle is coming."

Drakor leapt up from his bed. *She was back. Helta*, he had prayed the Earth female would not return. Despite Father's demands, this stranger signified trouble—to the mission, to his family, and to himself.

He joined his brother at the window and watched the vehicle roll to a stop near the front steps. The sound died away, leaving only the birds once again.

The door of the Earth vehicle opened. Erinprice emerged, her white skin glowing under the bright Earth sun. She wore yellow pants today that skimmed just past her knees, showing where her calves curved to the delicate bump of her ankle. A striped shirt hugged her firm breasts. But her arms were bare, other than some circular jewelry around her wrists that clanked as she walked.

She slid dark spectacles off of those sky-colored eyes and turned to shut the vehicle's door.

Drakor tried to fight it, but he could not stop the heat snaking its way through his veins. It circulated through his limbs before settling with a blazing snap in his groin. Perspiration tickled under his hair.

A knock sounded on the front door below them. Brundor turned away from the window, his smooth, unlined face eager. The Crossing, the years of searching for a lifemate, had yet to take its toll on him. "I want to meet her."

Drakor's gut knotted. "That would not be wise."

"Why not? You and Ankra have met her."

They heard voices below. Ankra must have let Erinprice into the house.

"This human cannot be trusted."

Brundor narrowed dark eyes. "You don't think you can trust me."

"I'll not deny that. You are at the age to start your Crossing. It can happen at anytime. Even on Earth."

"I can control it."

Drakor clenched his jaw, his rapid pulse evidence that he could not control the workings of his body. "No male can control the urges. I've been through it, I know what it's like."

"This isn't fair!"

"That's why Father should have left you at home." But no one listens to him. Brundor was like that ticking clock on the mantel. Some time soon the bell would ring and they'd all pay the price. An Elliacian male needed to be secluded during his Crossing into manhood. He needed a master to show him how to dominate the sexual urges rampaging through his body.

Helta, Drakor couldn't even control himself around this Earth female. He hated this place, this cool atmosphere and strange creatures.

Drakor crossed the room. "I'm going for a walk." He had to get out of this house and away from Erinprice. "Stay here."

His brother tied his long hair back with a leather string. "I'm going to get out of this house one day."

"And I hope it will be when we all go home."

Brundor flopped down on his bed again, reaching for the balled up paper. "Hey, Drakor, why is your face damp?"

"It's warm."

Without waiting for a retort, Drakor left the room and hurried down the steps. He expected to see Ankra and Erinprice on the couch in the front room, but saw neither. The room was empty.

With a sigh of relief, he headed outside and down the wooden porch steps, his gaze fixed on the ground. He'd wander the creek in the back woods, cool down his face with the chilly water.

"Hey!" a female cried, right before he crashed into her.

Their contact stopped him cold. *Great Sun!* In an instant, his skin burned, his arousal stiffened. He looked down into the pale eyes of Erinprice and backed away. The railing pole blocked his retreat.

Her pupils dilated. "Are-are you okay?"

Drakor nodded his head, but could not speak. A tingle began at the base of his spine and raced downward to his toes before circling up to his nipples.

She touched his forehead, her round jewelry tinkling in his ears. "You are hot. I think you might have a fever. You should go inside and lie down. Have something to drink."

His mouth dried. "No."

She licked her lips then traced her fingertips down his face, wiping the increased gathering of perspiration. "Your face is flushed. You really should go in and rest."

The longing amplified inside every cell, every fiber. His hands prickled with the need to grab the swell of her hips.

Clenching his jaw, Drakor grabbed her wrist and thrust it away from his face. A blaze sped from his palm to his groin, sparking a near explosion. Great Sun, she almost unmanned him!

"I-I am not ill," he choked. "Leave me."

"Oh, okay…I just had to get something from the car." She reached up and tucked a strand of hair behind her ear, exposing her throat. "Are you sure you don't want me to get a cool cloth or something?"

Drakor wet his parched lips and shook his head.

"You should consider wearing shorts in the summer," she continued. Why the *helta* wouldn't she stop this talking and leave him alone? "It is really hot out here and those pants look heavy."

He swallowed and squeezed his eyelids closed. Shadowed dreams of the past several nights swam before his eyes. He saw her writhing beneath him, her skin glistening. Then her mouth was on him, nipping his neck, kissing his abdomen, moving downward…

Great Sun!

Drakor squeezed his hands into fists, fighting the painful throb of his flesh. He must take control over his body's impulses. Why couldn't he remember his teachings, his mind control knowledge?

A gentle breeze cooled the dampness on his skin, but it also brought her scent to him. His mouth watered.

"Are you really sure you are okay?"

Drakor opened his eyes, tried a fierce stare, but raw lust zapped his intensity. "Go. Now."

He watched as she swept past him and up the porch steps. With her hand on the door, she turned back. Her sky-colored gaze swept down the length of him. Did she notice the swelling at his groin?

"You really are wearing far too much clothes for June."

His dream…her naked body…his naked body hovering over her …Drakor's stare lingered on her bare ankles, then rose inch by inch to her gleaming white neck.

He couldn't do it. He couldn't stop the voracious hunger. Restraint slipped, then disappeared entirely.

Breathing ragged and lips parted, Drakor started up the steps toward her.

ഇൗ

Erin stood immobile.

An instinctive fear blasted through her as she watched him approach, his dark eyes smoldering. But then she realized his intent and her breath caught in her throat. Muscles weakened. Pulse intensified. Breasts ached.

Noises of insects and birds vanished. She heard nothing but the whoosh of her heartbeat and the creak of the wood under Drakor's weight.

What would he do once he reached her? Her mouth watered with anticipation, but she could not permit this attraction—no matter how much she craved it.

Erin dashed inside the house and slammed the door shut.

"Is everything okay, Erinprice?" Ankra smiled at her from the bottom of the stairway.

"Um…" Should she tell her Mr. Sexy was heading up the stairs with a distinct look of lust on his face? Somehow, Erin doubted a sister wanted to hear that. She sure didn't want to hear it about Greg. "Everything is fine. But why do you call me Erin Price?"

"You told us that was your name."

Her breathing finally slowed. "My first name is Erin. Last name is Price. Just call me Erin."

"Two names?" Ankra pushed her hair over her shoulder. "Ah, yes. Forgive me. Come."

Erin's reporting instinct kicked in. First, they had that odd unused kitchen and now they assumed her two names were one? Those little things, combined with Drakor's tight need for secrecy, burrowed under her skin. Erin was beginning to believe there might be more of a story in the present owners on this land than the previous one.

She followed Ankra into the front parlor room and sat on the lovely striped couch, her pulse not quite normal. This agonizing desire for Drakor

25

reminded her of a crush she had her senior year of high school. It was one-sided, just her lusting after the substitute teacher, but she couldn't stop thinking of the guy.

"Erinprice...um, Erin." Ankra's long finger tapped on her leg. "I would like to ask you something. A favor."

Ankra's dark eyes reminded her of a doe. Sweet, innocent, beautiful. This girl was a sheltered treasure, hidden away from the real world, perhaps waiting for just the right man to rescue her like a knight in shining armor.

"Of course, anything," Erin replied. Anything that would get her closer to this family, bring her closer to finding her answers. Maybe these people didn't know a damn thing about her John Doe. But then again, maybe they were a story onto themselves.

A long, black strand fell across Ankra's eyes. "I want to meet a man. Will you help me find a boyfriend?"

This girl needed help meeting a man? No way. "You can't be serious."

Ankra only blinked, looking completely serious.

Where would she find a knight in shining armor in this town? If one was here, she would have known about it long before now.

The front door creaked open. Erin tried to prevent herself, but she couldn't stop glancing up.

Drakor stood in the doorway, his face shining and damp. Dark hair slicked away from his jaw and curled over his collar. Raw, male power radiated from long powerful legs, the muscled strength of shoulders and arms. His wild stare drew her in, seized her breath, curled her toes.

Awareness charged.

Suddenly, that knight shining in his armor took on a whole new meaning.

Chapter Three

Erin slowed the car as they approached the rainbow façade of the Victorian. "You sure you want to go to a dance club?"

Ankra gathered her bags. "Yes, please, very much so."

Unfortunately, large, crushing crowds were never Erin's thing. All that smoke and sweat and lame propositions just turned her stomach. But Ankra had begged to go to a place where she could meet other men. Besides, Erin had done far worse things for a story before. Far, far worse.

Erin swallowed against her tightening throat and forced the memories away.

Going to some stupid techno dance club really wasn't that big of a deal. Although Erin sensed the true mystery lay within Drakor, not Ankra. He was the one who was so secretive. He was the one who originally did not want her entering the house. He was the one whose words told her to leave but whose steamy eyes asked her to stay.

She should ask him to come to Mickey's tonight. Then she could gauge his reaction to the place, as well. See if he would make the same odd comments Ankra had. The girl had no idea about what clothes to buy, what types of music there was, or even what a wine cooler was.

Yes, Erin would get Drakor to go with them. Maybe she'd even get the chance to nose out if he knew anything about John Doe. She had to start somewhere. Time was ticking away on her deadline.

Erin opened the car door and stepped out into the late afternoon. "Would you fetch your brother for me?"

"Of course."

As Ankra went inside, Erin waited in the serene tranquility near the front steps. Two yellow butterflies danced then disappeared into the brush of wild honeysuckle. This spot was so far removed from the main road, from any other neighborhood, it almost felt as if she were in another world.

"I am here."

Erin turned. Drakor stood at top of the steps. He wore shorts and she gave a quick glance of his thick, muscled legs covered in fine, dark hair. They looked strong enough to bear her weight as he held her against the wall, moving inside of her…

Damn, she had to stop this. What had gotten into her? She'd never felt this promiscuous, this horny, around a man before.

"Um," she began, starting up the steps. But then stopped as his scent swirled in her bloodstream like chocolate syrup in milk. "Your sister wants to go dancing tonight."

Drakor leaned against the front door of the house. "Yes. She mentioned this inside."

Damn, Erin was a chicken. Where the hell was that bravado? That courage that got her the toughest interviews?

She cleared her throat, searching for an excuse. Anything but to have it sound like she was asking him on a date.

"A chaperone! Yes, we could use a chaperone."

A dark eyebrow lifted. "I do not understand."

Did she have to explain *everything* to these people? "This place we are going…" *has lots of drunk guys who will attack your sexy sister,* "…is very crowded and loud and well, I'd just feel more comfortable having a man there with us."

A few beads of sweat glistened on his forehead. "Ankra will not cause trouble."

"Maybe not, but your sister is a pretty girl. You should come along and watch out for her." *And give me more insight to who you are and how it can help me.*

Crickets sang in the bushes. Erin climbed a few more steps toward him until she could feel the heat emanate from his body. Despite the unrest he caused within her cells, Erin continued to press forward. She had to make him come along. "You need to come with us. I'd feel terrible if something happened to her."

"I can't." His gaze sliced through her. "It is impossible."

Impossible. The man was impossible. And yet his resistance was so strong he might as well wave a flag above his head saying, *I've got something to hide!*

Erin shoved her hands on her hips. Damn it, he was coming tonight or he could just sit down right now and tell her everything she wanted to know. They could skip the sleazy bar/club scene altogether.

"I realize you aren't from around here, but in these parts brothers watch out for sisters." God, could she really be saying this? Greg drove her nuts with all of his overprotecting crap.

Drakor glared at her, like a wary lion backed into a corner. A vein throbbed on his forehead. "You do not understand."

No shit, Sherlock. "Help me to understand then."

But he just clenched his jaw.

Even when cornered, the man was so tempting. His finely shaped muscles angled and turned, the form exquisite as if carved in marble. Lips, scowling yet sensual, pleaded for her touch. Power and strength radiated from him with a raw wildness.

Erin wiped her palms on her thighs. "Are you saying you won't come with us tonight?"

He shrugged, but did not grant her an answer.

"Fine," she bluffed, changing tactics. She trotted down the steps and headed for her car. "I'll get my brother to come. I know he'll do me a favor if I ask."

Erin just about reached her car when Drakor came barreling down the steps to her. "Wait." He came up behind her, so close she could smell the crisp scent of his deodorant. His body heat enveloped her in a cocoon.

"What?" Her nerves danced with anticipation of his touch.

But he only said, "I did not know you had a brother."

ഇറ

Drakor licked his lips. The curve of her shoulder glowed beneath the light of the sun. His gaze skimmed down her back to the gentle rounding of her bottom. What would it be like naked, hot beneath his palms? He could slide in and out of her, hands firmly on her hips.

But then Erinprice—no, Erin, Ankra had said—turned to peer at him, her eyebrows raised. "Yes. Why?"

"I would like to meet your brother."

She blinked, her face paling. "Oh…really?"

As much as he wished to leave this planet, he was bound here until he could locate Alaziri. Father told him one of his duties was to find any valuable inventions on this planet. And if Erin was not going to leave them alone, perhaps she could be of use to them. From the Resource Books, they'd learned that males invented many of the items in use. Here was an opportunity to meet one without having to speak to a stranger. He could get the information he needed, find Alaziri's body, and then they'd be gone from this place.

"Yes. Bring him here."

She tucked her short hair behind her ear, tempting him to run his tongue along the outer curvature. "Um…well, he could, but he might think it was rather strange…"

"You come out here to visit us."

She leaned against her car and folded her arms under her breasts. His tongue tickled with urgency to take one in his mouth. Liquid fire scorched his bones.

Her slight shoulder lifted. "Okay, whatever. How about you come tonight to the dance club and I will introduce you to my brother?"

Drakor nodded.

Her eyes crinkled for a bit, but then she nodded. "Does this mean you've changed your mind?"

He stared at the rising moon, its light illuminating a thin band of clouds. What was he getting himself into? He should speak with the brother, but he could not allow himself to be too close to Erin. The allure of her body was becoming too much for him to manage. It perplexed him. Once he reached adulthood, his entire life was focused on finding his *Mharai*. He'd been celibate for years now, his desire doused by the successful emergence from his Crossing.

He couldn't understand how a human could do this to him. One thing was certain—he must not give in to the cravings.

"You will drive us," he said as several winged creatures flew over their heads into the darkness.

Erin glanced up. "Bats."

He said nothing, instead perusing the long column of her throat. His pulse kicked up a level.

She looked back at her car. "You don't have your own car?"

"No." They had no Earth vehicle. Though Drakor assumed he could figure out how to maneuver it, his father thought it would not be wise if they were caught by the authorities in one. Thus, they were left with walking or Transporting. That, of course, would cause immediate attention if not done discreetly.

Erin shrugged then tucked her hair behind her ear. "I'll get my brother to drive us in his car. It's a hell of a lot bigger." She opened the car door and slid inside. "See you in a few hours."

Again, without allowing him to reply, she started the vehicle, gave a quick wave, and turned the car around.

He stood watching, while the dust kicked up after the tires. His groin throbbed, desperate and tender. He might bear the night if was far apart from Erin in a large building. But what the *helta* would he do while trapped in the tight space of an Earth vehicle?

31

Drakor sprinted up the steps and into the house. He had to practice the control he learned during his Crossing. He'd nearly failed this afternoon. He could not allow for that again.

No matter how many weeks separated him from losing his desires once and for all.

&)C&

Erin closed the door to her apartment and sagged against it. Blank white walls stared back at her. She should paint, hang up a picture or two, but this place was supposed to be temporary, not her home. Once she got her groove back, she'd move to the big city again and settle down.

So did she have a date with the mysterious but sexy Drakor? No. Not if he was hiding something she needed to know. As hot as that man was, he was hands-off as far as she was concerned. She'd been down that road once. And got lost.

Erin blinked the sting of tears away and tapped on Shellbert's container. The hermit crab didn't look up. Not that he normally gave her much sympathy.

Okay, so maybe Evan Moreland was a class-A jerk. He had been a sexy guy too, sexy enough to lure her into his bed. Sexy enough to make her lose sight of her story. Sexy enough to nearly get her fired when it all blew up in her face.

Erin clenched her jaw, that old familiar rage and humiliation bubbling up in her throat. Evan said he'd been set up. Or that's what Evan's story was when she interviewed him. Over the course of the in-depth exclusive, the man seduced his way into her bed. She ended up leaving her morals and ethics on the floor with her panties. Without realizing it, her articles grew more slanted, less objective. During the day, she fought his cause for innocence. At night, she kept him warm.

Then, he accepted a plea from the district attorney.

Damn him! That admission of guilt ruined her credibility. She looked like the biggest fool in the industry.

Erin left the big city then and moved back home. But the *Virginia Sentential* would never take her far, or recreate the success she once had. She needed something bigger.

And she did not need to screw it up by getting involved with the subject of her investigation. No matter how much she ached to have him inside her.

Erin dropped her bag and picked up the cordless on her way to the bedroom. Her brother picked up on the third ring. "Greg here."

"I hope you don't have plans tonight."

"Why? We have a date?"

"Don't be an ass. I need you to come along with me somewhere."

"I have poker, you know that."

Erin slipped off her capris and underwear. "It's to go Mickey's, okay?"

"Mickey's? Whoa, I didn't think that was your style."

"Look, I'm about to get in the shower. You coming or not?"

She heard the music volume lower in the background. "Who's going?"

"My new friend, Ankra..." She didn't need to tell him about Drakor. He'd just ask nosey questions.

"Oh?"

Erin went into the bathroom and turned on the water to warm it up. "You told me you wanted to meet Ankra and here's your chance. Take it or leave it, but this is your only opportunity and I won't ask you again."

Greg laughed. "Okay, okay. I'll go. No need to get your panties in a twist."

"Good. And you're driving."

"What?"

"I'll drive home if you drink too much, but my car is way too small. Pick me up at eight thirty." She turned off the phone and stepped into the shower.

It took three outfit changes before Erin decided on a pair of nice-fitting jeans and a plum-colored shirt. She lowered the zipper, hoping for a hint of cleavage. Nope, her size B's were not cooperating. Even a push-up wouldn't help her tonight.

She slid the zipper up a few inches and shrugged. Who was she trying to impress, anyway?

At eight forty-five, Greg pounded on the door.

"Okay, Brutus, I'm coming." She swung the door open and reached for her purse.

"Look out now!" He whistled. "Don't you look hot."

"Ugh. That's really kind of gross coming from your brother. You understand that, don't you?"

He shrugged. She looked him over. He wore jeans like her, and a button-down striped shirt. His blond hair was slicked back with some type of gel or something. She had to admit he was a good-looking guy. But she wouldn't go so far as to say he was hot. Yuck.

Erin ushered him outside and locked the door. "Let's go."

They climbed in his silver SUV. He turned down the music and backed up. "So I get to find out where the weirdos live, huh?"

"Oh, Greg, don't go screwing this up for me. This could be something really big."

"I know. A family lives in a painted Victorian out in the middle of nowhere and don't have glasses in their kitchen."

She reached in her tiny purse for her lip gloss. "You're patronizing me again."

"I just think you push for something when it might not be there."

Erin slid the window down and put her hand out into the rushing air. "You said 'might not be there.' What if it is? You'll get to see. You can be the judge."

He pulled onto the highway and they rode in silence for twenty minutes until Erin pointed them down the dirt road. Greg pulled the SUV up in front of the barely-lit house.

"Don't they have electricity?" He craned his neck out the window.

"It looked like gas lamps to me, but I've never been here in the dark." She glanced out her window and saw nothing but blackness until her eyes lifted to the twinkling stars and half moon.

"I've got to admit...this place looks a little creepy. Remember the *Adam's Family?*"

Erin chuckled. "Wait until you meet them."

They got out of the car and went up the porch steps. She grabbed Greg's arm. "Please, above all else, be nice. Don't tease them and do not try to fix me up with Ankra's brother. I'm looking to do an article on them, remember?"

He lifted an eyebrow. "Now I wouldn't do that. Besides, what did you say his name was?"

"Drakor."

Greg wrinkled his nose. "Where on earth did these names come from?"

Erin grinned. "See, and that's just the start."

She knocked, her stomach clenching with junior high nerves despite her every attempt at reasoning it away.

Drakor opened the door, his large body filling the front hall. He wore black khakis and forest green polo-type shirt. His dark hair still looked wet and curled under his ears, the scent of his shampoo awakened a thrumming low in her belly.

"Holy shit," she heard Greg say under his breath.

Ankra had come around the other side of her brother and smiled at Greg. She wore tight black pants and a sparkly red top. Her hair hung long and loose down her back and her beautiful eyes flashed with her grin.

Erin nudged him in the door. "This is my brother, Greg Price."

Ankra extended her hand and Greg brought it up to his lips.

Jordanna Kay

Erin rolled her eyes then glanced at Drakor. He watched the polite kiss then turned to her. Sweat sprouted on his forehead, his chest rose and fell in a quick rhythm. Those compelling eyes raked over her hips, her stomach, then lingered at her breasts. His tongue darted out and moistened his lips. Finally, his gaze lifted to her mouth, staring at it with such passion, her breath froze in her throat.

Awareness crashed through every cell in her body, caving her knees. Erin grabbed a hold of the doorpost for support.

Maybe it would be a better idea to keep her focus on the dead guy. John Doe didn't talk, couldn't lie, and he most certainly couldn't screw her. Not in either sense of the word.

Chapter Four

Drakor's heart crashed against his ribcage. He should turn away, but he was immobile. The curve of her hips, the soft swell of her shirt, the tempting pull of her lips...

Erin's light eyes blinked at him and her lips shone like a crystal from Elliac's northern caves. A searing urge to kiss her ricocheted through him.

Her brother started down the steps. "Why don't we get going?"

Drakor swallowed and followed them out to the car. They reached the vehicle, a larger one than Erin's. She pointed to the front.

"Why don't you ride up front, Drakor? Your long legs will have much more room up there."

As long as he wasn't next to Erin, he didn't care where he sat. He climbed in the front seat, while she and Ankra got in the back.

"So," Greg said after they drove a while, "what do you do, Drakor?"

He didn't understand the question. Too many things to remember, too many cultural references to comprehend. Eventually these humans would grow suspicious. "Please rephrase the question."

"What is your job?" Erin prompted from the back seat. He could still feel her presence, smell her mouth-watering scent.

"My profession is to do research," he answered, hoping they wouldn't pursue the conversation.

Greg tapped the steering wheel a few times with his fingers. "I own my own company. Developing software."

Drakor remembered that software had something to do with computers, a piece of equipment humans had recently developed that had a major impact in their lives and economy. So, insisting on meeting Erin's brother had been a wise decision. Perhaps this software could help them on their quest for a cure.

"Tell me more."

"Started Invasion Shield about three years ago. We develop software to detect security breaches on personal computers. I just hired a new guy a few months back and we've already started development on intrusion detection software that will rock this field." Greg gestured behind him with his thumb. "I tried to get Miss Stubborn back there to come on board, but she won't have any part of it."

Erin cleared her throat. "I don't want to sit in front of a computer all day."

"Right..." her brother said, with a mocking tone to his voice. He turned down a city street and slowed the vehicle. "Help me look for parking, will you?"

Drakor glanced out his window, searching for an open space between two cars. At least, that's what he thought he was supposed to do.

"Over there," Erin said, pointing over the seat between him and her brother. "Next to the white Toyota." Her fingertips brushed his shoulder, creating an instant burn on his skin.

After Greg parked the car, Drakor was the first to hop out. The sign for Mickey's lit up like the luminous red sunsets from home, flashing over a black door. People milled around out front, laughing, smoking, kissing. There were meeting places on Elliac, but nothing remotely similar to this.

Drakor handed his money to the large male at the door as the booming music reverberated in his body. Smells of alcohol, sweat and smoke invaded his nose and overloaded his brain.

For a moment, he sagged against the front window of the club, his entire body under assault from the surrounding sensations. Drakor closed his eyes, the pounding music thumping with his pulse. Acrid odor from a passing cigarette battered his nostrils.

But then he smelled Erin. He took a deep breath, welcoming the more pleasant aroma. It swirled within his bloodstream, comforting his taut nerves…until he grew erect.

Drakor's eyes snapped open.

Erin stood before him, her head tilted and eyebrows raised.

"Sick?" she shouted over the noise, but a knowing smile played on her lips.

He shook his head.

She shrugged then disappeared into the crowd. Drakor followed her into the depths of the building. The loud music pulsated through his blood. Colorful lights flashed among the crush of dancers.

Greg and Ankra were on the dance floor. He watched his sister move with a grace and ease so foreign to him. Greg's gaze devoured every inch of her. Their bodies jerked, turned then slid against each other.

Drakor swallowed and moved forward, squinting in the dark. He finally saw Erin seated at the bar, stirring a pink colored drink.

Erin took a few sips of the drink and rested her chin on her hand. She didn't seem interested in watching the dancing or in talking to her neighbors. Instead, she stared off somewhere he couldn't see.

A tall male came up next to her and began to speak. With the noise of the music and the crowds, Drakor could not hear their conversation, but he did feel a twist deep in his gut. Even though Erin did not look interested, shaking her head and returning to her drink, Drakor's stomach pitched.

"Hi!"

Startled, Drakor turned. A female with vibrant red hair, painted red lips, and large eyes smiled at him. "You been here before?" she asked, moving closer. "I come all the time and haven't seen you."

"First time."

"How about a dance?" She traced her finger along his forearm. He stared at her shining red fingernails, then let his gaze follow the path up her arm. The cut of her shirt offered him a view of rounded white skin. When he finally looked up at her face, her lips were curved in a grin.

She leaned against him, her voice in his ear. "You like what you see? It can be yours later."

How he wished he could have release. Since his Crossing nearly six years ago, he had not felt a sexual urge. Then a few days ago a stranger walked into his life and now his body was a mess. He thought of nothing but Erin. He'd endured nearly a constant state of arousal in the past day.

But only his *Mharai* could relieve him of this bittersweet agony. And it couldn't possibly be Erin.

Words whispered in his ear, "Come with me."

Drakor wanted to challenge his body, see if another Earth female could tangle his emotions and inflame his blood. It couldn't be that Erin was the only one.

He let the red-haired female lead him to a deeply shadowed corner of the room. She pushed him back up against the wall and pressed her large breasts against him. Her lips brushed across his cheek as her fingers trailed down his backside.

He felt nothing. Absolutely nothing.

Where was that urgency? That blistering desire taking over his rational thought?

Drakor pushed the female away from him.

"What's wrong?"

Scowling, Drakor moved away from her warmth and headed for a seat at the bar. That female did nothing to entice him, nothing to make his erection throb or his mouth water. If that were the case, then it wasn't *every* Earth female who unraveled the thorough teachings of his Crossing.

Drakor swallowed and scanned the row of full barstools, but Erin was gone.

ॐ

The only way to get rid of the guy bugging her at the bar was to walk away. Erin left him slurping on his beer and headed up the stairs. She hadn't seen Drakor since they descended into the darkness of the dance floor.

She squeezed past the dancers and jostling guys and went for the front door. The bouncer stamped her hand and she slipped outside into the cooler air.

A few people milled around along the sidewalk, all of them with someone else. She went to a planter holding a large tree and perched on the corner.

Some night this turned out to be. Greg was all over Ankra. And Drakor must be all over some other girl. Or they were all over him. Face it, as good-looking as he was, he'd be heading home with someone tonight.

She should feel relieved. Involving herself with Drakor would be like another death sentence to her career. But, damn, she melted into a puddle of horniness whenever he was around.

Erin smoothed her lip gloss over her lips, relishing the cool summer breeze.

"Well, lo and behold, who do we have here?"

Erin cringed at the sugary, southern voice. "Oh, Rita, could that be you?"

She turned to see her nemesis from the *Sentinel* standing near the curb, her arms crossed over her large bosom and her lips smacking the ever-present gum. Dyed-blonde hair twisted with a curling iron and a sleek outfit to upstage any model made Rita the queen of Mickey's ball.

Why the hell did Erin have to make do at this small town paper and put up with bitches like Rita?

"I didn't think you came to a place like this," Rita sneered.

"Why not?"

The diva bounced a curl in her palm. "Aren't you more of a corner barfly kind of girl?"

"Why, I would be, but you've laid claim to every one in the city."

"Listen, you little wench, you can think you're all high and mighty, but I'm going to bring you down." She put her hands on her hips. "I had my meeting with Rockford on Friday."

Erin caught her breath. Oh shit. Not Rita too.

"What?" Rita scoffed. "You mean you didn't expect a little competition for the mid-July exposé he's running?"

Erin shrugged. "I'm not worried." Though, in fact, she was concerned. Rita was Rockford's pet. The man practically drooled every time the woman walked by his office.

"Well, Erin, let's just say that we know which one of us is going to make the front cover and which one of us will be writing obituaries."

"You're a bitch."

Rita raised her eyebrows and smacked her gum. "That may be, my dear, but the best bitch will win. And I've already got my story picked out. And it will blow you right out of the water."

"I have an idea I'm working on." Well, maybe. Really nothing more at this point than a few strangers who built a really pretty house right on the spot where a John Doe no one cared about died.

"An idea, huh? 'It's a good idea to spay and neuter your pets' has been done already."

"Get lost."

"Absolutely." She grinned and her white teeth glimmered under the Mickey's neon sign. "It would be my pleasure now that I've ruined your night."

Rita turned on her heel and joined some friends waiting near the front door. Erin slid off the planter and banged her elbow.

That did it. She had enough. She needed to find Greg and the others and drag them out of there. Who cares if the night was still young? She knew dance clubs weren't her thing, yet she tried to be a sport. Now she just wanted get home and think through her plans. So far, her brief encounter with

42

Drakor and Ankra had given her no new clues as to the mysterious death of John Doe.

Erin left the relative quiet of the sidewalk and joined the throngs in Mickey's flashing and deafening rooms.

She went down into the darker dance floor where she had ditched the guy at the bar. Across the room, she caught sight of Greg near one of the mirrored walls. His back was to her and she knew he held some girl in his clutches. She tapped him on the shoulder.

"Go away whoever you are," he said without looking back.

Erin stepped around him and saw he had one hand on the girl's hip and another cupping her face. It was Ankra.

Her stomach knotted. "Oh, this is really great, Greg."

"Go away, Erin, I'm having the night of my life."

"Yeah? Well, I'm not. I want to leave."

He didn't take his eyes from his captive. "Catch a lift with someone. I'm not going anywhere."

Typical. Self-centered Greg strikes again. Yeah, he'll do people favors, he'll be a nice guy. But only if there's something in it for him. She could never just ask him for help.

Erin pulled his arm from Ankra's face. "You're supposed to be chaperoning her from leeches, not be one of them!"

He yanked his arm from her grasp. "Am I bothering you?" he asked his shining-eyed partner.

She shook her head.

Erin threw her hands in the air and groaned. "Oh, that's just great. Give me your keys, asshole. I'll wait in the car."

He reached in his pocket and held them out to her. "Have a good nap."

Erin snatched the keys and stormed across the room, pushing through the crowd. Once out the front door, she made a turn for the car. But the familiar wide flare of muscular shoulders made her pause.

Erin inched her way closer. With the light from the streetlamp, she could see wild, dark hair curling over the collar of a green shirt. Drakor stood against a streetlamp, his arms folded across his chest.

Why was he out here alone?

Curious, but not wanting to intrude, she crept up behind him and stood nearby. She was about to say something when, without turning around, he spoke.

"Greetings, Erin Price."

෫)උ3

All around him the air buzzed with nighttime insects and whispers of people walking by. He smelled their sweat and cigarettes. And yet nothing could compare to Erin.

Drakor squeezed his eyes closed but he could not prevent the explosion within his cells. Opposite to what that other Earth female had caused, Erin's closeness created a maelstrom in his senses. His mouth watered, his palms itched, his flesh hardened. Of course he knew she stood near him.

But why her? No one on his planet had ever found a mate anywhere but Elliac. The very few who never found a mate at all were so unusual, they were ostracized, forced to live in a separate colony. He had spent the last several years searching for his *Mharai*, waiting to find her, to end this tortuous celibacy. Now only a few weeks were left until he reached the birthday when it would be too late.

Erin Price could not be his lifemate. She was human. It was impossible. So why then did he hunger for her with such a voracious appetite? He wanted to take her nipples into his mouth, run his hands over the swell of her bottom, sink himself deep inside of her.

He heard Erin step off the curb and stand before him. He opened his eyes, drinking in the delicious sight of her.

Her eyebrow rose. "I assumed you would be inside dancing, having a good time."

"I was searching for you." His gut writhed. Desire, desperation, and fury all mingled in one burning throb.

"Oh? You were?" Something in her voice caught him. She sounded surprised, yet enthused.

"I was concerned. I saw a male disturbing you at the bar and then I didn't see you again."

"Wow, Drakor, you were worried about me?" She shoved her hands in her pockets and he caught a glimpse of the valley between her breasts. "Did you notice that my own brother has no such worries?"

His neck felt damp. "Your brother is with my sister."

"I know. I'm really sorry about that. Here I bring him along to act as a chaperone and he's the one all over her. It's really embarrassing."

"It should not embarrass you. You cannot control what he does."

"No, but I feel bad about his actions." She glanced at the ground, her light hair swinging across her cheek.

Drakor fisted his fingers to resist brushing the strands from her face. His lips tingled with the desire to taste whatever glistened on her pretty little mouth.

He clenched his jaw, scrambling for the lessons from his Crossing. Once he knew how to force his body into submission, to resist the cravings. Images of Elliac, of his hillside home, of anything other than her, collided and merged in his brain.

Sand. Rocks. Stars. Sun. He tried to block his desire with the thoughts of the ordinary.

It failed.

One look into Erin's sky-colored eyes and his arousal pulsated. *Helta*, he had to have her. Or he had to get off this planet.

She raised an eyebrow. "Are you okay?"

Drakor could not find his voice, not with his sensations spinning out of control.

Erin angled her head. Her lips sparkled brightly under the streetlamp. "Shall I take you home?"

Great Sun, yes. Drakor nodded.

Chapter Five

Erin threw her shoulders back, trying to ignore the tingle racing down her spine, leaving her breathless. Though Drakor never said or did anything to make her believe he wanted her, she could feel a sexual hunger radiate from his stance. Her legs turned to jelly right there on the sidewalk.

She pulled her gaze from his powerful stare and dug around in her purse for Greg's keys. "Let's, um, get going."

She started down the sidewalk but someone blocked her path. Rita.

"Who's this big hunk of a man?" The bitch gestured toward Drakor.

"A friend of mine. Is there something else you wanted to annoy me about? Or can it wait until Monday?"

Rita gave him a seductive glance over and smacked her gum. "And I thought Mickey's was out of your league. You are way in over your head tonight, my dear."

Erin felt the color rise on her cheeks. "I'm not your dear and how about minding your business for a change?"

Rita took a few steps toward Drakor. "If I minded my own business all the time I wouldn't be a very good reporter, would I? You should take notes on that."

Drakor stood his ground, his hands in his pockets. He watched Rita with guarded eyes. "You must be a friend of Erin's."

"A co-worker would be more accurate," she answered. "Are you two about to leave? That would be a shame."

47

"Yes." Erin forced away the tightness in her chest. She shouldn't be bothered if Drakor found Rita attractive. But for some reason, it really pissed her off. "We are leaving. Do you mind?"

Rita lifted an eyebrow. "Are you taking him home for the night?" She ran her fingers down his arm and squeezed his biceps. "Oooh! I think we all know that little Erin here is just going to drop you off at your door and drive away."

Erin narrowed her eyes. "And?"

"I could keep him company a little longer."

Taking a deep breath, Erin continued down the sidewalk. "Take your pick," she called to Drakor. "This ride is going now."

For a few minutes there was no sound behind her. She turned the corner and walked toward Greg's car, her heart slamming in her chest. Since Rita had moved into town about six months ago, she'd gotten the best leads, made the most contacts, enjoyed the fun social life. She'd bettered Erin in everything.

Drakor was Erin's story, damn it. He would lead her to solve the mystery of John Doe. Hell, he might have a mystery of his own to share.

The tapping of heels clicked behind her.

"Don't think you've won the war," Rita sneered, coming around to block Erin's progress. "There are many battles left to fight."

Drakor was nowhere around and Erin didn't know what she was talking about.

"There's only room for one of us at that paper. It's going to take someone with ambition and guts. Do you have what it takes? Oh look, here comes your boy now. He's far beyond you, my dear. Don't think his intentions are sincere. He's using you for one thing or another."

Drakor's easy, powerful stride brought him beside her. Rita waved good-bye. "Ta ta, you two. And, Erin, I saw your brother inside with some sleaze-bag. I've got my trained eye on him and it doesn't look good."

Erin's jaw dropped. Why did Rita care about Greg and why didn't Drakor defend his sister? He said nothing…only watched Rita walk away.

"Why didn't you say something to her? She just insulted Ankra."

"I believe that female is not your friend."

"No, she isn't."

He shrugged. "Then her opinion does not matter."

Hell, he had a point there. "Let's go." Erin climbed in the driver's seat.

They said nothing to each other on the way home. He pressed himself against the car door, his face shining and his cheeks flushed. Dare she ask him if it was lust that caused him to behave this way? She wasn't quite that bold.

When they pulled up to the house, Erin saw someone move away from an upper window.

"Who was that?"

He sighed. "My younger brother."

"You have a brother, as well? Who else lives here?"

Drakor got out of the car. She watched his long, lean body take two of the porch steps at a time. He hung his head then leaned against the mauve-colored post. He stared out into the trees, where courting fireflies lit up the shadows.

"My entire family lives here," he said at last. "My parents, Ankra, younger brother and sister."

"Oh!" Certainly not what she expected. Some reporter she was. She had come to this house to investigate her John Doe and somehow the sight of Drakor made her forget everything she'd learned in Journalism 101. "How old are your younger siblings?"

"Brundor is…" he hesitated and then said, "seventeen sun-cycles. Sitora is five."

"Sun-cycles?" He really was strange sometimes.

His dark eyes settled on her face. "Earth years."

Erin snorted. "Oh, sure, that makes more sense."

The way he talked, it seemed like he was from another planet. Crazy, of course.

And now her instincts told her nothing felt normal at this antique house in the middle of the woods. This man, with his gripping gaze and secretive nature, and his sister, with her voluptuous figure and naiveté, had to be something more than foreigners. She had to find out what. Could she use her feminine charms to get him to divulge his secrets?

Someone with ambition and guts, Rita had said. Erin once had them both in spades, but she didn't trust herself anymore. Ambition and guts had nearly ruined her, how could she know what was right anymore? Especially when thoughts of kissing this man kept her awake at night.

She noticed Drakor staring up at the half moon. "Kind of cool, huh?"

He turned those intense eyes on her. A tingle raced down her spine.

Erin cleared her throat, then started babbling. Anything to keep her focus. "I especially love it when it's full and hangs really low and huge. It's like you can reach right out and touch it. The craters are so clear I think it's just beyond the trees. If only I could climb to the top of one of them, I might actually be able to reach it." She sighed. "How cool would that be to walk on it, to explore something other than this planet?"

Drakor started to say something but stopped. His muscles flexed as he dug his hands in his pockets. In the distance, crickets sang.

She stared at his profile, the dark shadows erasing all traces of details. She could only see the small ridge along his eyebrows, the strong jutting of his nose, and the rounding of his lips.

He was beautiful. Breathtakingly handsome. But who was he really? She felt compelled to find the truth.

"Drakor?"

He blinked once and then slowly turned to look at her. There was no mistaking the blistering need in his bottomless eyes. All rational thought fled as desire engulfed her, stripping away her self-control and leaving her desperate for his touch.

"This is a mistake." Drakor had not meant to say it aloud. He could read her thoughts as if she'd whispered them against the curve of his ear. Erin wanted him to kiss her. Great Sun, he yearned to satisfy her request.

"Yes, it is," she agreed.

He watched her lips move as she spoke, longing to consume every part of her. But it would mean giving in to the bizarre notion that Erin was his lifemate.

His pulse drummed in his ears. His breath caught with anticipation. His body trembled with restraint.

"Oh, God...I can't...we shouldn't..." She closed her eyes and swallowed. The sweet scent of a summer flower swirled in his nose with a heady rush.

His gaze traced a path down her supple lips to her smooth throat, gleaming beneath the moonlight. Her breasts rose and fell, nearly touching his chest, their nipples pert. The air hummed, sizzled.

Drakor brushed his thumb across her jaw, her smooth skin warming him like a thousand suns. A whimper chimed in her throat and she leaned toward him.

Blood roared through his veins. Desire erupted in a breathtaking explosion.

He could deny it no longer.

Drakor brushed his lips against hers, tasting her longing. Erin opened her mouth and he plunged forth, diving into unknown yet somehow familiar territory.

Her hands skimmed up his arms and rested upon his shoulders. Warm currents eddied under his skin. He was at once on fire and tranquil.

Drakor slid his palms down her back and cupped her bottom. She released a moan, buried her fingers into his hair, pressed her body against him.

His flesh throbbed, knees weakened. He wanted Erin more than anything he'd ever wanted in his life. Nothing could penetrate this haze of lust, this scalding desire pulsating deep within his bones.

Her tongue stroked his, suckled it, spiraling waves of pleasure down to his toes. His hands and feet went numb.

Drakor leaned a hand against the post, helpless. He had to put a stop to this now, or he may not be able to stop it at all.

Haltingly, he pulled away. Her glazed eyes blinked at him, the moon shining like a white spot in their center. Kiss-swollen lips grinned at him.

He cleared his throat. "This was a mistake."

"But it felt right."

Too right. That's what bothered him. "I should not have touched you."

Erin shrugged a shoulder. "It was glorious. But you're right, it was a mistake."

Then why did it feel so terrible when they parted? His body screamed for her. And it yet was more than raw passion. Her caress released a peaceful river in his veins. She both calmed and excited him, created and destroyed him. It was as if she were made just for him.

Great Sun, no!

Erin tapped his arm. Her breasts rose and fell in rhythm with his heart. She swallowed, smiled, then jogged down the steps. "I need to go back to get Greg and Ankra."

Drakor nodded, unable to form words.

She waved out the window and turned the car around. He stood watching her until the vehicle's red lights blinked in the distance and then disappeared from view.

Drakor glanced up to the half moon, hanging just above the treetops. Erin had marveled at its beauty. She wished to touch it, to walk upon its surface. How little she and the other humans knew of rest of the universe. Why could they not believe that other life forms existed in the far off sky?

He swallowed, his throat tight and dry. The pain at his groin, in his heart, inside his skull had eased, but only slightly. He almost wished he had not kissed her, that he had not given in to his body's demands. But the brief moments of pleasure had been practically nothing compared to the contentment and peace he experienced. He would give nearly anything to have that feeling again.

Anything but believe his lifelong mate was a human.

ɛͻʕȝ

Two headlights cut a swath of light along the dirt road as Erin drove Ankra back to her house. Or rather she took her to the Victorian for the girl to retrieve clothes. Supposedly Ankra believed Greg was her knight in shining armor. Proved how much this naïve girl knew.

The moon was higher and seemed much further away now. The house stood completely dark when they pulled in front of it.

Erin and Greg waited in the car while Ankra ran inside.

"I guess you like her," Erin mumbled.

"She is something else," he answered, sighing.

"Be nice to her. Promise me again."

"Erin, what is the big deal here anyway? It's not like she's your best friend. You only met her a few days ago and you're snooping around their house for a story."

Her throat tightened. Exactly why she shouldn't have kissed Drakor. But, damn, did it feel good.

"You won't tell her, will you? About me looking for a story."

He leaned forward and rested his chin on the back of her seat. "Aw, come on, I'm not that much of a jerk. Though I hope you don't ever have me in the position to choose."

Erin raised her eyebrows and turned to look at him. "Does that mean you might actually be with her longer than a week?"

Greg chuckled and winked. "We'll see how tonight goes…"

"Gregory Price!"

"I'm just kidding, Erin. You really need to get laid."

She rolled her eyes. "Here we go again."

"Look." He pointed to one of the upper windows. A dull light glittered behind the curtains and a shadow moved in front of the window. "Could that be Drakor? Maybe he wants you to come inside."

"Give me a break." She squinted up at the figure. Was that him? Was he looking out to see if she had come back?

Didn't matter. That one kiss was an aberration, just to see if he'd allow it, if she could use her feminine wiles to get some information from him. But he'd pulled away.

The shadow moved from the window and the light dimmed to black. Whoever had been watching decided there was nothing worth seeing and went back to bed.

Erin closed her eyes, wishing the night was over and she was fast asleep in her bed. She heard Greg lean back and they waited for Ankra in silence.

She must have fallen asleep because the back door opening caused her to jump.

"I am sorry I took so long," Ankra said. "There has been a problem in my house tonight."

Erin turned to look back at her, but caught sight of Drakor walking toward the car, like a lion on the prowl. In spite of herself, Erin felt heat flood her belly, her heart quicken.

He tapped on the glass. She rolled down the window. "I need your aid."

"What is it?"

He inhaled sharply. "My father and I had a disagreement and I find that I cannot stay in the house tonight." His eyes flicked back to the rear seats. "I ask to stay at Greg's house tonight, if possible."

"Huh?"

Erin looked back to see that Greg's face was buried in Ankra's neck and he wasn't even paying attention.

"He wants to know if he can stay at your house."

Greg's eyes widened and his face paled. He obviously didn't like the request. No doubt he thought having Ankra's brother in the next room would interfere with his plans. He did have a point there. "Uh, Erin, can't he stay with you?"

Her mouth dried, anticipating being alone with Drakor. The things he could do with his tongue. And those hands…

It was a very bad idea.

"I have a one bedroom apartment. Where would he sleep?"

"On the couch?" Drakor offered.

Even if he slept on the couch, her hormones would have her out there within minutes. The man was raw, wild. Hot.

"I-I don't know."

Greg kicked the back of her seat. Selfish asshole. If he wanted Ankra alone that badly, he could do her a few favors in the process. "Can I talk to you a minute, Greg? Alone?"

He groaned but nodded. Ankra slipped back out of the car and Erin put the window up.

She turned to stare at him. "Now, you listen. Having this man sleep on my couch tonight is not the wisest thing in my opinion—"

"Aw, it could be good for you. As long as you don't pull something like you did with Evan."

She clenched her jaw but let the comment pass. "I will do you this favor…if you promise to pass on any of Ankra's suspicious or odd behaviors to me."

"What? Are you talking about when we …"

Erin quickly shook her head. "No. Unless there is something particularly odd. Just general stuff. Things she says, things she doesn't understand. Where she says they are from. That kind of stuff."

"Erin," he whined, cheeks flushed from the night of dancing. And Ankra's neck, no doubt.

"Drakor is not staying with me unless you agree."

"Fine. Whatever. There will be nothing to report, I'm sure."

She reached over the seat and banged his leg with her fist. "But if there is something, you *will* tell me, right?"

"Fine. Can we just go now? I'm going to be too exhausted to do anything at this rate."

"Won't that be a shame?"

Erin knocked on the window and waved for Ankra and Drakor to climb in. Ankra went back to her usual spot next to Greg and Drakor climbed in the front seat. Just the clean scent of him, the swirl of his body heat, made her skin tingle. An ache expanded deep in her belly, begging for his touch.

She clenched her thighs together. This was turning into one hell of a night—no matter which way she looked at it.

৪০ঞ্জ

Drakor heard the shower start in Erin's bathroom. He got up from the couch and wandered about the room, hoping to distract himself from thinking of her naked breasts, white thighs, and slick rump. It was useless. Already he was hard.

He shouldn't be here.

After learning that Ankra was going back to Greg's house, his father insisted Drakor follow suit. They argued. Mostly about how painful it was for him to be near her. And also about how Erin was after something from them. She spelled trouble. But that only made the reason to check out where she lived all that more important.

And he couldn't argue with that.

Drakor squatted down before a shelf. He pushed a power button and music filled his ears. He found the volume control and reduced the noise. Perhaps this would drown out the sound of water tapping Erin's body.

The shower stopped and Drakor turned the music down even further. He heard her humming along with some clanking noises. She dropped something on the tile floor a few times and uttered a curse. It made him grin.

He moved closer to the bathroom door, ready to spin away if it opened. But he needed to get a sense of her mood, to gauge how to play the rest of the evening. He was willing to use that kiss, and her obvious pleasurable reaction to it. There was no way his family was going to end up like Alaziri. He'd find out what Erin knew and then be away from her.

Drakor glanced in the bedroom. The tousled sheets and thrown clothes told him she did not care for tidiness and structure. He spotted her white, lacy undergarments and his erection leapt.

"What are you doing?"

He turned to face her. Her light hair was wet and combed back from her face. She wore no make-up, but her face glowed. A thick white robe wrapped her body, a knot in the front the only thing holding it together.

"I came in looking for a pillow." He went past her. "I will wait for you on the couch."

Drakor headed straight for the couch, sank on the cushions and rested his head back. He assumed she would redress and come out with the pillow and blanket. But she sat on the table in front of him and tapped his knee.

He slowly lifted his head and stared at her. She was still in her robe and the front gaped open revealing a hint of her naked skin. Liquid heat blasted through his veins. He gulped.

"I'm sorry you got in a fight with your dad." Even in the dim light, he could see her lips shining, beckoning him.

Drakor shifted in his seat, but his arousal pressed against his pants. "Where is your father?"

"He and my mom were killed in a plane crash eight years ago. I was in college." She went silent for a moment and then took a deep breath. "It's just me and Greg now."

Drakor cleared his throat and pulled his gaze from her alluring skin. "Your brother owns his own business. What do you do to earn money?"

Erin tucked strands of wet hair behind her ear. A whiff of sweet flowers made his mouth water. Light sweat beaded on his forehead.

"I write for the local newspaper."

His gut burned but he didn't move. Journalists, they were called. On the list to avoid. *Helta*, she could expose them!

"I'm on assignment now," she said quickly. "Investigating dance clubs. That's why I wanted to go to Mickey's tonight. To do some preliminary work."

It sounded plausible, but still it concerned him. He would have to keep his guard up even more. Yet, she may be a good person to help him locate Alaziri. "Would you know of missing persons?"

Erin's eyes flew wide but then she gave a careless shrug. "I may be able to find out information. Are you searching for someone?"

Drakor tensed. He wasn't certain how much he should share with her right now. "I have a friend I have been unable to locate. I don't know where to turn."

She lifted her chin. "Ah. Well, let me know how I can help."

His shoulders loosened. Already he'd learned that Erin was a journalist, potentially dangerous to their secret. But she might be able to help him find Alaziri. Coming here was not such a bad idea, after all.

Drakor reached out, covered her hand with his own.

Her breath hitched, the air tightened. Heat blazed from her skin to his palm.

"I want to say no, but…" Her statement drifted in the hot space between them. He lingered over the words, savoring her surrender.

He lost himself in her sky-colored eyes. Just tonight. He needed to feel that soothing contentment again. He didn't understand it, but right now he didn't care.

Erin moved from the table to beside him on the couch. "The mistake …I…let's make it again."

Drakor leaned forward, his pulse echoing in his eardrums. He eased himself on top of her, lying them down along the cushions. She mumbled something as his mouth captured hers, but the words were lost.

$\mathcal{SO}\mathcal{CR}$

Erin held her breath as that finely formed chest pressed her down onto the couch. She could feel his heart beating wildly against her breasts. Her nipples poked forward, rubbing against the rough fabric of the robe.

Drakor shifted his legs and his arousal dug into her thighs. Oh God, she wanted that inside of her. Now.

Thoughts of Evan and that catastrophe flitted away as Drakor's tongue licked its way up her neck. Right now her body had a need and only one man could fulfill it.

Erin threaded her fingers through his wild, dark hair. He moaned. Jerked his hips.

She arched her back, reaching up to him. Drakor separated her robe then captured a breast with his hand. His thumb circled around the tip, spiraling desire deep within her belly.

His lips left hers and blazed a trail down her throat. She quivered as they reached her nipple. A strangled cry caught in her throat as her body flooded with molten fire. His tongue flicked the tip, spiraling her higher. Higher.

He switched to the other side and Erin wriggled her hips against the sweet tension. Drakor pulled her robe further apart, first eyeing what lay beneath and then lightly kissing her skin.

"Yes, go on," she urged.

His face hovered above hers, his dark eyes hooded. A small white circle dotted the center of each. He blinked but the white spots remained.

Erin reached around his back and tugged at his shirt. She ran her fingers along the taut muscles on his back, surprised by the smoothness of his skin. "Take it off."

He pulled the shirt off. A small gathering of dark curls tickled her breasts. She giggled and he lifted his head again.

"This brings me great pleasure."

"Mmm," she agreed, "me too." So good she was afraid she'd want more after tonight. She couldn't allow that. Just tonight.

His hand moved inside her robe, his tongue down the sides of her neck. Spiraling waves of bliss crashed through her, tightening that desperate ache.

Erin pulled him back down on top of her and his warm fingers encircled her hips. She would give herself to him. She would let this night be like no other. Only one thing stood in their way.

Her voice trembled. "Do-do you have a condom?"

Chapter Six

Condom. A thin protective sheath to prevent venereal infection and/or conception. There were no venereal infections on Elliac and females could control their conception.

Drakor grimaced and sat on his porch step, staring at the fading sun. The thought of using something like that disgusted him. It was unnatural. Like so many other customs on Earth.

But it wasn't necessarily the lack of having a condom that had been his downfall with Erin, it was that he didn't know at the time what it was. She kept prodding him to see if he told the truth. When she finally believed that he in fact had no idea, she pushed him off. Although desire and disappointment lingered in her gaze.

Of course, it was impossible to sleep afterward. His body throbbing in pain, he could do little but squeeze the pillow. Alternating surges of hot need and agony swept through him and it took every measure of control he had not to storm into her room and take her as she lay sleeping. Though she'd have awoken before long.

An insect buzzed by his ear. He waved it away as the door creaked open behind him.

"I have a job for you, Drakor."

He looked up at his father. "Go on."

"Test the shuttlecraft. It has been idle for too long and I want to make sure it is in working condition."

Mother and Sitora stepped outside.

"Where are you three going?"

"We are taking Sitora into town for a short trip."

Drakor stood and looked around. "It is late in the day already and we have no Earth vehicle. Do not tell me you mean to Transfer."

Father picked Sitora up into his arms. "I have read about something called a 'taxi.' We will walk down to the main road and then look for one there."

As foolish as that sounded, it was better than using Elliac's mode of transportation. They only needed to put in a specific code into their Transmitters and then they would be transported to the new coordinates.

His father wiped the sheen from his forehead. "While we are gone take Brundor with you into the craft, show him what to do. He needs to learn."

His brother needed to learn a lot, but his pride and stubbornness stood in the way. "Yes, fine, but Greg should be returning with Ankra soon. What if he sees it?"

"Then you must be on the look out. The invisibility shield will activate in less than a second, as long as the craft is in working order." He tugged on Mother's arm. "Let's go."

Drakor watched them walk down the dirt road until they were out of sight. Then he went in to get Brundor and some tools.

"So you spent the night at her house," Brundor said as they went out the back door.

"Yes." Drakor entered a code in his mini crystal screen and the shuttlecraft appeared before them.

"Well? Tell me. How did it go? What was she like?"

Drakor ignored him and keyed in another code to open the hatch. It creaked open and dropped to the ground.

"You were there all night. Something must have happened."

Drakor climbed onto the ramp and started up into the interior. The only light was from the sun filtering in through the thick windows.

Brundor was at his heels. "You have to answer something." He jumped out in front and blocked the hallway. "Can I have her next?"

Drakor grabbed a hold of his brother's collar and slammed him up against a shiny console. An unfamiliar anger and protectiveness tightened his muscles. "Don't ever touch her."

Brundor eyes widened and then blinked at him curiously. "You act like she's your *Mharai*. No other female ever made you act this way."

Drakor growled. He wasn't going to believe that and he wasn't going to let anyone else believe it either.

"No, of course, she isn't. I just want you to stay clear of her." He let him go and made his way up to the front. He glanced around to make sure all was in place then slid into the pilot's seat.

"I won't touch her, but I will find someone else. I can't take this the way you can."

"Sit down, Brundor. You can handle it if you give yourself the chance."

His brother dropped into the co-pilot's chair and scrutinized all of the knobs and buttons in front of him. "That's easy for you say," he muttered, running his fingers along the silver metal. "You have your own female now that you can use whenever you want."

Drakor felt his face heating again. But he said nothing. The control he'd learned at his Crossing did more than help with sexual urges. Although they didn't work for that when Erin was around. No. Around her he was blazing heat like Elliac's sun. And harder than any crystal he'd ever found.

He wasn't quite even sure when or if he would see her again. She said almost nothing to him the entire morning, other than to offer him breakfast. He politely refused, watched her eat a toasted slice of bread, and then they left her home. Erin never even got out of her vehicle when they got here, she just drove away.

He should be ecstatic. Maybe he'd driven her out of their lives for good. He wouldn't have to worry about her investigating them. But instead emptiness burrowed into his gut.

"What are these for?"

Drakor glanced over at the buttons Brundor was itching to touch. "Lights. Exterior, interior, landing, spot, outer illumination. Go on and try them one at a time." He stood. "I'll go outside and make certain they're coming on."

Drakor leaped off the hatch and circled the craft. "Go on," he called. "Hit the buttons from left to right. One at a time. Wait for an okay from me."

Brundor hit the first button and the landing lights blinked on below, shining on the dry grass and clover with enough force to burn the edges.

"Good," he yelled. "Turn it off. Next one."

The spotlight in front flashed on and an enormous white circle landed on the rear of the house. So far, all systems go.

"Good, try the next one."

A row of lights blinked along the bottom half of the craft. Drakor walked the perimeter of silver vehicle, checking each light individually. He could barely see if these were on. He'd need true darkness to gauge their functionality.

He came around full circle and opened his mouth to call to Brundor, but a noise caught his attention. Drakor could hear a vehicle's engine and it wasn't the shuttlecraft.

"Brundor! Get out!"

"We just started. There are three more buttons to go."

"Get out! A vehicle is heading our way. The shuttlecraft is in full view."

The engine rumble grew louder and Drakor's heart slammed inside his ribcage. "I've got to make it invisible! You need to get out."

"What's the code? Let me do it," his brother called from somewhere inside the cockpit.

In the next instant, he hadn't a choice. Greg's truck came into view, kicking up the usual dust and dirt. Drakor fumbled for the crystal screen, entered the code and backed away from the craft. A second later, it vanished.

With Brundor still inside.

ഇ)രു

Erin swallowed the last of her lousy and very cold coffee. She watched Rita smile, chew her gum, and flirt her way into Rockford's good graces. It didn't matter that the door to his glass enclosed office was shut. Body language told its own story.

Her boss opened his door and ushered Rita out. They laughed with an ease that made Erin nervous. She bit her lip and resisted the urge to sprint to the bathroom.

"Ms. Price," Rockford turned to her, "your turn."

Erin swallowed, grabbed her spiral notebook and followed him in inside. He sat in behind his desk, the brown pleather chair squeaking loudly under his weight. She pushed the door closed and edged toward the open seat.

"Go on, sit down."

She carefully lowered herself to the seat. Meetings like this always made her nervous. Especially when Rita went before her. How could she compare with her? Rockford knew Erin's history and had given her the chance, but she could always see the doubt lurking in his gaze.

"Well, what have you got for me?" he asked in his raspy, oversmoked voice.

"Sir?"

"A story, Ms. Price. Do you not have the start of a story?"

"Uh…" She glanced down at her notes, which were basically just a listing of the odd things she could gather from Drakor, Ankra and the house. It didn't amount to much of a story right now. And so far she had nothing really to connect them to her strange John Doe.

He coughed and then cleared his throat. She glanced up at his red, beefy face. His small eyes stared at her. "Ms. Dixon informed me that she told you of my plans for next month."

Erin nodded. "Yes, she said something to me about it."

"So you know that one of you will have not only the front page, but also a full spread if your story makes the grade."

She nodded again. "What about the one who doesn't make it?"

Rockford shifted his chair and reached for today's paper. He held it up to her. "I don't need two big egos around here." He flipped through to one of the back sections. "But I have an opening for a fact checker."

The blood hummed in Erin's ears and her throat tightened. She would not go backwards. Evan already did enough damage to her career, she wasn't about to let Rita send her tumbling downhill again.

"Am I making myself clear, Ms. Price?"

"I understand, sir. What is the deadline?"

"I want to see a rough draft in three weeks."

"Three weeks?" She scanned her meager list. There wasn't enough here right now to caption a photograph. Maybe she should find another story? Maybe there really wasn't anything unusual about Drakor. And yet, she could not forget the odd manner in which he shielded her from his house and family. Or the fact that he lived in the same spot her John Doe had once lived. Hell, the man had absolutely no idea what a condom was.

She would have to talk to Greg about his night with Ankra. And she would have to go back to that vibrant Victorian house at the end of a dirt road. If she could just find a way to do some serious snooping.

"Ms. Price?" Rockford pushed himself up from his chair and looked across his desk to her lap. "Care you tell me what you have in mind?"

She tilted the sheet toward her chest. "Do I have to?"

He sighed. "Do you have something there? Are you working on an idea?"

"Yes. I still have a lot of work to do, that's all."

"Two Mondays from today I want an outline or a rough draft of what you are working on." He pointed behind her out the glass door. "Your competition has already begun her investigation. I suggest you get moving on yours rather quickly."

Erin nodded. "Yes, sir."

She left his office and went back to her small desk. She had to get out of this itty-bitty town and back into the real world. She had ambition, goals, and right now the very real need to prove she was still a kick-ass journalist.

She needed to call Greg. If he had a lot of information for her, it would save her having to go out to the house. She wasn't up to seeing Drakor after what almost happened.

Even a day and half later, she wasn't sure if she was disappointed or relieved that they never finished what they started. While she was safe from making the mistake she did with Evan, her dreams had gotten a lot more erotic and left her wholly unsatisfied when she woke.

Erin picked up the phone and dialed Greg's office.

"Invasion Shield, Inc., may I help you?"

"Hi, Cindy, it's Erin. Is Greg available?"

"He didn't come in today. Called in, saying he had some things to take care of and we could reach him on his cell in case of an emergency."

Erin coughed. "He didn't come in?"

"Nope, didn't sound sick or anything. Maybe you should try his cell phone. You have the number, right?"

"I have it. Thanks."

She hung up and stared across the room. Rita looked very busy. On the phone, taking notes, checking something on her computer. Oh, it would be great to find out what her story was. How nice if it was as half-baked as her own.

She picked up the phone again and twisted her chair away from Rita. She dialed Greg's cell.

He answered on the third ring. A loud noise like water or wind blasted in Erin's ears.

"Greg here!"

"Greg, what are you doing? Where are you?"

"Hello? Is this Erin?"

"Greg. What's that noise?"

"Sorry, I can't hear you!" He hung up.

Erin felt her cheeks heat. She stared at the phone in her hand. He just hung up on her. And where the hell was he anyway?

"Problems?"

Erin glanced up into Rita's sharp eyes. "It's nothing."

"How was Saturday night? Did your friend get home safe and sound?"

Erin shivered, remembering his kiss on the porch. And later, when his hot body covered hers, when his expert tongue stoked a fire under her skin.

"He got home just fine," she managed to answer.

Rita lifted an eyebrow. "Well, if he's looking for someone else to show him the town, pass along my number."

"I'll be sure to do that."

Rita pulled a piece of gum from her pocket, unwrapped it and popped it in her mouth. "Was that your brother you were trying to call?"

"Is it your business?"

"Everything is my business, my dear."

Erin clenched her teeth. She'd like nothing more than to strangle this woman right now. Ever since Rita Dixon got here, she'd taken everything important away from Erin. Greg was all that was left. And Drakor.

She got to her feet, a thought suddenly occurring to her. "Are you doing a piece on Greg or Invasion Shield?"

Rita chuckled and snapped her gum. "You can read my story on the front cover next month. Have a nice day." She turned and went back to her desk, shaking her head the whole way.

Erin groaned. She had to get out of here. She had to get more information on her story. She had to figure out if she really had a story or if she was wasting her time.

She snatched her bag and headed outside into the summer heat. The thick air in the parking lot dampened her neck. Heavy clouds blew in from the west. Great. A storm.

Erin pulled out her cell phone and called Greg again. With no one else in the parking lot, she could yell to make herself heard.

He got it on the second ring. "Erin, is that you again?"

This time the background was quiet. "Yes. Where were you?"

"At Blackrock Falls."

"That was the falls I heard? What are you doing there?"

"Minding my own business. What do you want?"

Erin leaned against her car door. "I need to talk to you. Remember what you promised?"

"Oh, come on…"

"I have to do this story, Greg. It could be the start of something big or the end of my career."

His voice dropped to a whisper. "Hold on." He covered the mouthpiece for a few minutes and then got back on. "Sorry, I had to get out of the car."

"Why? What are you doing?"

"Listen, I'm with Ankra, okay? I wanted to show her the falls. We were about to head to lunch when you called."

"Well, isn't there something to tell me about this weekend?"

"You want to know how late the night went? When I took her home the next day?"

Erin pulled her notebook out of her huge purse and leaned on the hood of her car, using it as a table. "Don't be an ass. Can you give me anything unusual? Anything to go on?"

"Hmmm…well, she seemed really annoyed that I used a condom."

"Gregory! I do not want to hear that!" Ick. Hearing about her brother having sex was almost as bad as imagining her parents doing it.

"Okay, okay." He laughed. "But after what happened in college, I wasn't about to take chances."

Erin winced. How could she forget about Sarah and the pregnancy? Those weeks were hell on Greg and their parents. He almost quit school to marry her and then Sarah came back from a weekend at home saying she had miscarried. Greg suspected an abortion, but whatever happened, the two of them broke up. It was no wonder he refused to have sex without protection.

He cleared his throat. "You said to tell you anything unusual. That seemed awfully strange to me."

"Will you move on, please? Anything else?"

"Erin, I didn't really take notes. Can we get together for dinner later this week and I'll try to come up with something?"

Great. He wasn't going to be a big help, was he? She'd have to come up with some plan on her own.

"Fine. Let's meet at The Onion Bloom for dinner tomorrow."

"I can't. I have a commitment."

"When can you meet, Greg? We need to chat."

"Can it wait until Thursday night?"

She groaned. Typical Greg, agree to help out when he had the need, but then do whatever he could to back out. "Fine. I'll plan to meet you there at six thirty."

"Hey, Erin?"

She closed her notebook and shoved it back in the bag. "What?"

"I almost forgot about this. Don't think I was still drunk, but I could have sworn I saw something yesterday when I dropped her off."

Erin dug around at the bottom of the purse for her keys. "What do you mean? You saw something."

"It happened so fast. I might have really imagined it."

"What? What was it?"

His voice dropped lower again. "Something shiny and silver and huge in their backyard. It was there and then it was gone."

"Greg, what are you talking about? I can barely hear you and I sure can't understand you." She shifted the bag and bent to unlock the door.

"Listen. It looked like something out of *Star Trek*."

"A spaceship?"

"Yeah. It looked like a spaceship."

Her keys clattered on the asphalt.

Chapter Seven

Drakor glanced up at the sky. Dark clouds formed overhead and he smelled the rain in the distance. This would be the first precipitation they witnessed since arriving on Earth. He knew from his studying that the amount of rain depended where you were on the planet, but this little town didn't have much during the hot months.

At home, the showers and storms came almost daily. Elliacians had learned to live with the often violent weather outbursts. They built their walls extra sturdy or burrowed underground. But more than the storms, they all suffered if outside for over an hour. The sun could severely burn both skin and eyes. First they had adapted to it with their darkened skin, then they learned to avoid it. Now it seemed, they couldn't get enough of it to strengthen their bones.

He pushed aside several yearling trees as he walked on the dry forest ground. He had found no evidence of their arrival on Earth. Nothing had fallen off the shuttlecraft. At least, not that he could see.

Drakor looked ahead as the sound of crunching grass came near. Brundor called out to him.

"What is it?"

"You have a visitor."

By the look on his brother's face, Drakor knew who it was. Of course, who else would be here to see him? He tried to deny the energy coursing through him. The past twenty-four hours had actually been a relief. He felt no cravings or urges. His body could rest. All that would change in a few minutes.

Suddenly, Drakor remembered that it was Brundor who delivered the message. He stalked over to his brother, who leaned against a large tree. "Tell me you did not touch her."

"No. But I should have to get you back for yesterday."

"That again? You refused to leave the ship. I had to make it invisible. You know that."

Brundor crossed his arms. "All you had to do was give me the code. I could have done it." He shuffled his feet in the dirt. "You act like you're in charge."

"When Father isn't around, I am in charge."

"Yeah, well, you said you don't like the old customs from home, so why don't you forget this one too? I shouldn't have to wait for you to die or join with your *Mharai* in order to have some power."

Drakor clenched his teeth and pushed his way past. "Power. Social status. Self-importance. You sound just like Father."

Brundor grabbed a hold of his arm. "How can I prove I am old enough to handle things if you two won't let me?"

Drakor shook him off and continued toward the house. When would Brundor mature into a man? He still seemed to be several sun-cycles from it. What kind of a fool was he to risk their exposure so he could punch in the code?

Drakor stopped short. He had almost forgotten to step around the shuttlecraft. Though visually undetectable, physically it was still there.

He came around to the front of the house and his gaze settled on Erin's small vehicle. The windows were all the way down and steam rose from the hood. He went closer. She wasn't in it but he could smell her essence on the seats.

"It's small, I know, but it gets me around."

His pulse jumped at the sound of her voice. He turned and leaned against the car, hoping it wouldn't be difficult to keep his distance today. "You might want to put up the window. Rain is coming."

"I know."

She stood up on the porch, dressed in light brown pants and a striped shirt. She clutched a notebook to her chest and sunglasses covered her eyes. Nonetheless, his body reacted as if she were nearly naked beneath him. He hardened at the memory.

The sound of shuffling feet caught his attention and he saw Brundor come around from the back of the house, a scowl set in his features. His heart lurched when he saw his brother head for the steps. *Move, Erin, move.* With the mood Brundor was in, there was no telling what he might do.

Instead, she stuck out her hand as his brother started up the stairs. "Hi. I'm Erin Price. You must be Drakor's brother."

Drakor held his breath. He wanted to rush over and yank her out of harm's way and yet he wanted to see if Brundor could prove himself. So, he stood poised, ready to act if necessary.

Brundor stared at her hand and then up at her face. An awkward and tense moment passed. Finally, his brother ignored her greeting and continued up to the door. "I am." And with that clipped response, he then went inside the house.

Drakor released the air in his lungs and looked over at her. She looked perplexed for a moment and then scribbled something on her paper. What was she doing? She's a reporter, someone who investigates and reports for the media.

She was dangerous.

"Did I forget something at your home?" Drakor leaned against her car.

She started down the steps and he tensed. "Um, no. I was hoping you could help me with something."

Thunder echoed in the distance.

"I'll try, I guess."

"Remember that story I was doing about Mickey's?"

He nodded. Her scent swept over him as she came closer. His body temperature rose, making the humid air feel like a steam bath.

Erin jumped up and sat on the hood of her car. "Ouch!" She slid off again and rubbed the back of her pants. "That was hot."

Drakor drifted away from her. He wanted to rub the spot for her, he wanted to feel it under his bare hands again. *Helta,* he wanted to drive himself deep inside of her…

Erin tucked her hair behind her ear. "Anyway, can we go somewhere and chat? I want to ask you a few questions. How about inside?"

"Not a good idea." More thunder grumbled. Closer this time. "My family is inside and I really don't—"

"Your family?" She touched his arm. "I would love to meet them."

He tried not to flinch, but the contact burned him. She pulled her fingers away and stared at them. "You feel warm again. I know it's hot out here, but…"

Breathlessness engulfed him. His knees weakened. Without thought, he reached out and pulled her hard against him. Her notebook fluttered to the ground. "It's you. Whenever I'm near you…"

Despite the startled look in her eyes, he could feel her body respond to him. He inhaled the sweet scent of her desire. She relaxed against him, pressing her cheek to his neck. "I should stay away from you," she whispered, and he suspected she didn't mean to say it aloud.

He wrapped his arms around her, clenching his hands to stave off his urges. "Great Sun, I should stay away from you, too. But whenever you are near me, I can't help but want to hold you. Touch you."

He wanted to kiss her, to devour her with his lips and tongue. But he remembered the night on her couch, he remembered the pain from not completing the act. He couldn't do that again. He couldn't stop himself again.

A thunder crack made her jump. She backed away from him as the raindrops started. Bending to retrieve her notebook, her gaze rested briefly on his groin. He saw her swallow.

"I-I need to get behind you. To close the windows."

He stepped out of her way and went around to the other side. They rolled up the windows and ran up the steps of the porch, just as the storm crashed overhead.

Erin laughed when they reached the door and the sound poured through him like the heavy rains on the drain spout. An image of being on Elliac and running through the storms flashed in his mind. She laughed like this, and he pulled her into an embrace, allowing the rains to drench them. Then, during their mate-union, they stood under the heat of the sun and pledge themselves to each other. To be with one another only. Forever.

His chest constricted and he reached for the door handle. That vision would never be a reality. Erin was not his *Mharai*.

But his real one—the only one he could ever have—would be lost to him within a few days time.

ℴℴ

The first thing Erin noticed on entering the Victorian this time was the smell. Some type of freshly baked sweet bread made her stomach growl.

Drakor noticed it too. He lifted his nose and sniffed the air, his eyes widening. His sexy mouth twitched and she couldn't understand why he looked annoyed. It smelled heavenly to her.

He ushered her into the formal parlor and pointed to the flowered Victorian couch. "Please, sit. I will return in a moment."

Once he disappeared up the central staircase, Erin opened up her notebook. Scribbling quickly, she added to the notes she made earlier.

Brother rude. Would not make eye contact. Would not shake hands. Face sweating and red, but outside air is warm. Seemed to want to avoid meeting me. Looks very similar to D. Dark hair and eyes, olive skin. Tall, though thinner.

House. All Victoriana artifacts, either accurate reproductions or antiques. No personal items, such as photos, magazines or books. Have not yet seen rooms other than kitchen, foyer, and parlor. Grand, wooden staircase in center of house. D. often disappears up there, presumably to meet with family members.

Need to find shiny spaceship? in backyard.

Heavy footsteps came down the steps and Erin snapped the book shut. She looked over to see an older version of Drakor walking toward her. His face was rounder, fuller, almost puffy looking. Dark circles surrounded his sunken eyes. She knew immediately that he wasn't well.

"You must be Erin Price."

She scrambled to her feet and held out her hand. "Yes, sir. You must be Drakor's father."

He nodded and shook her hand. "Please, sit down again."

She did and he sat next to her on the couch. Drakor chose the cream-colored chair across the table. The thunder roared overhead and lightening flashed behind him out the window, creating a halo affect around those strong, sculpted shoulders. Her pulse quickened just thinking of how they felt under her fingertips.

"I never got your name, sir," she said, holding the closed notebook firmly on her lap.

"Mutazor."

Another strange name. Was that his first or last name. She never did learn the surname for Drakor and Ankra. Somehow it just never seemed like the right time to ask such a question. Especially when they'd never offered it to her. But if she was going to do this article, if she was going to get all the information on these people she could, she had to ask.

"I'm sorry. Is that your given name or your surname?"

He looked at her blankly, then turned to his son. But Drakor could not answer either, he just looked uncomfortable and cleared his throat.

"I am not sure I understand," his father finally admitted.

"Well…most people have a name that was given to them by their parents at birth. That's their first name. Then, they have a family name, which is called a surname. Many people often have a third name, which is between the two. It is called a middle name." Both men blinked at her. She continued, "For instance. My first name is Erin, my surname is Price, and the name in the middle was my great-grandmother's, Oriana."

Drakor gasped but then his face turned stony.

"Ah," his father turned his attention back to her, "so you wonder if we have a name other than the one we've told you already?"

"Yes."

"No. My name is Mutazor. Thus, all my sons will have a single name, but it will end with the 'or' sound. My wife's name is Carolita, so all daughters are named with the 'a' sound at the end."

Erin wished she could take notes, but she'd have to force it in to her memory instead. "Or" sound for males, "a" sound for females.

The wind pushed the rain against the house and she had to shout over it. "You have no family name that all of you share?"

"No, this is our culture. We name according to the custom I just told you."

Now was her chance. Despite the book closed firmly on her lap, she had the opportunity to get as much history as she could here and now.

"That's an interesting method for naming. Where is your culture from?"

Drakor made some sort of groan, but Erin continued to watch his father. He, too, tightened his hands and stiffened his shoulders. He flinched at the crash of thunder. "Far away."

"What country? You know, most European countries have the custom of given names and surnames. I really have yet to hear of a place that doesn't."

"You wouldn't know of it," Mutazor mumbled. He looked away and glared at his son.

"We choose not to speak of it." Drakor's bewitching eyes stared her down, dared her to ask anything further. "We have left that place and do not want to speak of it again."

Erin didn't quite believe him. Their secret loomed above them like a mist. She could clearly see it there but could not grasp a hold of any solid matter.

"Can you at least tell me the name of the country or city? It would be interesting to read up on it on the internet."

Mutazor shook his head. "No. We have told you enough already. Please, excuse me." He stood slowly, in obvious pain, and waved at his son. "Drakor, please come with me upstairs a moment."

Once they got to the top of the stairs, Erin yanked open her book and quickly jotted down notes on the strange naming custom and nervous behaviors of Mutazor and Drakor.

Once done, she shut the book and tapped her fingers, waiting for them to return. She glanced over at the large vase of flowers, the heavy mirror on the wall, the clutter of knick-knacks so common in Victorian times.

She got up to wander the room when the smell of the bread tickled her nostrils again. She had to find it. Maybe she could have just a small piece. She'd been stupid to skip lunch.

Erin followed the scent to the kitchen. She knocked once then pushed the door open. A thin woman with dark hair pulled up into a tight bun looked up at her. Her startled dark eyes widened. She seemed too petrified to say anything.

"I'm Erin Price." She was about to hold out her hand for a handshake, but it was probably futile. "Are you Drakor's mother, Carolita?"

The woman remained immobile, but there was shuffle behind her and then a little girl appeared.

"Hello," Erin said to the angelic face, which of course was adorned with large dark eyes and had dark flowing hair down her shoulders. If nothing else, all the members of this family looked alike.

"I'm Sitora." The little girl smiled.

The woman shushed her and pushed her back.

"I won't hurt you." Erin spotted the sweet bread on the counter. Her stomach growled. "I'm Ankra and Drakor's friend."

Sitora peeked around her mother's skirt and smiled again. Erin crouched down and covered her eyes. Peek-a-boo worked with babies. Certainly it would work with a five-year-old, right?

The child giggled and they played. Erin kept waiting for her mother to pull her away, but she let them continue.

The wind outside splashed the rain against the window. Erin stood at the sound, glad she wasn't out driving in it. A storm like this had taken down the plane that killed her parents. Trees bowed in the wind and the purple sky shifted and blinked with the lightening. The ground looked completely soaked, it might even be flooded soon if this downpour didn't let up.

She looked again at the wet grass and stepped closer to the windows. The trees, the yard, the grass—everywhere dripped with the rain. But in the center, not too far from the back of the house, an enormous spot on the ground looked different from the rest.

This huge, uncovered area didn't glisten or bend with the weight of raindrops. It was dry.

Chapter Eight

Drakor closed the door to his father's room and let out his breath. He knew Erin's questions would arouse suspicion. But Father decided that gleaning information from her—on how to heal their people or even how to locate Alaziri—was enough to justify her seeking information from them. But was she really here to do research a story on the dance club or was she after something far more dangerous?

He went down the steps and headed for the parlor. The room was empty. Her notebook sat on the couch. Dare he take a peek at what she had in there? Drakor glanced around for her and went around the corner to check the bathroom. It was empty too.

Shrugging, he took the opportunity presented to him and flipped open the book. Brief, messily written notes were littered on the pages. He could barely make out some of the words. What he did understand confirmed his fears.

His stomach knotted and his throat tightened. Erin was investigating them.

He heard the kitchen door swing open and footsteps come down the hall. He shut the book and stood, but it was just his mother and Sitora.

"In the kitchen," Mother hissed as she pulled his little sister up the steps.

"I like her." Sitora's eyes beamed.

Drakor waited for them to reach the top of the stairs and then headed for the kitchen. He pushed the door open to find Erin's staring out the back window, with something in her hand.

He went near her, but not too close. He struggled with wanting to send her from his house and wanting to pull her tightly against him. Every ounce of blood pumping through his body wanted her as close to him as possible.

Drakor cleared his throat. She jumped and turned to look at him.

"Oh, I didn't hear you come in the room."

He did not respond, merely stared at her. It was as if he could see through those layers of clothing to the supple skin underneath. His mouth watered for her taste. But his gut clenched at her threat.

Erin shrugged then took a bite of the item in her hand. Her eyes shifted again to the backyard.

Something of interest held her attention and he tried to find it. He saw the tall trees swaying back and forth. The layered, dark sky blowing overhead. Silver sheets of rain angled through the air toward the ground. Blades of grass flattened under the downpour.

Drakor gulped. He knew what she saw. The area under the shuttlecraft remained dry. But did Erin know what she saw? Did she know why the grass remained untouched?

He pulled his gaze from the yard to Erin again. She finished off the item in her hand, looked around for something and then licked her fingers.

"You liked that." He must distract her.

"Very good. What's it called? Maybe I can get the recipe from your mother."

Drakor didn't know what the recipe was. He didn't even know his mother tried to bake something. She must have bought the ingredients yesterday when they took Sitora to town. But why?

"You wanted to talk about Mickey's."

Erin's sky-colored eyes blinked a few times. She bit her lip and he again had the urge to be the one nibbling it. He had to stop that. He had to stop thinking of holding her, of touching her. She was human. She could expose them. No amount of desire for her could change that.

"Yes," she finally answered. "Let's go sit down out front again."

Drakor pushed the door open. "After you."

But as they started down the hallway, the front door swung open. Ankra walked in, followed by Greg.

"Afternoon," Erin's brother said, running his fingers through his wet hair.

Ankra smiled and went to the staircase. "I will return," she said.

Drakor watched her go up, jealousy pounding his heart. He knew she had mated with Greg. He could tell by her behavior, by the way in which her body moved, by the permanent grin on her face.

Drakor sighed and glanced over at Erin. She and Greg were whispering to one another in the far corner.

"Erin!"

Ankra stood at the top of the steps and Erin passed by him to find her. "Yes?"

"Will you come upstairs for a moment?"

Erin went up the steps and Drakor had to look away from her retreating back. He heard the door to his sisters' room shut and so he headed over to Greg.

"Interesting place, here." Erin's brother glanced about the room.

"Yes. I need information from you."

Greg folded his arms across his chest. "Sure, shoot."

"Where does one buy a condom?"

"What?" Greg coughed.

Drakor did not want to use one and probably wouldn't. But if he was ever in the position he found himself Saturday night, he wanted to have one for Erin to see. Then, maybe, he could convince her that he did not need one. He wasn't human, he couldn't pass along any disease to her, much less impregnate her with a child. Of course, he couldn't tell her that.

"You...you want a condom?" Greg's wide eyes and pale complexion showed he had not recovered from his initial surprise. Was it such an odd question?

"Yes. I need the location of where to purchase one."

"Well, at the drugstore or the grocery store." He took a step closer and lowered his voice. "Do you need one for Erin?"

Drakor did not answer what he thought was an obvious reply. "I will accompany you when you go to these stores again."

Greg nodded and turned his gaze out the front windows. The sky color had lightened from a lead gray to the silver of the shuttlecraft. Rain still fell, but had eased considerably. Erin's small vehicle glistened with drops that reflected the sun. Somewhere, behind the house, the clouds must have separated.

"Look." Greg pointed past the vehicles.

A rainbow arched from the dirt road to a spot behind the tallest tree. Drakor's stomach roiled and chills skated down his spine. Rainbows were uncommon on Elliac, despite the frequency of storms and blinding heat from the sun. Thus, their appearance often sparked suspicion and concern. Superstitious people would hide inside their homes until the curving shaft of colors disappeared. Folklore told a rainbow's appearance prophesied a tragedy to the viewer.

Greg leaned closer to the window, moving the heavy curtain aside. "That's so cool."

Drakor took a deep breath. He shouldn't worry. They weren't on Elliac, they were on Earth, where rainbows were viewed with awe and excitement.

But if that were the case, then why was dread snaking its way into his heart?

ಸಿಂ

Erin couldn't stop tickling Sitora. The little girl giggled until she nearly fell off her bed. It seemed strange to have a grown woman like Ankra sharing a room with such a small child, but neither sister seemed to mind.

As was typical in the rest of the house, the bedroom looked as if it were torn out of a Victorian Home magazine. An ornately carved mantle, similar to the one in the parlor, covered an unused fireplace. Busy wallpaper and border ran around the room, while the hardwood floors were covered with several throw rugs. Ankra and Sitora each had their own four-poster bed roofed with a green canopy.

This house was like a dream or a bed and breakfast or a museum. Erin still couldn't understand why Drakor and his family lived here, nor how this house was built. Tomorrow, she would have to verify the land and tax recordation.

"Maybe I should check on Greg," Ankra said. She gave her sister a stern look and then opened the bedroom door. "I'll be back up in a moment."

Once Ankra was gone Sitora rushed over to Erin and plopped down on the floor next to her. In a low voice, she asked, "Why do you use a kitchen?"

"What?"

"The room downstairs with the sink and the stove. Do you use it a lot? What can you make in there?"

Erin cocked her head. She didn't understand Sitora's questions. "Your mother just made some delicious bread in there, using the oven. Doesn't she cook and bake for all of you?"

"Mother just wanted to try it. She's never used one before."

Erin just didn't understand why these people were so clueless with such a basic necessity of life. If they didn't know how to use a kitchen, did that mean they were so wealthy at one time that a servant did all the work?

Since she couldn't come with a useful response, Erin decided more tickling was in order. She ran her fingers along Sitora's neck and the girl squealed and scooted away. They scrambled along the floor after each other, until Sitora crawled under her bed. Erin flattened onto her stomach to go after her.

But instead of reaching her target, her gaze landed on something else. Under the chest of drawers, she saw a small flat screen. It looked like the PDA

Greg carried, but about half the size. She couldn't see any buttons on it anywhere, in fact, it appeared to be nothing but the screen itself.

Her reporting instinct kicked into high gear. Was it broken? Were there more pieces to it? More importantly, did it hold information that could tell her about this odd family?

Erin stretched her hand toward it, but it was so far back toward the wall she couldn't get it.

"You can't get me!" Sitora taunted in her accented voice.

Erin reached out for the small screen again. If she only had a few more inches…just two or three…

The door of the room slammed shut and Erin yanked her arm back.

"They are leaving!"

Erin got to her feet and faced Ankra. "Who's leaving?"

"Greg and Drakor. My brother wants something at a store and your brother is taking him."

"Oh." Erin had to admit she was a little disappointed. She hardly got five minutes with Drakor since she got here and she certainly never had a moment to discuss Mickey's. Not that it really mattered.

Oh damn! She left her notebook down there!

Erin ran past Ankra and burst out of the room. She took the steps two at a time and got to the bottom just as the guys were heading out the door.

"Hey, did you see the rainbow outside?" Greg said to her, pulling his keys out of his pocket.

"No." She turned to look out the window in the parlor room, but a hand clamped on her arm.

"Don't."

Erin's gaze fell on Drakor. His face had the usual sheen and ruddiness, but his eyes stopped her with their fear. She wanted to ask him why he cared about something like that, but she couldn't. Something about the way he held her seeped concern under her skin.

She couldn't understand how a rainbow could cause her harm, but it mattered to him and it just didn't seem worth debating.

"Okay," she whispered. "I won't look."

He relaxed. "Perhaps we will work on your story another day."

Her story? Oh, he meant the one about Mickey's. "Of course, another time. I'd really appreciate your help."

Drakor let go of her arm and followed Greg outside. Once the door clicked shut, Erin raced to the couch and snatched her notebook.

How could she be so stupid? It had been sitting here since she went to the kitchen for the bread. Damn, what if Drakor looked through it? If he saw the notes on himself he may not want to see her anymore. It didn't seem that way, not when he just mentioned helping her with her story another day. It didn't seem like he read through it at all.

Clutching the notebook to her side, Erin headed back up the steps to say good-bye to Ankra and Sitora. The door to their room was closed. She went to knock on it when one down the hall opened.

Erin looked over to see Brundor ambling toward the stairs. He stopped when he saw her standing there. He glanced around and then came over to her.

"Where is my brother?" His voice was low, edgy.

She noticed sweat collecting on his brow and color blooming on his cheeks. His dark eyes bore down on hers, hot and desperate.

Erin's stomach pitched, her heart raced. But she'd be damned if she was going to let this guy see her fear. "He went out. I was just going in to see your sisters."

Brundor closed the gap between them. She was no comparison to his tall, lanky frame, though she knew enough evasive moves to bring him to his knees.

"They can't keep me locked away forever."

His hot breath on her face brought the taste of bile up her throat. He reached out to her face and Erin squeezed her eyes shut, ready to yell the moment he touched her. She wouldn't cause a scene if it wasn't necessary. No, she had too much invested in this family now to see it all shot to hell with hysterics.

But nothing happened other than Brundor's triumphant laugh echoing in her ears.

⁗⁗⁗

"You do have cash with you, right?"

Drakor patted his pants pocket. He had plenty of human money. Father had seen to it that they each had enough to purchase whatever was necessary. Long ago Elliacians had given up physical money. All transactions were electronic. Most children had never seen a coin or paper note before.

They entered the drugstore and the aisles of clutter and flashy packaging startled Drakor. Where were the electronic monitors to display the items? The keypads to place an order and compute the financial transactions?

He shook his head and followed Greg down an aisle. All items to his left looked like objects for babies. Diapers, bibs, pacifiers, toys, shampoos. He stopped and stared at the smiling baby on the food jar. For a moment, Drakor's throat tightened and his chest ached. It seemed a child would not be in his future.

"Come on," Greg called from the next aisle over. "They're down this way."

Drakor caught up with him, pushing away the thoughts of children and home.

"Mr. Price?"

A short male approached them. Though clearly an adult, he looked several Earth years younger and his nervousness proved it. Brown eyes darted to Greg and then to his watch. A light-eyed female came up to him and laced her arm through his. She looked familiar, like someone he met recently.

"Jay?" Greg went over to the stranger and shook his hand. "A surprise to catch you out here. And who's this lovely lady?"

The red-haired female smiled and chewed something in her mouth.

"This is Renee, my girlfriend."

She stuck out her hand and Greg shook it. "Nice to meet you."

The short male nodded and licked his lips. "This is my boss, Mr. Price."

Greg turned and waved him over. "This is a friend of mine, Drakor." He lowered his voice. "I never did get your last name."

Not that again. He ignored the comment and nodded, saying nothing.

Greg clapped the male on the shoulder. "Jay, here, is the one I was telling you about. He's a bright guy."

Jay gave a half-smile that did not reach his eyes. A few beads of sweat formed on his forehead. "Oh, well, we'll see. Once the patent comes through…"

"Don't be so modest." Greg laughed. "Your idea is absolutely brilliant. I wish I'd hired you three years ago. We'll get that patent and then you'll have a mighty large bonus." He turned to the female. "I'm sure you'd be happy about that."

She winked and continued to chew the thing between her teeth. The sound tickled Drakor's eardrum and he suddenly remembered who she reminded him of—that female from the dance club. The one that Erin didn't like. This wasn't the same person, but they were very much alike.

"So you took the afternoon off?" Greg asked.

Jay squirmed and wiped the sweat off his forehead. "I-I had some things to do today. You weren't in the office to check with, so Cindy told me to just go."

"Hey, Jay, it's not a problem. I blew off the day myself. We'll get back in the groove tomorrow."

Jay nodded. "Yeah, I've got some other stuff to show you when we get back to the office."

Greg tapped Drakor's shoulder and whispered, "All the way at the end of the aisle. Take your time. I need to chat with Jay for a few minutes."

Drakor walked away from the trio. He scanned the shelves as he went by. Pain relievers, medicines, vitamins. One bottle caught his attention. It read, *for stronger bones.*

He picked up the container and read the label. Two of its ingredients, Calcium and Vitamin D, aided in keeping bones healthy and strong. Was this the same medicines the Researchers developed on Elliac?

He needed to bring this back. If their mission could easily be solved by these pills, then they could return home quickly. Father could be reevaluated and examined by a healer.

Drakor followed the aisle to the end. Many colorful condom boxes vied for his purchase. Each had a different name and some unique quality about them, but they all shared the same description. *If used properly, will help reduce the risk of unwanted pregnancies and catching or spreading HIV infection (AIDS) and many other sexually transmitted diseases.*

Which one of these did Erin fear? Other than the bone crippling disease on Elliac, all other infections and viruses had been eradicated. He could not pass anything on to her. And he certainly didn't believe he could get her pregnant. Not only would she have to be Elliacian for that to happen, she'd have to be his *Mharai.*

He could not be convinced that Erin Price was his chosen mate just because her middle name had both of his parents' lineage name sounds in it, or that he craved no other female, or that he felt a mystical sense of contentment when he touched her. She was human. And no Elliacian had found their mate anywhere but home.

Drakor sighed and yanked a small box off the hook. It didn't matter which one he bought. When he could get close enough to her again, when he could complete his duty for this mission, when he could feel the satisfaction his body yearned for, he would *not* be using one of these protective sheaths.

He would just have to find a way to fool her.

Chapter Nine

"I'll have a Coke."

"You sure you don't want a beer?"

Erin slid Greg a glare. The past few days had been excruciating and as much as she would like to relax, she couldn't afford the luxury. Time was ticking away and her goals and dreams were slipping away with it.

Once Drakor's brother had spun away from her, mumbling something about proving his strength, Erin had not been back to the house. Not that she was afraid to go, she just never had a good enough excuse.

"A Coke, thanks," she told the waiter. He shrugged and left the table.

Greg closed his menu and shoved it next to the ketchup and BBQ sauce. "This meeting is probably a waste of time, you know."

The dim hum of voices droned around them. Thank God she hadn't picked a more kid-friendly place. She couldn't handle loud squealing and crying right now.

"Humor me, will you?"

Erin took out her notebook and opened it to an empty page. Not that there were so many pages full of notes. She'd spent the last several days sketching out theories and angles to base her story on. But without any hard evidence what did she have but mere speculation?

"Just tell me anything odd Ankra might have said or done, okay?"

Greg sighed. He leaned back and laced his fingers behind his head. "Let's see…she talked about her father and how he was sick."

"How is that strange?"

He shot her an annoyed look. "Listen, I'm just going to tell you the things she said and did. You can figure out whether it means something or not."

"Okay, okay." Erin took the cap off her pen and started to scribble notes as he talked.

"She said something about friends not being able to walk and being deformed. I didn't really get that part and she didn't elaborate."

The smell of onion soup made Erin's stomach growl. When was that waiter coming back to take their order?

"So I've got that her dad is ill, which I noticed myself, and people she knows can't walk and are deformed. Did she say how they were deformed? Like skin and facial problems, humps on their backs, what?"

He sniffed the air. "Mmm, something smells good. Like I said, she didn't elaborate and I didn't ask." He leaned forward and stared at her from across the table. "I've had more important things on my mind when I've spent time with her."

Erin rolled her eyes. "Yes, screwing her. But you've gone out with her to Blackrock Falls, you've taken her to lunch. So don't give me that line that you spent all your time in bed with her."

The waiter arrived with their drinks. Once they gave him the dinner order and he disappeared, Greg took several swallows of his beer. Erin watched him, waiting patiently for the alcohol to loosen him up. He'd be much more willing to help out once the beer softened his edges.

When about half the bottle was gone, Erin resumed her questions. "So what did Ankra think of the falls? Of the restaurant you took her to?"

"Well, she was really worried about being outside so much. I asked her if she put on sunscreen and she didn't know what it was. I stopped off at the drugstore and bought some for her. I explained what it was and that it would protect her skin from the sun."

"Did she feel better afterward?"

He shrugged. "I dunno, but her skin felt real good right then."

"Come on, Greg. Stay focused, will you? You're like a damn horny rabbit."

He licked his lips. "Where's my carrot?"

Erin took several sips of her Coke. It was either that or kill him. "Did she like seeing the falls? Once you put the lotion on her?"

"Said she'd never seen one before. Said they have rivers and lakes and mountains and stuff, but she doesn't travel much where she's from."

Erin's heart kicked up a notch. "Did she say where she's from?"

Greg gulped more beer. "Nope. Just kept saying that the earth was a fascinating place."

"What's that supposed to mean?" She wrote the statement in her book.

"Dunno."

"Anything else?"

"Not really."

She tucked her hair behind her ear and took another sip of her Coke. "Anything at all?"

He raised an eyebrow. "To me, the weirdest thing is that she got very upset when I put on the condom."

"Oh, Greg …"

"You said 'anything,' Erin, so I'm telling you something. Write it down."

"I don't want notes on your sex life."

"It's strange. You should realize that."

How well she did realize it. Her night with Drakor ended because he didn't have one to put on. Hell, he didn't even know what it was. "Maybe she just didn't realize what it was, Greg."

"Well, that's odd too, isn't it?"

Oh, yeah… "But maybe she's on the Pill and so she wasn't worried about you getting her pregnant. Or maybe she just doesn't like the way they feel. Can we stop talking about this now?"

He shook his head. "I don't buy it. Not with the hell she was raising over it."

"So, did you give in to her?"

"Hell, no. I don't care what she says about only being able to get pregnant when she chose to, I'm not risking it. There's no way I'm supporting a baby right now."

Erin looked up from her notes. "Did she say she could get pregnant when she chose to?"

"Something like that."

Could Ankra really control her biological functions? No. She must have been referring to contraceptive usage. Either she was on the Pill or used an IUD or diaphragm. That must have been what she meant.

Greg drained his beer. "Not to change the subject, but you do know that her brother really likes you."

"What makes you say that?" She bit her lip, hoping to stop the erratic heartbeat slamming in her ears.

He gave her a grin. "Men can tell these things. Have you seen him recently?"

"As if it's your business, no, I haven't. Not since that day you took him to the store. I haven't been back over there."

But she needed to. She never did have that talk with Drakor about Mickey's. Not that she gave a damn about the dance club, but she did need information from him. Or another chance to look around the house. Maybe she could get a hold of that tiny PDA-looking thing under the dresser.

Greg lifted his eyebrows. "I'll bet he's anxious to see you. You should go back over there."

"What's up? What did he tell you?" She narrowed her eyes. "Where did you go that day?"

He waved the waiter over. "Another beer." He turned back to her. "Drakor needed some things at the store and he needed a ride."

"So? What is the big deal? What are you gushing on about?"

"Trust me. If he's anything like his sister, you won't be sorry."

"You're drunk."

As much as she wanted to be disgusted at his suggestions, Erin couldn't help the quiver that tickled her stomach. She remembered all too well the skill of Drakor's fingers and tongue. The weight of his body and the firmness of his hard muscles. Hell, she hadn't thought of much else since last Saturday night. Already shivers danced under her skin, tickling her nipples and warming her belly.

"I'm not drunk. I just know when a man is hot for a woman."

She shook her head and sighed. "Oh, that's great. So he wants to screw me. That doesn't necessarily mean he likes me."

"Yeah, he's a tricky one, but I think there's more to it than that. I think you should go back over there."

Erin put the cap back on her pen. She knew she wouldn't get too much more out of her brother tonight. "Even if I did go back there, we couldn't do very much in that house with his whole family there, could we?"

Greg laughed, his blond hair falling into his eyes. "So just pick him up and take him back to your place."

"What's the matter with you? You think just because you have a new girlfriend, I have to have a boyfriend?" She closed the notebook and shoved it into her overstuffed bag.

Greg leaned across the table and grabbed her wrist. "Erin, you need to get laid more than any person I know."

She put her nose in the air and yanked her arm away. "I have a story to do. If I go back over there it's to look for evidence."

"Evidence of what?"

She leveled her gaze at him. "Something out of *Star Trek*. Like a spaceship, perhaps?"

೫つೞ

"Is this what the Researchers gave you to take?"

Drakor handed the bottle to his father, who stretched across the bed with a cloth on his forehead. Between the vomiting and the headaches, he grew more ill with each passing day. Father hadn't been well enough to even speak to him for the last three.

"Perhaps. They have different names here on Earth." Father squinted at the words. "Builds and maintains strong bones."

"So it seems that humans need to have help with this sort of thing too."

"Yes. But I wonder if their dosage is the same. And since it was on the shelf at a local store, I'm guessing it must be optional." He lay back again after the effort of speaking.

"Probably because they still carry the gene to process it."

"Yes, probably so." Father took the cloth and wiped it over his face. "Will you get your mother for me?"

"Where is she?"

"In with your sisters."

Drakor turned to go. It was difficult to see his father this way. Wasted and swollen at the same time. His life robbed by the very same drugs supposed to make him healthy. If only they could finish this mission and get back to Elliac. Perhaps the Researchers would discontinue Father's medicines. Perhaps Father would listen to them.

"Drakor?"

"Yes?"

"After you get your mother, go in and speak with Brundor."

His chest tightened. "Why?"

"He and I talked and he wants to see you."

Drakor sighed and went to get his mother. Then, he entered the room he shared with Brundor. The lights were off and the room quiet. He could hear a few crickets singing in the distance outside, but nothing else in the room save for Brundor's breathing.

"Are you awake?"

"Yes. Come in and shut the door."

Drakor pushed the door closed and leaned against a mahogany pole on his four-poster bed. He folded his arms over his chest.

"I have convinced Father to let me go out."

"It's a mistake."

"Why won't you believe that I can control myself? You never believe me." In the gray shadows of the room, Drakor could see Brundor thrust his arm in the air. "Father gave me this."

"You have a watch. Does it tell you the Earth time?"

"Don't know. Don't care. All I know is that it permits me to leave this house."

It was a fool's mechanism. Something they used during the Crossing to trick the mind into believing its power. If Brundor believed the watch would give him control, it very well could. "Are you going to leave it on when you come near females?"

"I can control myself around them, you know. I don't even have to have this watch."

"You can't possibly have the strength it takes to control your urges. Especially with your impatience."

Brundor sat up, his back to the open window. "I knew you wouldn't believe me. Ask your girlfriend."

"What did you do to her?" Drakor's stomach clenched. A surge of protectiveness rippled through him, startling him, and he had to grip the pole to hold himself back.

"I didn't do anything. That's my point."

Drakor's breathing increased to a pant. Adrenaline galloped through his veins. "Tell me what happened, Brundor."

"The other day you left and I saw her at the top of the stairs alone."

"And…" Control. He must retain control.

Brundor shrugged. "I came up to her. I didn't touch her, don't worry. But I wanted to prove to myself and to you and Father that I could be near an Earth female and not touch them."

"I would have killed you." Why did he just say that?

"I know you'd kill to defend your *Mharai*. I'm not stupid."

"She's not my *Mharai*." Drakor forced the words from his lips. But his body fought his statement. He could barely contain the impulse to strike his own brother. Mates protected each other without hesitation on Elliac; it was as natural to them as breathing.

Brundor relaxed again on his pillow. "Go on deceiving yourself. Every sign there is points to her. But it sure is some rotten luck."

Drakor sucked in a deep breath. "The Fates would not have done that. If I am to have a *Mharai*, she is waiting for me on Elliac."

"Okay, sure. So, when will you take me to that dancing club you and Ankra went to?"

"What? I'm not going to…" He let the words die away when a familiar sound rumbled in his eardrums.

Drakor took a step closer to Brundor's bed, closer to the window. He saw a flash of dual lights and then they darkened. But the sound of the motor did not die away. He squinted and saw the vehicle swerve over toward the line of trees, rolling under their cover of darkness. Then, the hum ceased.

"What are you looking at?"

"It's nothing." But it was something.

"Well, can I go?"

"Yes, fine. We'll discuss it later." He turned away from the window and headed for the door. "I just remembered that I have a report to write up. Don't wait up for me."

Brundor chuckled. "Better you than me."

Drakor slipped out the door and headed for the staircase. But his mother called to him.

"Fetch your father a glass of that milk."

He stopped and turned to face her, his eyes hard. "What is milk, where would I find it, and why does Father need it?"

The lines around her eyes deepened. She wrung her hands. "Drakor, please. We are doing all that we can to find a cure for the illness on Elliac and for your father."

"He should stop taking the drugs. That might work better than Earth food. Haven't our bodies moved beyond processing nutrients through our mouths? Won't eating and drinking make him worse?"

She blinked several times and he was surprised to see tears in her eyes. "I believe he may be dying. He asks for the milk. It's a jug of white liquid in the cold appliance with the door. Will you get it for him?"

Drakor nodded, his throat closing. He proceeded downstairs to the kitchen. Why did his father want to go backward in technology instead of forward? Humans were so far behind in commerce, education, science, health. Elliacians died from only a handful of causes: prolonged exposure to the sun, old age, suicide from the embarrassing bone deformities, and the death of a *Mharai*. Though the latter stemmed from an ancient custom and a false belief that mates could not survive alone, most Elliacians continued with the practice.

Drakor opened the door on the tall appliance and found the white jug of liquid. He filled a glass with the creamy sustenance and then his eyes caught the flash of a beam in the backyard.

He went closer to the window and watched again. There. A small circle of light flickered through the trees.

Drakor brought the drink up to his parents' room and then, without a word, raced outside to follow the intruder.

The warm night air enveloped him as he stole into the woods. His eyes could see better in the dark than a human's and the three-quarter moon provided ample glow to lead his way. He crept up behind the person until he was nearly at the creek.

It was definitely Erin. He could see the outline of her curved legs and the swing of her chopped hair. She held something small in her hand, turned it over a few times, and then dropped it into her bag. She turned to look behind her and he took a few steps closer.

"Erin."

She jumped at the sound of his voice. "Oh, my God! Drakor, is that you?"

"Yes." He moved closer still. His blood pulsed. Awareness soared. "Did you lose something?"

"Um...yes, a few days ago. I didn't see it out front and so I thought an animal might have brought it in the woods."

He didn't believe her. At the moment, it didn't matter.

Erin patted her bag. "I guess I should be going. I was trying not to bother anyone."

Drakor stood just a step away from her. Her scent crashed through him, bringing his arousal to full attention. "We never discussed the dancing club. You said you needed to talk with me for the article."

She tucked a few strands of hair behind her ears. "Oh, um, sure. I can come over in the morning or something."

Tonight. He needed to be with her tonight. Helplessness at his father's illness, the lack of information on Alaziri, the aching knowledge of his birth anniversary only a few days away...Great Sun, he needed her warmth right now.

Drakor cupped Erin's jaw with his hands. "Perhaps we can go back to your home. Now."

Erin blinked up at him and licked her lips. "Um-I..."

He rubbed his thumb over chin, paying no heed to the burn on his skin. "Erin, do you need me or not?"

A shadow moved across her face. She stared at him without words, her gaze almost a question. But then she took a deep breath. "Yes. I need you. Let's go."

Chapter Ten

"Drakor, wait!"

They both turned to see Ankra running toward the car. She had a small bag in her hand.

He stopped but did not turn, his body tense.

His sister pulled him away and Erin leaned against her car door. She didn't know what Ankra was after but it was obvious what Drakor wanted from her tonight.

His hand on her face, his intense eyes staring at her under the moonlight. Her traitorous body clamored for him. Having him over again was a huge mistake. And yet, like she thought before, it was just one night. Her three years of celibacy would be over. It's not like she was going to give up her story, her career, her future over one night in bed with Drakor.

Erin reached into her bag. Her fingers moved aside the papers and pens and closed around the small object she found near the creek. She'd probably would have never seen it if her flashlight hadn't reflected off its casing.

Small and rectangular, its surface felt slightly bumpy and somewhat plastic-like. There could be a light bulb inside, but what would this be used for?

Drakor came up before her and she quickly dropped the item as if she'd been caught putting on her mom's lipstick.

"Ankra wishes to see your brother tonight." An edge sliced through the words.

She looked at them both, surprised. "Does he know she's coming over?"

Ankra shook her head. She appeared ready to weep.

"I'm sure he won't mind." Erin moved out of the way and opened the door for her.

They rode to Greg's house in silence, though Erin couldn't shake the feeling that Ankra was anxious and upset and Drakor was annoyed. But she didn't dare ask either of them any questions.

The street was quiet and the houses dark when Erin pulled before Greg's door. Good thing she had an extra key to his house since she doubted their knocking would wake him.

The three of them slipped inside the foyer and Erin knocked on one of the walls. "Greg!"

No answer.

She took a few steps up the staircase and knocked again. "Greg, wake up. I have a surprise for you."

Still nothing.

"We'll be down in a minute," she said to them and went up to the top of the steps.

Erin banged on his bedroom door. "Greg. It's Erin, wake up."

She pressed her ear to the door and waited. Damn, he could sleep through the implosion of his own house. She didn't want to go in his room. What if he slept naked? Ugh. But since he wasn't answering her, she didn't have a choice.

She opened the door and snuck inside the dark room. His loud breathing told her he still slept and she saw him stretched out on the bed, luckily under covers.

"Greg!" she whispered, not wanting to startle him.

He shifted on the bed but didn't wake. Erin went next to the bed and kicked the mattress. "Damn it, Gregory Price, wake up!"

"Huh?" He blinked at her, reached for something under his pillow and sat up. "Get out, whoever you are!"

Erin's heart lurched into her throat and she backed up to the wall. "Is-is that a gun?"

He lowered his arm. "Erin, is that you?"

"Yes. Why-why do you have a gun?"

"Oh shit." He shoved it back under the pillow. "I was hoping you'd never see that." He raised his knees and leaned his elbows on them. "What are you doing here, Erin?"

She swallowed, her heart still slamming in her ears. "First tell me why you have that damn gun."

Greg brushed hair out of his eyes and sighed. "A few days ago there was a break-in at the office."

"What?"

"Not too much was taken. It just looked like some files were gone through and one or two desks had their locks picked open."

Erin let out the breath she was holding. "Why didn't you tell me before? We even had dinner together and you didn't mention it."

"I didn't want you to get all worried about it."

"So what's the gun for?"

She saw him shrug a shoulder. "I thought that if they were looking for something at my business, they might come to my house next."

"Were you going to shoot them?"

"Nah. Just scare them off." He leaned over and glanced at the clock. "Hell, Erin, it's almost midnight. What are you doing here?"

She sighed. "I was at Drakor's place, snooping through the woods for some evidence—"

"Of the spaceship?"

"Of whatever I could find." She reached into her bag and pulled out the object. "I did find this." She handed it to him.

"Turn on the light, will you? I can't see shit in the dark."

Erin flipped on the light on his bedside, praying he had clothes on under the sheets. Thankfully, she saw cloth at his waist. He must sleep in his underwear.

"It looks like a light of some sort." He flipped it over in his hand.

"That's what I thought. What do you think it belongs to?"

"I don't know." Greg tried to put his fingernail along the edges. "There aren't creases or cracks. How does this thing open?"

"I haven't had much time to look at it."

"Is this why you came here and woke me up?" He looked up at her. "To show me this?"

"No." She took the light from him and stuffed back into the purse. "Drakor saw me out there and asked me if I wanted to talk about my story—"

"Your story? The one you're doing on him?"

"No. The one I made up about Mickey's. I needed an excuse to talk to him and go over there, remember?"

"Okay. So, why are you here?"

"Well, as he and I were leaving—"

"He wanted to work on the story with you tonight? In the middle of the night?"

Erin lifted her chin. "That's what he said."

Greg grinned. "That's not what he meant."

Hell, she knew that. It hadn't been so long that she would forget what a man's heated gaze or urgent caress meant. It was probably why he was so annoyed with his sister for coming along and delaying the moment.

"Anyway, as he and I were getting in the car, Ankra came running out to us."

"Ankra?" He sat up straighter.

Erin yawned. She was getting sleepy. Drakor might not be getting what he came for. "Yes, she said she needed to come see you. She looked upset."

"Why?"

"I don't know. But she's waiting with Drakor downstairs."

"They're here?"

She nodded. "Get dressed, will you?"

Erin headed for the door and Greg jumped out of the bed. He slipped on a pair of shorts he grabbed off the dresser and followed her down the stairs.

In the living room, they found Ankra huddled on a corner of the couch and Drakor standing next to the window, staring out at the moon.

"What's going on?" Greg asked.

Ankra leaped from the couch and ran over to him. She fell against his bare chest. Startled, Greg wrapped his arms around her back and held her.

"What's the matter?"

She wouldn't answer.

"Drakor," Greg turned to Ankra's brother. "Why is she crying?"

"I do not know." He didn't turn to look at them but Erin could see the tenseness in his shoulders. "She will not tell me."

"I cannot," his sister moaned. "Father will not let me."

Drakor swung around and glared at her, his eyes narrow and fierce. "Father is keeping something from me."

Ankra whimpered and squeezed her eyes closed.

Drakor stormed over to where she stood with Greg. "I am responsible if something happens to him. He cannot keep things from me."

She opened her eyes and looked at him. "He…he says you would not understand. That you refuse to believe."

Drakor's whole body stiffened and his features hardened in rage. "What isn't he telling me, Ankra? I will not leave you here alone until you tell me."

She sniffled and finally nodded.

Drakor took a hold of her arm and pulled her from Greg's embrace. "I need a private room."

"Downstairs," Erin suggested. "There is an office with a door."

He lifted his gaze to hers. Never before had she seen such a raw combination of anger, disappointment, and yearning. He then disappeared down the steps with his sister.

"What in the world was that all about?" Greg looked at her.

Erin shrugged. "I don't know, but they certainly get stranger and stranger, don't they?"

"You ain't kidding."

ഇ)രു

Drakor pushed the door closed behind them until he heard it latch. "Tell me, Ankra." He turned to glower at her.

She sat in the chair before the human's computer and crossed her arms over one another. "We cannot return to Elliac until the mission is complete."

"I know that."

She looked away from him. "It isn't complete yet."

Drakor shifted and glanced around the room, seeing nothing but white walls and shelves of books. "I need to find Alaziri, I promised his family—"

"No." Ankra drew her feet up on the chair and put her chin on her knees. "I'm not referring to you. I'm talking about me."

Drakor's stomach clenched. A muscle ticked on his jaw. "I found those capsules at the drugstore. They should be enough to take back to the Researchers."

"It takes more than capsules," she said against her legs.

"Ankra, you must explain what Father didn't want me to know."

She lifted her colorless eyes to him. "You've paid no attention. On Elliac or here. You and Brundor are so concerned about your needs, about finding a *Mharai* to satisfy yourself with that you have barely an idea of what it is like for those crippled at home."

He crossed his arms. "I do see how they suffer."

"You didn't want us to take this mission. After all, it got in the way of your search for a *Mharai*. Only when you realized we could give Alaziri the proper burial did you concede to come along."

Drakor felt heat rise to his face. "The anniversary of my birth is only a short time away. If I have not found her by then I will be forever alone. How would you feel in my place?"

Ankra lifted her chin. "I could sacrifice myself and my happiness if it meant healing others."

"How very noble of you, sister. And how does this fit into Father's secret?"

Her gaze slid away from his again. "As I said, those capsules you found will not be enough to save Elliacians. They need more, something stronger, something that is forever a part of them."

"Which is?"

"They need the working gene."

Drakor laughed. "And how did the Researchers suppose we bring back DNA? Are we to take the blood of these humans? To kidnap a human and bring them with us?"

She squirmed and pushed the chair away from him. Her discomfort caused the gnawing anxiety to swirl in his gut.

"Tell me, Ankra. These word games are only angering me."

"I…" she cleared her throat, "I am to bring back the genes within me."

"How would you?" But even as he said the words, the knowledge slammed into his brain like a hurtling comet. An offspring. Her mission consisted not just of mating with a human male, but to become pregnant by him.

Drakor turned and leaned his arm against a metal cabinet. "No." He leaned his head on his forearm. "Tell me it isn't possible."

"We don't know if it is possible or not. But we must try." Ankra got up from the chair and stood next to him. "How else can we be sure to have the genetic material?"

"But-but your *Mharai?*"

She shrugged. "Who knows if I have one and if I do, hopefully he will understand that what I did was for the good of Elliac."

Drakor's throat tightened, his pulse pounded. "And you are here now because you have not accomplished this yet?"

"Correct." She sighed. "Though I continue to try."

"It is the condoms?"

"He refuses to mate without one."

Drakor swept passed her and sank into the chair. "Humans resist unwanted pregnancies and venereal diseases. They have not evolved the way we have."

"I know, but it is prolonging our stay." She blinked and tears filled her eyes. "Father's health is failing and he will not leave Earth until this is done."

"So he will sacrifice his life, as well."

Ankra wiped at a tear. "This mission is so important. He took it as a great honor. He hoped you would feel the same."

Drakor closed his eyes. How could he be the same as his father? Humans were light years behind them in technology. How could such a culture provide them with the missing link they so desperately needed?

Even if Erin did not discover their true identities, someone else would. The government would come and entrap them or kill them, just as they may have killed Alaziri. Every moment on this planet was a risk to their lives. Humans feared the unknown. They would not understand.

No. Drakor would not have permitted his family to make this sacrifice, honor or not. "I cannot agree that this is the right way."

Ankra sighed. "That is precisely the reason Father did not want to tell you."

He looked up at her. "Greg is human and you are not."

"How do you know when or where our bloodlines have separated? Perhaps we aren't so different from them."

"He isn't your *Mharai*. How could he get you with child?"

"Perhaps with humans it doesn't matter. After all, they choose their own mate on Earth."

"So how will you accomplish this when you have thus far been unsuccessful?"

She flipped her hair over her shoulder and gave a small smile. "I have been reading about human female reproduction. I will lie to him and tell him that the time of my conceptual abilities have well passed, so the condom is not necessary."

"What is the human female time of conception?"

"Somewhere around four days."

The answer cheered him. Hopefully he would discover that this would not be Erin's fertile time and he would not have to fool her not to use the condom. Drakor still did not believe he could get her pregnant, no matter what his sister, his father, or the Researchers said.

"Why do you lust after Erin if she is not your *Mharai*? You have clearly come tonight to mate with her."

"I do not know the answer."

But he could not turn back now. He wanted to satisfy the desperate cravings they started last week. He wanted to feel the serenity their intimacy gave him. It could very well be the last time he would ever feel desire or inner peace.

He needed deliverance, distraction, desire.

Drakor stood and went to the door.

Ankra quietly cleared her throat. "She is not like some of the other females on this planet who can mate without giving something of themselves."

He paused, his fingers on the knob.

"Erin will be heartbroken when you are gone from here."

Drakor clenched his jaw. An uncomfortable feeling climbed his throat. "You cannot possibly know this."

"I am a female, Drakor. I understand her. I see it in her eyes. As I have said, we are really not very different from humans. It is only you who fail to believe."

He forced a laugh and shook his head. "This is nonsense. There are countless differences—"

She put her hand on his arm. "You scoff at the humans and you hold yourself apart from the Elliacians. Where do you belong, Drakor? Who *do* you hold allegiance to?"

Her words slashed through his heart. He twisted the door handle and straightened. "Myself." He headed back up the stairs.

Chapter Eleven

Erin didn't know what to expect. When he first mentioned coming back here his steamy gaze sent her heart fluttering, her knees weakening. But now, after that brief visit to Greg's house, Drakor's mood had abruptly shifted.

He still had that ever-present sheen on his forehead and color on his ruddy cheeks. But his dark eyes stared at her with more than longing. He seemed confused, uncertain, almost despondent. What had he and Ankra talked about?

Erin opened the door to her apartment. Maybe she should ask him if he was all right or if he'd rather she take him home. But when the door closed behind them, Drakor ensnared her waist with his arm and yanked her against him. His warm breath sent shivers down her spine.

Her heart pounded beneath her breasts. Her nipples ached for his tongue.

He kissed the outside of her ear and she closed her eyes.

Was she ready for this? Last week she pushed aside her caution to use Drakor, to use sex to ply secrets from his lips. But now she'd learned more—not enough—but more. And she had to use any means necessary to get this piece nailed.

One night wasn't going to ruin her career again. She just had to separate feeling from, well, feeling. Emotions from sensations.

But she wasn't quite ready yet. It was too soon. She hadn't even put down her purse. Plus, she needed chocolate. Big time.

Erin broke free of his well-muscled arm and headed straight for the kitchen. Inside the fridge she pushed aside an old bag of salad, a half-eaten yogurt, and leftovers from the dinner with Greg. Ah, there it was.

Erin snatched the can, shut the fridge door, and grabbed a spoon from the drawer.

She turned to find Drakor leaning against the doorway, his powerful arms folded across that luscious chest, and a predatory glint in his midnight eyes. She held out the can. "Frosting?"

He shook his head. "What is that strange creature?"

She followed his gaze. "That's Shellbert. He's my hermit crab."

His face remained blank.

"I know, not much of a pet, but it's all I got the time and energy for." Erin pointed to a chair with the spoon. "Have a seat."

Drakor pulled his gaze from the plastic container and sat. His wild, seductive stare unnerved her. Butterflies danced in her tummy. Awareness swirled deep between her legs. She flipped off the top of the milk chocolate frosting and carved out a heaping chunk.

Erin dropped into the chair next to him and licked a taste off the spoon. "Mmmmmm…this really is good. You should try it."

Drakor cleared his throat. "No, thank you."

"You've had frosting before, haven't you?"

"Erin, I need to know if my brother caused you any harm."

Well, that sure was a change of subject. "Harm? Um, no, but he did spook me a little."

He sat up straighter and his eyes hardened. A vein pulsed on his forehead. "Tell me what transpired."

"He saw me in the hallway and approached me. I didn't know what he was going to do." She focused her attention on the lump of chocolate on her spoon. "But then he laughed and said he wouldn't dare touch me or something. You would kill him."

Brundor must have been using a figure of speech. Certainly Drakor would not kill his own brother.

"He did not touch you?" His controlled voice cut through her thoughts.

"No. He mumbled something about proving his strength and then he left. Do you know what it was all about?"

His jaw worked but his shoulders relaxed. "I am relieved that he did not cause you any harm."

She took another lick off the spoon. "I'm fine. Seriously."

Drakor wiped his palms on his shorts. "You like that food product."

Food product? He always came up with something to remind her of how odd he was. And now her stomach took a dive. His oddities were why she was so interested in pursuing a story on him and his family. Their secret. Drakor was the main subject of her investigation. Just like Evan had been.

He raised an eyebrow, his sexy lips curved in a grin. "I like the look on your face when you taste it."

Damn, he sure knew what to say, how to entice her back under his spell. Her better sense told her to get him out of the apartment, but every cell in her body throbbed for his caress.

"Really good chocolate is almost as good as..." Sex. That's why she was eating it now. Trying her hardest to satisfy her lust with the chocolate rather than Drakor's capable hands.

"As good as...?" He was going to make her say it.

Erin licked her lips then planted herself on his lap, straddling his legs. "Why don't you decide for yourself?"

"No."

Erin held the spoon in front of her mouth. With all of the provocative lure she could muster, Erin slowly licked the frosting, encircling it with her tongue.

His breath caught. Dark eyes drew half-closed, the odd white circles returning. His mouth tensed, then his lips parted. Hot fingers clamped down on her waist.

A delicious shot of anticipation shivered through her. She liked this game. "You will try some now." Erin held the spoon before his mouth.

Drakor hesitated, but then slowly opened his mouth. He took a small nibble and then closed his lips. She heard his tongue moving around, as if feeling the texture and absorbing all of the flavors.

"Well?"

He didn't answer her with words, but opened his mouth again. She obliged him by placing the rest of it inside. The spoon came back empty.

"Surprising." He sounded astonished.

"That's nothing. You should try Belgian chocolates, they are to die for."

Drakor said nothing, but yanked her hips hard against him. His erection pressed against the aching spot between her legs. He reached into her hair and he pulled her face to his.

Erin tossed the spoon over his shoulder and it clanked in the sink. He smelled sweet, like the frosting. Ideas of where she could lick that confection off of him whirled through her thoughts.

"I would have never expected that," he whispered against her cheek. "You must tell me how I can repay you."

Erin could think of a hundred ways. But what she wanted most, besides his lips on her mouth and his hard body on top of her, was to know who he really was. Where did he come from? What was that thing she found behind his house? Did he have anything to do with the mysterious life and death of John Doe?

She put her hands on his shoulders and the firm muscles moved beneath her palms. Her hands moved down to his sculpted chest, where she could feel his heartbeat thumping under her fingertips.

Her fingers traveled lower, sliding across his stomach to the top of his waistband.

Drakor moaned and pulled her hips again, grinding her pelvic bone over his rock-hard arousal. A jolt of electricity ricocheted throughout her bloodstream, curling her toes.

Oh God, this spaceship business had to be nonsense. This was clearly a man underneath her, not some freaky space alien. A man whose tongue found the sensitive spot on the curve of her neck, whose hands cupped her bottom as if they were already naked.

Hot tremors spiraled down her legs. To hell with her past, her mistakes, her regrets. She had to be naked with him. Right now. But…didn't they come here for another reason?

"The story on Mickey's—" She closed her eyes as his lips suckled the hollow spot at the base of her throat.

His palms cupped her breasts, kneaded them. "It can wait."

Erin moaned. Oh God, how could he be this good? How could he make her forget everything but him? "Yes," she murmured. "It can wait."

"I must tell you that I won't be able stop this time." His thick voice echoed through a hazy veil of lust. "Once we start, Erin, I won't be able to stop."

He'd better have brought condoms with him, because she sure as hell didn't want him to stop.

∽ଚ୍ଚ

The last time.

This could be the last time he ever felt this way. If they didn't return home soon, he would never find his true *Mharai*. But he needed Erin now. Needed her to take him away from the worries and disasters of his family.

Great Sun, he needed the comfort and peace only she could provide.

Drakor slid his tongue along the curve of her shoulder. He knew this spot made her squirm. She moaned and wriggled, her pelvic bone deliciously sliding on his erection and her breasts pressing up against his chest.

Control. He clenched her shorts. He must retain control.

"We should move into the other room." He whispered the words against her shoulder.

He heard her gulp. "Yes. The bedroom."

Drakor scooped his hands under her bottom and stood, lifting her with him. She wrapped her legs around his waist and he carried her into the bedroom. He laid them atop her messy blankets and positioned himself on top of her. He wanted no opportunity for her to change her mind.

The light from the streetlamp filtered through the curtained window above the bed. A shadow split her face so that he could see one eye, a little of her nose and her pretty little mouth. She smiled an invitation.

He captured her lips, smelling and tasting the sweet frosting again. His first bite of actual food and it was like Erin herself—one taste and he craved more.

Erin parted her mouth and he plunged his tongue inside. Hot blood roared through his veins, intensity surged in his bones.

Drakor released her mouth and kissed her soft throat. Erin's hands reached into his hair, her breasts rose toward him. He pulled on her shirt, yanking it free of her shorts and slid a hand over her silky warm skin.

His mouth watering, Drakor lowered his lips to her bare stomach. His arousal strained, ached, begging to be free of these pants. Not yet.

A sweet and intoxicating floral scent lingered on her skin. His tongue, awakened from a lifetime of sleep, sought to taste the flavor. Drakor dipped it into her navel. Erin moaned, clenched his hair.

Ah, a sensitive spot like her neck and he would use it for all its worth. Drakor held her hips so she could not slide away and teased the small bump with rapid flicks of his tongue. She bucked and twisted beneath him, her panting rising to a tortured pitch.

"Oh God, it tickles. Drakor…"

He could die with this heat. Like being outside on Elliac for too long, his body blazed and his throat dried. But he didn't want to stop. He couldn't.

Drakor released his hold on her and sat back on his heels. He pulled his shirt over his head and tossed it to the floor.

He trailed his fingers up her white thighs until he reached the button at her short pants. They slipped off her legs to reveal underwear with small flowers. He left them and reached for her shirt, pulling it over her head and out of his way.

Now she lay before him in only her underclothing. Despite the low light in the room he could still marvel at her body. The magnificent shadowed curve of her hip. Her fair breasts, trapped beneath a white-laced bra. At the wet skin now glistening on her stomach.

Drakor swallowed. No turning back now.

He lay along side of her and traced his fingertip from her lips, down her throat, between her breasts, over her navel and inside her underwear. He found the warm folds of her skin and slipped a finger inside. Erin gasped, arched her back.

Restraint slipping, Drakor plundered her lips with his tongue while his fingers stroked dampening heat between her legs. She twisted, tightened, whimpered.

Drakor slid his hand out from her underwear and moved on top of her. He removed her bra and tossed it off the bed. Then, moving quickly, he suckled at her yielding skin. Her small, pale nipples stiffened under the flick of his tongue.

His erection pulsated. He couldn't hold out too much longer. But he wanted her to ask for it, to be so overwhelmed with passion that she did not ask for the use of the absurd condom.

Drakor slid further down, his tongue leaving a trail on her fair skin. Erin squirmed again when he teased her navel and he swallowed the chuckle in his throat. She bucked under his merciless tickle and he slipped the underwear off her hips.

"Oh, please, Drakor."

He looked up from his position at her thighs. Her head was back, exposing her throat. Her round breasts slanted sideways, slightly bouncing with each deep breath she took. Outside the window, someone walked in front of the lamp, causing an elongated shadow to travel along her body like the second hand on an old Earth clock.

Drakor closed his eyes, but the sight of her still burned in his view. *Helta,* he didn't want to feel this deeply, need her this badly.

She is not like some of the other females on this planet who can mate without giving something of themselves. Erin will be heartbroken when you are gone from here.

Ankra's words haunted him and he rested his cheek on her leg. He should leave now before it was too late. She was human. An outmoded, suspicious, disbelieving human.

And he needed her. Every inch of her supple, seductive body. Too soon the anniversary of his birth would arrive and he would be left alone. This night with Erin could very well be his last time. Only she could soothe his soul.

"Drakor?" Her desperate voice echoed in the room. "Are you putting it on now?"

She meant the condom. She hadn't forgotten. Nor was she watching.

"Yes." He kissed her thigh while he undid the button his shorts and dropped them to the floor. He reached in his pocket, pulled out the envelope and ripped a corner so that she heard the noise. How could he convince her that they didn't need it?

He didn't care that Ankra, Father and the Researchers believed a human could impregnate an Elliacian. That didn't mean an Elliacian could impregnate a human. Besides, she wasn't his *Mharai* and this would prove it. Hell, he didn't even know how to use the thing.

"It's torn," he lied.

"Torn?"

"You don't have another, do you?"

Drakor resumed his tastes of her inner thigh, licking his way up toward the crease of her leg. She was sweet. She was the stars. She was a thousand Elliac suns. He blew softly on the light-colored triangle of hair and Erin gripped the bed coverings.

"Oh God!"

The inferno in his veins exploded at her strangled cry.

Drakor moved himself over her, positioning himself between her legs. He kissed her with a savage intensity and she returned his hunger stroke for stroke. He rubbed the tip of his erection against her wetness, torturing himself more than her.

Erin reached around and grabbed his hips. She let go of his tongue. "Do it," she cried, "but you have to pull out."

Pull out? He could barely hold on as it was. He grunted a reply and sank himself inside of her. Her inner body converged on him with the sweetest agony. Somewhere, through a haze of desire, he heard her gasp then moan. Her hips rocked to meet his strokes and for the first time he feared he might end this too soon.

Drakor pushed himself deeper inside of her, the scintillating fire pulling him far away. He closed his eyes and visions of Elliac filled his mind. The haunting beauty of the red and bronze hills and the powerful echoes of the thundering purple skies.

But then the sound of her breathy whimpers filled his ears and he found himself back on Earth. He felt her pick up speed, grip him tighter, until she was moving not just up and back but side to side, as well. And, then, when he thought he could not hold back a minute more, Erin cried out and a hot wave flooded around him.

That was all it took. He thrust himself deeper into her, reaching, straining, connecting intimately with a human he once swore to hate until a pleasure so intense crashed through him that he lost all feeling in his fingers and toes.

Through the heavy veil of desire, Drakor heard her plea for him to pull out. With a tremendous effort, he slid himself out of her while the remainder of his desire shuddered from his body.

Drakor collapsed with his face buried in her neck, barely able to move, unwilling to think. Erin wrapped her arms around his back and kissed his cheek.

Jordanna Kay

"You must tell me how I can repay you." Her soft voice repeated his words back to him.

But Drakor turned his head away, squeezing his eyes shut.

She couldn't. Not now. Not ever.

Chapter Twelve

Erin needed to water her plants. Her Peace Lily had drooped over the sides of its pot and several of the Philodendron's leaves were yellow.

And she needed to go grocery shopping and return a bathing suit she bought last month and stop by the dry cleaners and go to the gym and get a birthday card and…

Oh God, she needed to see Drakor again.

Erin sat down on her bed and smoothed her hand over the blankets. She dropped back and spread her arms wide. Oh, to have him touch her again, to have his lips and fingers tracing circles on her skin. He could have kept her awake until sunrise but he said he was tired. Imagine that, she was willing to have more sex and he wasn't. It didn't matter.

She knew he was now putty in her hands. Next time she saw him, they'd have a delicious romp and then he'd tell her all she needed to know.

She should be tired after being up all night, but truth was she couldn't wait to go somewhere. Bubbles fizzled in her stomach, like drinking a fresh soda straight from the fridge. She felt nervous and excited and slightly lightheaded.

And she couldn't sit in this apartment another minute. Erin grabbed her bag from the kitchen chair and left for Greg's house.

"Is Ankra still here?" she asked a few minutes later on his doorstep.

Greg yawned and stretched. "Nah, she had to go back. Said her dad was sick. I drove her back a while ago and then went back to bed."

Jordanna Kay

He stepped aside and Erin followed him in. Butterflies still danced under her skin but she couldn't tell her brother about last night. Not only was it too weird, she couldn't stand his endless teasing.

"So, what's up?" he said.

"Did you ever find out why Ankra was crying last night?"

He took a few swallows. "No, nothing other than her worrying about her dad. That's all she'd say."

Erin slid onto one of the barstools. "Oh."

"What about you? Did Drakor go back with you? Did he tell you what they talked about downstairs?"

She glanced away from him, trying not to blush. "No. He didn't seem like he wanted to talk about it."

Greg cocked a blond eyebrow. "Did he want to talk at all?"

"Okay, that's enough of that."

"Oh, come on. I know if he went back to your place in the middle of the night something must have happened."

She lifted her nose in the air. "He was there the whole night last week and nothing happened."

Greg shrugged and took the milk out and drank it straight from the container.

"Do you have to do that?" Erin wrinkled her nose. "It's really nasty."

He gulped the remainder of the carton and tossed it in the trash. "Hey, that's why I live alone, okay?"

"Didn't Ankra want some while she was here all those times?"

Greg scratched his head and leaned against the counter. "Now that you mention it, I don't recall Ankra ever drinking it."

"Maybe she doesn't like milk or is allergic."

"No. I mean, she never drank anything. Or ate, for that matter. Hell, she never wanted to go out to eat. Kind of weird, huh?"

122

Erin's butterflies turned into bees. She swallowed. "I thought you took her to lunch that one day."

"I did, but she just sat there watching me. When I asked if she was hungry, she just shook her head."

"I'm sure she had to eat sometime." Erin tried to calm that investigative bubble wanting to burst. But she could so clearly remember Drakor refusing to eat when he was at her apartment. Refusing to try the frosting until she forced it on him.

No. He wasn't something from a spaceship. He looked like a man. He felt like a man. Hell, he even screwed like a man. There was some other secret he was hiding. She'd find it. Eventually.

"What's gotten into you?"

Erin looked up into Greg's questioning blue eyes. "Nothing. I'm fine."

He shrugged a shoulder. "Okay. Is that all you came over for?"

"Well…" She tapped her chipped fingernails on the tile countertop and desperately glanced around the room. Why was she here?

Because she couldn't face the apartment alone. Because she'd just had the best sex of her life and used the guy for her story. She was a tramp. And a damn horny one at that.

"Do you *really* think you saw a spaceship?"

ॐ

Drakor stormed out of the house, the welcoming heat enveloping him like a fog. He pushed his way past the young trees and deeper into the woods until he reached the creek.

Anger and helplessness surged in his veins, making his headache worsen. He squatted along the muddy banks and rinsed his hands in the cool water. He couldn't bear to hear his father throw up again. He couldn't watch his mother scurry to the kitchen yet again for some human concoction to calm his father's stomach.

It was that medicine the Researchers gave him. The ones that were supposed to prevent his bones from weakening, prevent his life from deteriorating in sickness. Now his father was dying. And he refused to leave Earth to see if he could be saved on Elliac.

Drakor swirled the bottom of the creek, sending up clouds of dirt and disturbing several tiny fish. He couldn't do this at home. After an hour in that sun, he'd be in the hospital. No amount of clothing or skin protection could help them. About the only redeeming thing on Earth was its weather.

And Erin.

Drakor walked over to the spot he saw her at last night. Was it only a few hours ago that he found her out here? So much happened in that time.

He fought the urge to find his way back to her. How he longed for the peace and contentment of her arms instead of the worry and anger of his father dying. The memories of himself inside of her haunted him throughout the day. Brundor knew instantly that something transpired while he was gone. And it only served to fuel his brother's jealousy and hunger.

The sooner they all got off this planet the better for all of them.

Drakor swatted at some insects swarming around his face and moved out of the trees and back toward the house.

Did he hear singing? There it was again. A soft, sweet sound coming from the far corner of the yard. His eyes scanned the area until he saw Sitora near the swinging tire.

He strode over to her, all the while her angelic voice soothing his torn soul. She held her battered doll in her hands while she tried to push it on the swing. He could see it was difficult for her to hold and swing at the same time but she didn't give up.

"Hello, Sitora."

She looked up at him and he could see the redness from the heat covering her cheeks. Her long hair hung limply over her shoulders and for a moment he wished he could pull it up the way Erin sometimes did hers.

Drakor pulled out a corner of his shirt and wiped the sweat from her face. "What are you doing outside?"

She shrugged and swung her doll again. "I don't like it inside."

"Why not?"

"Father is sick and Mother and Ankra are crying."

"I know." He looked down at the grass at their feet. "I'm sorry. Are you afraid Father will die?"

Sitora didn't answer him but resumed her song instead. It was a bedtime song from Elliac. He remembered it from his own childhood. He always thought that one day he would sing it to his own children. But that wouldn't happen now. He would never find his *Mharai* in time.

Drakor leaned against the tree, his chest squeezing with her off-key words. "Sing another song. Don't you know something else?"

"Will you push me on the swing?"

He couldn't do that now. Not with his father dying inside and his future crumbling within his spirit. "I can't, Sitora. Not now."

Her dark eyes glared at him. "Erin would."

His heart clenched. "What?"

"Erin would play with me. She's the only one who does. When is she coming back?"

Drakor felt his throat closing. He couldn't let himself think of Erin now. He couldn't see her again. It hurt him to leave her this morning, more than the agony of before when he could not touch her.

He swallowed and found his voice. "When did she play with you?"

"When you went somewhere with her brother. She played with me in my room. She tickled me." Sitora held her doll close to her chest. "No one else ever did that."

A warm sensation washed through Drakor. He had images of Erin holding a baby, chasing after a toddler, tickling Sitora. Images of her pregnant body enfolded in his arms.

No!

Drakor threw his head back against the tree trunk. A blast of pain ricocheted through his skull.

"Is she coming over again?"

He didn't want her to, but he knew she would. He never told her not to come. And since she was investigating them, she was due to return soon. He should have told her something to keep her away. But he needed her. His body needed her contact. And needed to see if she could help him locate Alaziri.

She is not like some of the other females on this planet who can mate without giving something of themselves. Erin will be heartbroken when you are gone from here.

Even if it were true, he couldn't worry about that. He couldn't let Erin discover who they really were. He couldn't let himself get lost in her embrace again.

"She isn't coming, is she?" Sitora said, blinking up at him.

"I don't know. We may be gone from here if she does come."

"I want her to come with us."

Drakor managed a smile. "That's not possible."

"Why not?"

"We cannot bring a human back to Elliac with us."

"Why not?"

"Because they don't belong there."

"We don't belong here."

He sighed. "It isn't the same. We are only staying a short time. And we've come for a reason."

"She can come for a reason and only stay a short time. You can bring her back."

"It isn't that simple."

"Why not?"

"Because it isn't. Sitora, you are too little to understand. Humans belong on Earth and we belong on Elliac. That's the way it is." Unless a child of mixed heritage comes back inside the belly of a sacrificial Elliacian.

She crossed her chubby arms over each other. "It doesn't have to be that way. You are just being mean."

Drakor glared at her, his exasperation bubbling. "I am not being mean. I just know more than you."

She put her nose in the air and stomped away. "If you really liked Erin," she said over her shoulder. "You would ask her to come back with us."

If he really liked Erin, he couldn't leave without her.

Sitora wandered around to the front of the house and Drakor watched her go. What else was there to do? Ankra would not say whether or not she had been able to convince Greg to leave off the condom. In fact, his sister did nothing but weep most of the day. And yet, she insisted that she'd rather sacrifice her body, her future, her very father so that she could help Elliac.

"Drakor!"

He looked up at the sound of his mother's voice. She called to him from the other side of the house. Immediately, he could see lines on her face deepened and the weak pallor of her skin. She looked about as ill as Father.

He hurried over to her. "What is it?"

"Your father. He is calling for you. You must come now."

Drakor sighed and followed her inside the house. He passed a weeping Ankra sitting on the top step and a shuffling Brundor near their bedroom.

Inside his parents' bedroom his father lay on the bed, his face shining and as white as the Earth clouds outside. Dark circles rimmed his glassy eyes and his chest rose and fell with too rapid a pace. The smell of sickness punctured the air and Drakor swallowed.

He moved close to his father's side and knelt down next to the bed. "I am here, Father. You've called for me?"

"Drakor..." He reached his shaking hand out and Drakor took it in his own, ignoring its coldness.

"I am here."

"You must take my place. Be the leader...the leader of this mission."

"I do not have the same values as you, Father. I cannot jeopardize the rest of the family for this. Is it not enough that we might lose you?"

His father winced. "I am already lost. I would have been lost on Elliac. You must save our world." He stopped and closed his eyes briefly. "It is up to you to bring back what the Researchers need."

A hot flush of anger bloomed in Drakor's chest. Human genes could not be the answer to their problems. How can a culture, a people, so vastly primitive, have what they don't?

"We will be discovered if we stay longer, Father."

He tried to shake his head. "You must prevent it. You cannot return home until-until it is complete."

Drakor let his father's hand drop. "Erin is a journalist and she suspects we are not as we seem. She could expose us." But would she? After last night, would she tell the world what she learned?

"You will do what-whatever it takes to keep her away."

"What if I can't?"

"Then you will become Alaziri. All of this will be for nothing."

Drakor stood, pain and outrage feuding in his heart. Everyone first thought Erin was his *Mharai*, now she was his enemy.

"Call the family in here," his father croaked. "I must say my good-byes."

Drakor forced down the lump rising in his throat and waved his family in. They gathered around the bed—Mother and Ankra crying and clutching hands and Brundor staring down at his feet. But where was his littlest sister?

"Where is Sitora?" Drakor glanced about the room.

No one seemed to hear as Father rasped out a few words of good-bye and that he would one day see them on the far side of the Sun. Drakor started for the door to find Sitora, when a sudden gasp blew from Father's mouth.

Mother wailed and threw herself across his body. Ankra sank to her knees and put her head on Father's arm. Brundor turned away, his shoulders sagging.

Drakor stared at them, his own heart falling for the man he never agreed with. This man who was his father. Then the ghostly image of the rainbow flickered before his eyes. *A tragedy prophesied to the viewer.* Father was dead and he was now in charge of this mission. If he stayed on Earth, how many other tragedies would ensue? If he returned home immediately, how much disgrace would shadow his family?

With his birth anniversary a few days away, was peace lost to him forever?

Chapter Thirteen

Drakor turned to leave the room, his family's overpowering emotions choking him. Right now he could not grieve, he could not mourn. Not now anyway. There were more important matters to attend to.

"No, don't go!"

It was Mother. Her dark, wet eyes implored him. Tear tracks scattered among the lines and wrinkles on her face and her bottom lip trembled. She reached out her hand.

"You must help me. Drakor, my son."

He held his breath, every muscle rigid, anticipating her next words with dread. "Help you?"

She nodded and gripped Father's gray hand. "I cannot stay here without him."

Exactly what he feared. Drakor squeezed his eyes closed and released his breath in a hiss. The dull ache inside of his skull continued to pulsate. "You don't have to do this, Mother. We are here for you."

"He is my *Mharai*. We are meant to be together." She sniffled. "Always."

Drakor leaned against the doorframe. "That doesn't mean you have to forfeit your life when he is gone."

Her weeping began again in earnest. "You don't understand the feeling. The connection. If you find your *Mharai*, then you will understand. You won't want to ever be separated."

Even his own mother thought he would never find his destined mate. Why would she? She knew nothing of his relationship with Erin, but she knew full well how soon the anniversary of his birth was.

Despite her plea, he could not help her kill herself. "I cannot do it."

Ankra rose from her spot beside the bed. She planted herself before him. "You would deny Mother her last wish as you denied Father his?"

Drakor set his jaw. "I did not deny Father his wish. I feared we would be exposed if we remained here much longer."

"I just need more time. And you should tell Erin the truth. If she really cares for you, she won't reveal us."

Tell Erin the truth? Just hand a journalist the story that aliens were on her doorstep, that she mated with an alien and so did her brother. He couldn't trust a human with information like that. Not even Erin.

"We will remain until you are pregnant and not a moment sooner, even if I have not found Alaziri. No one will reveal who we are or why we are here." He looked over at Brundor, who had sunk against the windowpane. "No one."

Ankra crossed her arms. "Are you going to help Mother, or not?"

He wouldn't let himself glance over at his mother, still leaning against her mate's legs. He couldn't bear to see the pain and entreaty on her face. "I cannot take part in her death. It was hard enough to be forced to take part in Father's."

Ankra's voice hardened. "Then I will do it and you can be the coward that you are."

Heat flared at Drakor's ears and his pulse intensified. "First I have no allegiance and now I am a coward. You should watch your tongue, sister."

Her eyes challenged him. "And you should care more about others than yourself sometimes."

"I care a great deal about this family. That is the whole reason I did not want to come, why I want to go. We are in danger here. Why does no one recognize this but me?"

She shook her head. "But your family is not worried about this the way you are. We believe in the mission. We feel it is an honor."

"You are only worried about not finding your *Mharai*," Brundor said from across the room. "If your birth anniversary were not so close, you would not be so concerned."

Ankra's raised eyebrow showed she agreed. Let them think he only worried for his own peace and happiness. He knew better, he knew he worried for their safety. They didn't have to like him. They didn't have to agree with him. They only had to follow him.

Drakor went over to Mother and took her hands. He helped her to stand. Her watery eyes asked for his compassion. He wanted to give it, he wanted to understand. But would he ever feel that way? Would he ever find his true *Mharai* and know the intimate bond?

He kissed both of her wet cheeks. "Join him on the far side of the Sun."

A small smile curved her lips. "You will look after Sitora?"

"Of course."

She clenched his fingers. "Do not let our deaths be in vain. Complete the mission, bring us back to Elliac with honor."

He kissed her forehead and took a step back from her, a sigh swallowed in his throat. "I will do my best," was the only truthful thing he could say.

Drakor glared at his sister, who returned the stare and then headed for the dresser. Brundor challenged him for only a moment and then shifted his gaze away. Had he divided them? Had his refusal to give Mother her *Mharai-death* driven his family from him?

They were all that he had left now. Ankra, Brundor, and Sitora. In two more Earth days his birth anniversary would come, making him thirty Elliac sun-cycles. Making him past the age of finding his mate.

Why should either of these two care? Ankra still had many cycles to go and Brundor had not even had his Crossing yet.

He growled, disgusted at their willingness to end another person's life. Maybe he really didn't belong with any of them.

"Brundor!"

His brother turned to face him. The small gleam of trepidation pleased Drakor. At least he still held power over one of his siblings.

He tossed his crystal pad over. "Activate the shuttlecraft."

"Now?"

"Yes, now. How else will we keep them until we can return home?" He waved a hand over to the bed, indicating his parents. Mother still lived and his heart tore at referring to her as dead. But he could not change her mind.

"What is the code?"

Drakor rattled off the code and the craft appeared outside the window. He knew it was risky. Erin or Greg could stop over at any time. Especially since this day was at week's end, when many humans did not have to work.

But what else could he do? He had to preserve his parents' bodies until they could return home and give them a proper burial. Earth's atmosphere would not permit proper preservation. His only choice was to bring them onto the shuttle. As soon as possible.

His throat tight and dry, Drakor tried to swallow but couldn't. He took a last look at Father's still form, lying lifeless on the four-poster bed. Then, at Mother, whose tearful eyes yearned for her peace. She would rather be dead than be without him.

That must be the true test of finding one's *Mharai*. No matter how Erin made him feel with desire or contentment, he could easily live without her. Couldn't he?

An unknown weight lifted from him. He had been right all along. She was not his lifemate.

He pulled his gaze away from Mother, his eyes blurring, and spoke to the other two. "Come find me when you need my help to move them to the shuttle."

Then, he turned from the room and went to look for Sitora.

ଃଠାରଃ

Erin threw her keys on her kitchen counter and dropped the grocery bags to the floor. Okay, so she couldn't stop thinking about Drakor. Who could forget such mysterious, steamy eyes? Just about any woman would have heart palpitations watching his thick, muscled body move. Like a lion on the prowl.

She opened up the fridge and put away the milk, eggs, and yogurt. Man, her fridge was bare. It's a wonder she had anything to eat all week. Okay, so he distracted her. But really she needed this story. No doubt Rita was nearly done with hers. She just couldn't go back to being a nobody again. Not after what she went through before. She'd worked too long and hard at this po-dunk paper to make something of herself again. After this spread, she'd be able to get out of here and have a life in the big city again.

Erin shoved the Ben & Jerry's ice cream in the freezer. The blast of cold air woke her from her daze.

She had to do more research on that Victorian and on the death of John Doe. The two just had to be connected. Mysteries and secrets like that were not mere coincidences. Not in her book anyway.

Erin grabbed her keys again.

The floor at her office building seemed deserted when Erin got off the elevator. She went past the rows of metal desks until she reached her own. Her usual pile of papers and folders stood next to her computer monitor. Some new junk mail lay on her chair and she tossed it in the trash.

She bent under the desk to flip on the power strip. Bam! Erin jumped at the door slam, banging her head on the desk. Who just came in? Please, don't let it be Rita. Anyone, but Rita.

The sound of footsteps brought the person close and Erin gradually backed out of the desk and sat up. Bronze, silk capris and a matching white and bronze shirt greeted her eyes. Oh, shit.

"Well, I must say that this is a first. Erin Price in here on a weekend?"

"Don't you have a hole you can climb into?"

134

Rita tapped her red manicured nails on the desk. "Touchy, touchy. I happen to be working on my story. And you?"

Erin nibbled her lip. "None of your business."

Rita raised her tweezed eyebrows. "Everything is my business."

The nerve of this woman. It would take someone like her to dampen her good mood. Erin felt the corner of her eye tick, that damn annoying reaction to Rita's presence. "Shouldn't you be doing something other than bothering me?"

Rita smiled. "I can find something to do. Give me your friend's phone number and I'll get busy."

"My friend?"

"You know, the one from Mickey's. Mr. Tall, Dark, and Extra Hot. The one that was way out of your league, remember?"

Out of her league, huh? It didn't seem that way last night when tongue was inside her mouth or his hot hands were—

"Dear Lord, are you blushing?"

Erin blinked. "Uh…no."

"Yes, you were. You have the hots for him, don't you? I think Ed in printing is a little more your type."

Ed. Sloppy, middle-aged, with a comb-over. That was her type? Rita thought she knew everything. Thought she was so smart. Well, this time, Erin had something on her.

"You don't know what you're talking about." Erin stuck her chin in the air.

"Oh?" Rita snapped the gum in her mouth.

"Mr. Tall, Dark, and Extra Hot has been spending quite a bit of time with me, thank you."

"What do you mean?"

"I mean I've been to his place, he's been to mine. Maybe he's not so out of my league."

Rita stopped chewing. "You're bluffing. There's no way he'd go for a girl like you."

Erin grit her teeth. "What's that supposed to mean?"

She waved her arm in the air with a flair. "Look at you. Short and pale, boring hair, bland face. What would he see in you?"

"He must see something because he spent the night with me last night."

"That's a lie."

"It isn't, you can ask my brother. Greg knows he was there."

Erin could swear that she saw Rita blanch. Her mouth dropped open and her perfectly made-up face shifted a few colors. Somehow, offering Greg as a back up was enough to have Rita believe her.

"He slept on your couch, right?"

Erin grinned. "That was last week. Last night he slept in my bed. Well, you know, not really slept…"

Rita straightened her back and sucked in a deep breath. Erin could tell she was not pleased that Drakor actually had an interest in her.

"Don't get cocky. I have something on your brother that will bring him down. And then you'll fall right along with him."

Erin's stomach pitched. "What do you mean you have something to bring him down? Is your story on him?" Oh God, was she the one who broke into his office?

Rita's lip curled into a snarl. "There's something illegal going on in that office and I'm going to expose it."

Erin gulped. "Whatever it is, Greg can't possibly have anything to do with it or know about it. You can't just ruin him."

"Oh, can't I? He should have a better rein on his employees." She raised an eyebrow then turned to walk back to her desk.

"Wait a minute. What employee? What are they doing wrong?"

Rita smacked her gum, obviously satisfied that she had the upper hand again. "He's about to be in a legal dispute over a patent infringement. You know, he really should be more careful."

Erin sank into her hard chair. Patent Infringement?

Oh shit, she had to go see Greg. She had to warn him. But why did she have the urge to see Drakor instead? Why was burying herself in his arms the first thing she wanted to do?

Either way she had to get out of here. She'd have to do her research later.

She grabbed her bag and keys and pushed away from her desk.

"Oh," Rita called across the room. "I still mean what I said before about your guy not having an interest in you. Sleeping with you really doesn't mean anything, you know." She winked and blew a quick bubble. "Like I said at *Mickey's*, a man like that is only using you. You can take my word on it."

For once, Erin could actually laugh. She was using Drakor. What difference did his motives make?

But as she hurried to the elevator, Erin couldn't help but wonder if Rita wasn't right. What did Drakor see in her?

ℰᴄℜ

Despite her impulse to lose herself in Drakor's arms, Erin rushed over to see Greg instead. He opened the door wearing a pair of old shorts and no shirt.

"Just watching a baseball game." He waved her in. "Want a beer?"

If she liked it, it might make her feel better. Or at least calmer. She shook her head. "We need to talk."

He went down the hall and back to his couch. "Didn't we just do that this morning?"

"This is very important, Greg. You've got to listen and pay attention."

"It's not about Drakor or Ankra again, is it?" He propped his bare feet on his coffee table.

"No. It's about Invasion Shield."

"Huh?"

"Your company. Something illegal is going on and you need to do something about it."

He still didn't look at her and watched the game instead. "What are you talking about? I'm not doing anything illegal."

"Not intentionally."

"Oh, that was a strike if I ever saw one. Come on, Ump!"

Erin kicked the table. "Are you listening to me?"

"Sit down, will you? You're making me nervous hovering about me like some mother hen."

"You should be nervous." She moved around to block him from seeing the TV screen.

"Get out of the way. You may be a pain, but you ain't made of glass."

"Ha. Ha. Very not funny."

Greg scooted down the couch to see past her. "Don't you have any other friends you can annoy? Can't you see I'm busy?"

Erin looked around for the remote but he held it on his lap. She stalked over to the set and pushed off the power button.

"Aw, Erin, come on. There was a man on third base and one out left."

Men! She growled at him and went to stand before him, crossing her arms. "Now you listen to me. Rita is investigating you and Invasion Shield. She says someone in your company is doing something illegal."

He gave her a helpless look. "That's impossible. She's just blowing smoke up your ass."

"I think she's telling the truth."

"Why do you believe her of all people?"

"Because she's so desperate to bring me down. I don't think she even meant to tell me. She was just pissed off."

"Why?"

"Because she wanted to go out with Drakor and I told her that he was with me."

Greg lifted his eyebrows and drank some of his beer.

"She didn't believe me at first and I said she could check with you that he was at my house last night. That got her all ruffled and then she went on about you and your illegal company."

He shrugged. "She just had her pride stung and looked for a way to get you."

Erin sat on the coffee table in front of him. "She was specific, Greg. She said something about patent infringement."

"Patent infringement? I don't get it."

"She said you should keep a better rein on your employees."

His eyebrows furrowed and he frowned. "But who would do something like that? Is someone selling me out? A junior engineer passing on our documentation?"

Finally he was listening to her. She sighed. "I just wanted to warn you. Rita is planning a huge article on it to expose you."

"She must really hate you."

"Me?"

"I can't imagine this story just popped into her head. She must have searched for something to get at you." He reached for the remote. "If it's even true."

"Are you saying you don't believe me?"

He pointed the remote around her and flipped the TV back on. The sounds of cheering echoed in the room. "It's her I don't believe. And you shouldn't either."

Erin got up from the table and moved slowly toward his front door. She had told Rita she didn't believe her, but in all honesty, part of her did. Her comments about Greg's legal troubles seemed too confident to ignore.

And her comment about Drakor using her? It didn't really matter, not when she was using him.

But, still, some part of her ached to think he only slept with her for some ulterior motive, that he might not really find her attractive.

There was only one way to judge for certain. She'd have to go see him.

Chapter Fourteen

About halfway between the spot where the dirt road began and Drakor's house, Erin saw a small figure walking toward her. She recognized the long dark hair and short gait. Sitora.

What was the girl doing all the way out here by herself?

Erin pulled the car off to the side as far as she could and got out. Sitora looked up and her face brightened instantly.

"What are you doing?" Erin rushed over to her. "Is everything okay?"

Sitora shrugged and tugged at her hair with one hand. In the other, she held a cloth doll. "Father is sick and Ankra and Mother are crying."

Erin squatted before her, sinking her knees into the hot, powdery dirt. "Drakor told me your dad was ill. I'm very sorry he is sick, I know that can be scary."

She pulled the little girl into her arms and held her. "Were you too sad to stay at home? Is that why you were leaving?"

Warm breath blew down her back. "I wanted to find you and you came."

Erin smiled. At least she knew she made an impression on one person in this family. She backed away and stood up, holding out her hand to Sitora.

"How about I take you back to your house?"

"Can I ride in that?" She pointed excitedly to the car. "Please?"

"Well, I don't have a booster seat for you, but how about you climb in the back?"

Sitora ran to the car and yanked the door open. She scrambled to the back seat. "Drakor says you can't come with us. But I want you to."

Erin reached behind the seat and pulled the seatbelt over Sitora's shoulder. "Go with you where?"

"When we leave. He says you can't come because you won't belong. I think he's being mean."

Erin stopped, her stomach twisting in a slow knot. "Leave? When are you leaving?"

The girl shrugged and squeezed her doll against her chest. "I don't know."

Questions swirled in Erin's brain. Where were they going? Why were they leaving? Was Drakor going to tell her? Did he know they were leaving all along?

Biting her lip, she turned to slide into the driver's seat. But a sight up ahead made her breath catch in her throat. Drakor walked toward them with long, purposeful strides. His wide shoulders were emphasized by the white shirt he wore and his dark hair lifted with his brisk movement. On the prowl. But the look on his face clearly stated he was after something other than the warmth between her legs.

"Oh!" whined Sitora from behind her. "He's going to take me back. Don't let him."

Erin got out of the car and stood next to the open door.

Drakor came up before her and she suddenly noticed the unusual paleness of his skin. His eyes were both red and hard. The rest of his features, set in a scowl, looked nothing like the man who had lain in bed with her last night.

"I need to take Sitora home." His voice was clipped, tense. The accent more noticeable than usual.

"I don't want to go!" the girl yelled from the car.

Drakor took a step closer and his scent tickled Erin's nose, reminding her of the taste of his neck. She tried to force it away but warmth still burned in her belly.

"Sitora." He put one hand on the windshield and leaned over the car door. "Father and Mother...they..." He sighed and Erin could swear she heard his voice crack. "You need to come home right away."

"No!"

Erin touched his arm. "Let me try."

Drakor leapt as if she had just burned him. He looked down at the spot where her fingers grazed his skin and she could see his breathing quicken. He stepped back from the car.

Erin swallowed and turned to the stubborn five-year-old in her back seat. "It sounds like it's very important that you go back. Perhaps your parents really want to see you."

Sitora looked down at her lap. "Will you come with me? Can I still ride in here?"

"Sure, no problem."

But when she turned to face the girl's brother, his cold stare had returned. "No."

"She feels comfortable with me." Erin walked toward him, stopping just before his statue-like stance. "It will make it better for her."

He bent low so Sitora could not hear. "Father has died. She needs to come with me." He straightened and looked over her head.

His father died? The crushing pain from her parents' death came barreling up until her heart felt as if it would tear again. She reached her arms around his back, as much to comfort herself as to comfort him. "I'm so sorry, Drakor. I know how painful it is to lose a parent."

She felt him tense immediately but he did not return the embrace. In fact, he cleared his throat and stepped away from her. "Sitora needs to get out of the vehicle and come with me."

"Drakor?" Erin's chest and throat tightened.

143

"This doesn't concern you, Erin." He still wouldn't look at her, his face remained impassive. "Go home."

She understood grief. Anger typically followed disbelief. But wouldn't he want her comfort?

"Sitora, out now!" He stormed over to the car. Erin wouldn't look back but she heard the little girl crying and Drakor physically pulling her from the car. He walked past her with Sitora thrown over his shoulder, a muscular arm holding her in place. "Go, Erin."

The girl wailed, fat teardrops falling to the dry dirt. She reached her arms out as if Erin could save her.

But Erin couldn't do anything. Drakor ignored her, dismissed her, completely rejected her. And he was leaving.

A man like that is only using you. You can take my word on it.

Maybe Rita's word was good after all.

ৡ০েপ্র

Drakor didn't realize how painful that would be. And he wasn't referring to Sitora's kicks in his stomach or howl in his ear. Seeing Erin gave his body a lurch he didn't expect.

She looked as extraordinary as ever, with her hair back from her face in some sort of a clip, her face pink from the sun and heat, her skin fragrant and innocently tempting.

Erin's touch on his arm made his body remember how she felt beneath him. It remembered how much he wanted her, how content he felt in her arms. Her presence soothed the pain in his head and the emptiness in his heart. And when she embraced him, it took every ounce of strength, everything he possessed to not capture her mouth with his lips.

But he couldn't. Erin was dangerous. To this mission. To himself. And if she came any closer to the house, she'd have seen the spacecraft.

No. He had to make her go. He had to make her realize that she wasn't welcome there. At least not today.

As they started up the steps, Sitora still wailing, Brundor burst out of the front door.

"Oh, there you are. We are ready. Ankra has already gotten the cloths."

Drakor sighed and lowered his sister to his waist. She wrapped her arms around his neck and he carried her up the stairs.

"Where's Mother?" she asked in a quiet voice. "I want to see her."

They entered the room where his parents lay side by side on the bed. He had to admit they looked peaceful, if not gray and sullen. But Mother had passed with a smile on her face and her hand clasped to her *Mharai*.

He put Sitora down on the floor but she refused to move from his legs. "What's wrong with them?"

Ankra suddenly noticed their appearance and rushed over. She scooped Sitora up and held her close. "They have gone to the far side of the Sun to be with one another always."

The little girl blinked, her large eyes glancing from one body to the other. Drakor watched her reaction. No tears over the deaths of her parents and yet she would not stop crying over being taken from Erin.

He pushed thoughts of Erin away. He had to shut that door and move onto another. One that could get them off of this planet as fast as possible. One that would keep them from harm.

"We had better move them into the shuttle," he said to the others.

Ankra whispered something to Sitora and then they both carried the coverings over to the bed. Each taking a corner embroidered with a large sun, his sisters covered first their father in a royal blue cloth. Then they repeated the procedure with a red one for Mother.

Once that was complete, Drakor waved Brundor over. On Elliac, the death procession required four men to carry the bodies of loved ones to their resting place. Here there was only he and Brundor. It would look less ceremonial, but they could get the job done.

Jordanna Kay

Drakor picked up his Father's shoulders, careful to keep the cloth covering the body, and Brundor lifted his feet. Slowly they carried the heavy weight down the stairs, out the door, and to the backyard. Neither one spoke as they lowered the body to the ground in front of the shuttle ramp.

They returned to the house and repeated the process with Mother. Ankra and a still silent Sitora followed.

Once the bodies lay next to one another on the ground, Drakor reached his hands out to the others. "Grab hands." But there weren't enough of them and they couldn't touch.

Drakor's veins turned to ice. Another bad omen. First the rainbow and now they couldn't join hands over their deceased loved ones. He glanced at his siblings' alarmed faces.

"It will be fine. We're on Earth, we can't always do it the Elliacian way."

Their faces relaxed, but only slightly. They all held their arms aloft, as if they could touch, even little Sitora. Drakor looked down at the covered bodies and then up at the sky.

This wasn't Elliac's powerful and relentless sun, but it would have to do.

"Oh, mighty Sun above us, please take our beloved parents into your fold. Welcome them with your heat and your glory. Allow them to remain forever together. They are *Mharai*. They are one."

The four of them lowered their heads and Drakor struggled with the rage inside of them. Their deaths, this mission, his entanglement with Erin. None of it had to be.

Drakor motioned to Brundor and they carried the bodies into the shuttles, one by one. A narrow slot in the far back of the craft was just long enough to fit both of them in it. Drakor sealed the door and locked it with a code. They would be preserved until they had all reached home again.

The four of them started from the backyard around to the front. Ankra and Sitora went over by the swing and Brundor played with the crystal pad in his hand until the craft disappeared.

Drakor had nearly reached the house when he caught a scent on the breeze. Erin's scent.

146

Immediately, his lungs ceased functioning. Cold dread enveloped his heart.

Then he located her. She stood mostly hidden by the trees but he could see her wide eyes and shocked expression. One hand pressed against her chest, just between her breasts. The other hand hung by her side, clutching something tightly within a fist.

Sitora's doll.

Chapter Fifteen

Erin tried to tune out the loud voices around her and flipped the small, rectangular light over in her hands. At least, she and Greg assumed it was a light. A light from the spaceship she saw parked out in the rear yard of Drakor's house two days ago.

A spaceship! Oh God. And she saw the four of them standing over two covered bodies in some strange ritual. Once the bodies were on the ship, Drakor's brother made it disappear with some small PDA-looking thing. Most likely the same sort of thing she saw under the dresser.

She had to pinch herself three times as she stared at the scene to make sure she wasn't dreaming. And then when Drakor saw her—she shivered at the look of alarm and rage on his face. It didn't take her but a half of a second to bolt back to her car and tear out of there.

But it all made so much sense now. How little they all knew about typical aspects of human culture. The odd words they used and the simple words they didn't understand.

Erin shifted in her chair and glanced around the office. Everyone was too busy to pay attention to her and yet she didn't want some nosybody like Rita coming over to ask questions.

The light's casing had smooth bumps on its surface but no seam in which to open it. In fact, no matter what she tried, it wouldn't shatter or crack. Right after she realized that she had just slept with a man from outer space.

Would he be considered a man? He felt like a man. Oh God, this all either made her sick or ecstatic.

148

Real, living aliens were not just small town Virginia news or even national news. Hell, this discovery was global! She could go way beyond the front page of this paper, way beyond being a local somebody. The sight she saw behind that Victorian house could surpass all her dreams.

But she'd need more proof than this hard case that wouldn't open. She was going to have to go back there and look for that thing under the dresser. And she would have to forget about ever sleeping with Drakor again.

Erin pulled out her notebook and started scribbling everything she could remember. She had been far too shocked yesterday to even think about writing it down. And she'd tried to get a hold of Greg but he wasn't at home, he didn't answer his cell and he never called her back.

Erin jumped as the phone rang and then picked it up. About time her unreliable brother called back.

"Ms. Price," said the building's receptionist. "You have a visitor."

Ah, so Greg realized the urgency and came straight over. Smart man, finally. "I'll be right down."

She hung up the phone, grabbed her notebook and bag and headed for the elevators. Rita gave her a superior glance as she passed. Bitch. But she didn't matter anymore. There was no bigger news than this anywhere, at any time.

The elevator doors closed and Erin smiled. No. Once she got the evidence, she'd look into the charges Rita insinuated against Invasion Shield. Erin would debunk that and then Rita would be left high and dry.

Oh, yes, despite having spent most of the weekend in shock and disgust, she was starting to feel much better already. She just needed to tell Greg about what she saw and then they could begin working on his issues.

The front lobby was empty save for the receptionist. "Where is my visitor?" she asked the girl.

"He's outside. Nice-looking guy."

Erin rolled her eyes. She was about to offer Greg's number to her now that he'd certainly want to move on from Ankra, but a call came in and the girl picked up the phone.

The front door opened into a hot wind. She smelled rain. She looked around the parking lot and didn't see anyone until she saw a figure inside her car on the far side of the pavement. Didn't she lock it? She must have forgotten. Erin ran over and slid into the driver's seat.

But when she turned to face Greg, her blood froze. "Drakor!"

His dark stare did not look menacing. More like resigned. "Hello, Erin."

"What are you doing here? Are-are you the one that came to see me here?"

He nodded. "We need to talk."

She looked down on her lap. Her stomach did a few flip-flops while scenarios of how he could kill her flashed through her brain. "What's there to talk about?"

"Your home." His voice was more quiet than she'd ever heard it. "Let's go there."

"No!" Being alone with him might have been the first thing on her mind on Friday but it was the last thing she wanted today. "Look, Drakor, I know what I saw and I know you saw me there. What's there to say?"

His fingers brushed her hand. She expected revulsion at his touch but instead she felt that familiar warmth and desire. She couldn't move any further away unless she got out of the car.

"I need to explain." He sighed. "We must go somewhere other than here."

Erin nodded. "Granny's."

He took his hand away and they rode in silence to a small diner.

The smell of greasy burgers and cigarette smoke greeted them at the door. They found a booth in the far corner, away from the noise of clattering dishes and shouting waitresses. Erin chose the seat facing the room. She wanted to be able to get someone else's attention if necessary without having to turn her back on him.

Drakor slid his large frame onto the red, pleather seat. He still looked paler than normal. Slight shadows encased his eyes and his mouth looked as though it had forgotten how to smile. No doubt he was truly worried about her discovering the truth. And he had reason to be.

She opened the conversation. "Well?"

He leaned forward, his colorless eyes reflecting her red shirt and masking all of his emotions. "Erin, you must keep what you saw to yourself. Tell no one."

Like *that* was ever going to happen. Especially after the way he treated her. The way he used her. He probably just wanted to experience sex with a human. And she was naïve enough to be his guinea pig.

"Why?"

She saw his jaw clench.

"Do you have any idea what your government would do to us?"

"I've watched *X-files*. It's probably not very pretty."

"*X-files?*"

Erin shook her head. "Never mind. Bad joke. Look, Drakor, I realize you are worried, but why should I listen to you? Why should I stop myself from having the biggest story of my career?"

The waitress stopped at their table. "Can I get you drinks or a menu or something?"

"Lemonade and a slice of chocolate cream pie for me."

She wrote it on her pad and turned to Drakor. "And you, mister?"

"Nothing, thank you."

"Nothing? Not even water?"

"Nothing."

The waitress shrugged and left the table.

"Why don't I ever see you eat or drink anything?" Erin asked, glad the opportunity had finally presented itself.

"Because I don't. No one from my home does."

"But your mother made that bread."

"She wanted to experiment. She thought it might help my father."

Erin hesitated, remembering his death. Her impulses were to reach out to him again, but she couldn't take the rejection. "How do you not eat or drink and yet grow and remain healthy?"

He leaned back against the cushion and spread his arms across the back. His gaze shifted to the streaked window. "The atmosphere and weather at home make it difficult to grow any food or keep livestock. We tried for a number of years but the yield wasn't high enough. Everyone was starving. And so the Researchers eventually developed capsules that would meet all of our requirements of nutrition and hydration. We take several in the morning and several at night."

He recited it as if he had it memorized from a manual. His voice inflected little emotion and he still didn't look at her.

"Don't you feel hunger?"

"Hunger?"

"Your stomach. Doesn't it hurt or cramp for something to be put in it?"

"These capsules were developed long ago, well before I was born. As infants we nourish from our mothers but we are eventually weaned onto the capsules. I had never before tasted food until..." Slowly, his gaze found hers again. "Until you gave me taste of it."

She remembered that frosting experience, his hard body beneath her and his steamy eyes penetrating to her very core. She had wondered whether he was an alien and deemed him human. Just goes to show what a lousy judge she could be.

"Eating is more than just nourishment. It is enjoyment. That's why there must be a million recipes—different combinations of food. Pizza and Chow Mien and Enchiladas and brownies." She tilted her head. "Have you never even seen or smelled it before?"

"Small amounts of food is still grown," he replied. "For ceremonial purposes. *Mharai*-unions, family deaths."

Ma-rye? "I'm sorry about your father."

"My mother died as well. She chose not to live without him."

Erin leveled her gaze at him. *Chose not to live without him?* What did that mean exactly? Part of her wished she could write this all down in her notebook and the other part of her felt a unique sadness. He shared that with her. They both had lost both parents at the same time. But now he was responsible for his three siblings.

She still couldn't believe she was talking to an alien. How could someone this handsome, this sexy, not be from this planet? And how did he know her language and speak it so clearly? How is it that an alien race resembled them so completely?

Oh God, her head was starting to spin again with the jumble of unanswered questions.

"Drakor, how come you know my language so well? It's too much of a coincidence that you would speak it on your planet."

His face changed instantly. His eyes hardened and his nostrils flared. "We have our own language. But there have been others that have come here before. They have gathered the information."

Her journalist mind raced. Others? Others have come before Drakor and his family? Where were they? Did anyone ever realize who they were?

"When? How long did they stay? Did they know English—?"

Drakor cut her off with a harsh glare. "My family has benefited from their work. Do you know of a man named Alaziri?"

No. She certainly would have remembered a name like that. "I can't help you there. Is he one who came before?"

His dark expression made it obvious something had occurred with the previous visitors. But she knew he wouldn't explain anything about it now.

But she had to know why he—and the others before him—were on Earth. Was it for trade? If that were the case, wouldn't they make their presence known and contact the government?

"Okay, I'll drop it. But why are you here? Why are you on Earth?"

His glare shifted to the paper napkin he kept twisting in his hands. "I can only tell you that we need something from Earth to help us at home."

"What?"

He shifted in his seat and it squeaked under his weight. "I can't tell you that."

"Why not?"

"Erin…" He looked at her again and reached across the yellowing, scratched table. His mood had softened and his hand trembled. He really was afraid. Or nervous.

But she couldn't let that hold her back. He used her. For what purpose she didn't know. But at least now all cards were on the table.

"One lemonade and a chocolate cream pie." The dish and glass banged down in front of her and Drakor pulled his arm away. "You sure you don't want anything, sweetheart?"

"No, thank you."

The waitress left and Drakor scooted out of the booth. "I'll be right back," he said with a pained voice and escaped out the front door into the afternoon sun.

សាଔ

Drakor found a wooden bench and dropped on to it, burying his face in his hands. Why did Erin have to bring the doll back at that moment? If only she had waited, even a few more minutes. But now he was forced with having to do whatever it took to subdue Erin, to pacify her into silence.

He didn't expect her to resist so much. After all, hadn't Ankra said that if Erin cared for him at all she wouldn't say anything? Hadn't they shared that night together? Didn't that mean anything to her?

Then he had this persistent headache to deal with. Ever since he spent the night within Erin's arms, a thudding inside his skull never ceased. Unless he was with her. It was as if his body continued to crave her. Like she was some drug he needed to be free of pain.

He groaned. How could it be that only a week or so ago he thought they would be off this planet within a few days? Now he was stuck here. Stuck until Ankra could get pregnant. But how would Greg ever want to see her again once Erin told him about what she saw? Would Ankra have to start over with another male? Would that keep them here on Earth even longer?

Vehicles sped by on the road and doors slammed in the parking lot. He lifted his head and winced. Earth's sun glinted off several windows, nearly blinding him as the pounding in his head returned full-force. Drakor sighed and went back inside the small restaurant.

Odd smells assaulted him again and he found his mouth starting to water. He saw Erin enjoying her pie, licking the fork with her tantalizingly smooth tongue. He swallowed and made his way over to her.

She looked up. "Are you feeling okay?"

"My head hurts."

"Oh, I have some medicine for that. Or do you not take medications either?"

He suppressed a growl. How superior she sounded. How much she thought she knew. Typical human. Had he thought she was any different than the others? Ankra certainly believed her to be, but his sister didn't judge character well obviously.

"We do have medications at home, but I would prefer to not take one made on Earth."

Erin lifted her eyebrows. "Oh? Afraid we might poison you?"

He didn't answer. It didn't matter. Now that he was sitting across from her, his headache began to ease. It would be wise if he changed the subject.

"What am I smelling?"

She took several gulps of the yellow liquid in her glass and then set it on the table. "Probably the burgers and frying onions. The grease is a strong scent."

"Burgers?"

"Hamburgers. It's a meat patty, made from cows."

"Cows. We don't have any of those. But I think I saw a picture of them before."

Erin smiled. "I could take you down a few country roads around here and you could see them in person. Moo."

He cocked his head. "Moo?"

"It's the sound they make. I'll tell you, it makes much more sense now. I'm almost relieved."

He stared at her.

"You know, that you guys didn't know the simplest words or ideas. I mean, I'd say that most cultures around the world know what a cow is, even if they don't eat it."

Drakor ignored her comments. He had best focus on something other than her suspicious and provocative remarks. He turned his attention to her half-eaten pie. Did that taste like the frosting she had given him only two nights ago? He licked his lips.

"I can order you a slice, if you want."

He glanced up into her unusual eyes, though on Earth they weren't unique at all. He just hadn't gotten used to all of the variety here yet. "Just the other day you let me eat off of your spoon."

"The other day I didn't know you weren't from Earth."

"Why does that make a difference now?" He leaned across the table.

Erin glanced away. "It just does."

Drakor captured her hand with his and lowered his voice. He didn't want to go down this path, put himself in a position to see her more often. But he had to do whatever it took to dissuade her. Or to distract her until they left.

"The other day you wanted me in your bed, you wanted me inside of you. The other day you told me that I had given you a gift. You didn't want me to leave the next morning." She tried to pull away but he held on firm. "Erin, the other day we found ecstasy and contentment together and now you won't even share your food with me."

She wouldn't look at him but he could see her eyes shining. "Yes, and then Saturday you pushed me away and out of your life."

He sighed. He had to be careful. He could either lose her or gain her right now. "Erin, my parents had just died, I was suddenly responsible for my family, I had so many things to take care of."

"You could have been nicer about it all."

"I don't know what to say or how to act in those situations."

"I feel like you lied to me."

"How did I lie? Did I ever tell you where I was from?"

"No, but—"

"Would it have made you feel better if I had told you that I wasn't from here? Would you have believed me? Or would you have thought me crazy?"

A small grin played on her soft lips. "Crazy, for sure."

"So, what else could I have done?" Drakor let go of her hand and touched her face. Heat flooded down his arm and drenched the rest of him. He hardened instantly.

She looked up at him and he swore he saw surrender. Or something close to it.

He released his breath in a trembling sigh. He hated to do it, but it seemed that this would be the best way to distract her. "I haven't changed any since the other night. Have you?"

Erin's mouth opened slightly. The pace of her breathing quickened. He traced her lip with his fingertip and the pain in his groin grew to a nearly unbearable pitch. He couldn't take this much longer. If she didn't reply soon, he'd have to climb over this table and take her on the bench.

"There is something between us, Erin. You can't deny that."

She stared at him, not moving, not answering and he wondered what was going through her head. What was she trying to determine? Why was she waiting?

Finally, she closed her eyes. "No, I can't deny it."

Drakor released his touch on her face, breaking the connection of intense desire.

At least he had this. The other night had not been a stroke of luck. She yearned for him the same. Perhaps the more often she lost herself in his arms, the less likely she would be to report on their existence. It was worth a try.

Now he could focus on something other than today's date. It was the anniversary of his birth and he had lost all chance to find his *Mharai*.

Chapter Sixteen

They rode to his house in silence but she could feel the heat emanating from him. Just about every time she had been around him in some way, his body sent off waves of heat and jolts of desire. Was that part of his world too?

She had agreed to drop him off at the house. It seemed like a good excuse to get there and now she needed one to get inside. What could she do to convince him to let her in? How could she weaken his defenses?

Once she got in there and had that small electronic thing in her hands, there was no telling what she could do with it. It looked like Brundor had make the spaceship disappear with it.

Drakor cleared his throat and she glanced over at him. He stared out his window, his face shining and ruddy. For the hell of it, she took a chance on asking him about John Doe. Now that there was nothing left to hide from one another, she could discover if he was connected to the other man.

"Drakor, do you know of the man who lived here before you?"

His back straightened. "I'm not clear on your question."

"Before your family built that big Victorian, there was a small cottage out here and a man who lived in it."

He wiped his palms on his legs. "You need information on this man?"

Erin shrugged. "He's a John Doe. I'm trying to find out his real name, that's all."

"John Doe?"

"Nobody knew who he was, what his name was, or where he came from. Other than he lived in that cottage. But the bank held no mortgage on it. He had no savings account." She tapped the steering wheel. "A real mystery."

"Where is the man now?" Drakor's voice was tight, edgy.

Erin opened her mouth to reply, but then the realization slammed into her brain. Her John Doe was Drakor's missing friend. The one he asked about that first night he came to her apartment.

She couldn't tell him he was dead. Not now. She had to sort all this out first, understand how all the pieces fit together. She had to find out why Drakor and his friend came to Earth.

Oh hell, time to suck it up and deal with the fact that Drakor wasn't human. Time to be a woman and use her feminine charms to get what she wanted. Plus, she needed to change the subject from John Doe.

The dirt road to the Victorian loomed up ahead but Erin ran her fingers up Drakor's leg until she reached the hem of his shorts. He gasped, jumping in the seat.

"Erin..." His voice sounded low and tortured.

She bit her lip to keep from smiling. "Hmmm?"

"Your hand. P-Please move it from my leg."

She left it there until she pulled in front of the house and she needed it to move the gear into park and yank on the brake.

Drakor reached for the door handle but she leaned across the car and put her other hand over his crotch. He shuddered, moaned, when her fingers brushed along his erection. Two could play at this game.

"Wh-what are you doing?"

She grinned. "I wanted to see if that something was still between us."

His sultry eyes finally locked onto hers. "And is it?"

Erin ran her fingertip along the hardness in his shorts and his whole body tensed. She moved herself closer to him, licking her lips. "I think it is."

She heard him catch his breath as his eyes fluttered closed. She must be torturing him. That was good. She'd get information out of him yet.

Leaning across the seats twisted her back but she couldn't let him go yet, not when she had him within her clutches. Erin scooted over the brake and landed in his lap. The very same place this all started two days ago.

Drakor groaned but didn't push her off. Erin wiped the sweat gathering on her forehead and wriggled a bit, just for good fun, rubbing her hip against him.

Suddenly, his hands captured her waist and his eyes flashed open. "You do this on purpose."

"Shall I stop?"

"Great Sun, no, don't stop."

She stared into his bottomless eyes, unable to ignore the incessant pounding of her heart. "How can you not be from Earth?"

"I do not understand your question." His husky voice rumbled his chest.

"You look, you feel, you taste, every thing about you seems human."

He drew in a sharp breath and his eyes narrowed. "I am *not* human."

Erin recoiled. "You say it with disgust."

Drakor shook his head, his hands sliding up her sides. "I did not mean for it to sound that way. But you must understand what's happened in the past…"

Despite her body's continued hunger for him, the mood had clearly been broken by his statement.

Erin reached to the seat behind her and snatched Sitora's cloth doll.

"Do not leave." His voice was pleading. "Historically, humans have treated others with—"

"I'm going inside to give your sister her doll," she said, deliberately interrupting him, and opened the car door.

"Erin, wait!" He reached across the seat for her but she slipped out before he could grab her. She ran up the front steps and knocked on the door. She tested the knob, but it was locked.

Footsteps sounded behind her and then Drakor had his hands on her shoulders. He swung her around.

"We need to talk."

"Why? Because you're worried what I might do if I'm angry?" And well he should be.

He stared at her and once again she was drawn into his mysterious gaze, complete with the odd white circles in the center. "Yes," he answered softly. "I don't want you angry. I want you to understand."

But it was easier if she were angry. Easier to steal that PDA-looking thing from him and write the story of her career when she wasn't thinking of the next time his lips would touch her neck.

He took a step closer and she swallowed. The scent of him saturated her, just as it did in the car. Her body tingled and her nipples hardened. Even now, even when she couldn't stand him, his essence broke through to her innate sexuality.

So this is how it would be. No matter that he was an extraterrestrial, no matter that he hated humans and used her, no matter that she would expose him to further her career—she would always be attracted to him. She would always want him. She just needed to keep a clear focus on that. But under no circumstances, would she fall for him.

The door opened behind her.

"Erin!"

She turned around to see her little friend. "Look what I've brought back for you, Sitora."

The little girl took her doll and gave it a hug. Then she rushed forward and squeezed Erin's legs. "I'm so glad you came back. Drakor said I wouldn't see you again."

She bent down and pulled Sitora in her arms. "Well, he can't seem to keep me away, can he?"

"Uh-uh!" The girl leaned away from Erin's shoulder and stuck her tongue out at her brother. "I'm the one that got the present today, not you!"

"Present?"

Sitora nodded. "Today is the anniversary of Drakor's birth. But he's too mean to get any presents."

Drakor's birthday? Erin looked over her shoulder at him. His arms were folded across his chest and his lips were set in a grim line. Instead of enjoying the day, he looked furious. As if he didn't want to be reminded of it.

"Your birthday?" She tried goading him into admitting why he fumed. "Most humans see it as a cause for celebration."

He glared at her. "I'm not human, remember?"

℘℃Ϟ

Drakor felt the heat of anger flush his face. He left his sister and Erin on the porch and stormed down the steps. It was probably unwise to leave Erin unwatched, but he couldn't stand before her any longer.

Damn this game they played. In the vehicle he had been so close to tasting her again, to having his fingers trail over her smooth skin, to cupping his palms around her breasts.

Then she had to mention him looking human. And he was stupid enough to allow his emotions to answer her. Of course she would be defensive of her people, he should have known better.

But then she had to provoke him again with the talk of celebrating his special day. What did she know of it? How could she even begin to understand what the day meant for him? From now on he would have no one. Once he returned to Elliac, he would have to carry the shame of *Unmhar*, mate-less. The shame would only double if he allowed them to return home without completion of their mission.

Drakor heard the door shut and shook his head. Now Erin was in the house unsupervised. Ankra was in there somewhere, but she did not know of Erin's discovery. He had told no one. No sense in worrying them, in making them fear her.

He started around to the back of the house, a few raindrops sprinkling around him. But when he reached the back his stomach dropped. The shuttle appeared in full view and the plank lowered to the ground. He ran forward, his heart pounding wildly in his chest. What if Erin had a camera with her?

Brundor stood at the top of the plank, looking oblivious to any wrongdoing.

"Get out now!" Drakor said from below.

"What's the problem?"

"What if someone were to see it?" *Again.*

His brother obeyed and came down the plank. He touched the crystal pad a few times to vanish the shuttle, then he started up the hill toward the front of the house.

Drakor caught up with him. "What were you doing in there?"

Brundor shrugged. "Stuff."

"What stuff?"

"Looking around."

He reached out and grabbed his brother's shoulder to stop him. "You can't just go in and out of there whenever you want."

Stormy, dark eyes stared back at him. The rain picked up in intensity but neither of them moved. "I am preparing for our trip home."

Despite the plausibility of the statement, Drakor doubted its truth. He had never known his brother to plan, organize, or prepare for anything. There was some other motive behind Brundor's actions and before long Drakor would find it out.

They made their way up the stairs to the porch but Brundor stopped before going in. He sniffed the air. A red hue appeared on his cheeks and he licked his lips.

Drakor felt his chest tighten. He recognized this look and he didn't like it. He grabbed his brother's arm and leaped back from the heat. Oh no. Not now. Not yet.

Brundor looked at him with wet eyes and a feral smile. "You said you weren't going to see Erin again."

The hair on the back of Drakor's neck stood up and he leaned closer. "She is not your business."

Drakor watched his brother swallow as a line of sweat sprang out on Brundor's forehead. "You promised to take me to that place. To meet the females. You have to take me."

"It's your Crossing. You've started it."

His brother ran his hands through his hair, dampening them with the sweat from his forehead. "I smell her." He lifted his nose again. "I know she's here. You told me you were done with her."

An electric rush blazed through Drakor's veins. "I said I probably wouldn't see her again, not that I was done with her."

"What's the difference?" He reached for the doorknob. "I need her."

Drakor reached around and thrust his arm between Brundor and the door. "You won't dare touch her."

"Why do you defend her? She is human."

He didn't know the answer, other than that Erin was the only female he could have. The only place he could forget his future loneliness was in her arms.

"If she is not your *Mharai*," Brundor continued, "then let me have her. You know how painful these urges are."

Twice in a male Elliacian's life they went through this immense pain. First during the time of their Crossing and second when they found their *Mharai* but could not mate with her. Both times the sexual energy searched for a release and rebelled against a forced withholding.

But once through the Crossing, which in itself caused both agonizing restraint and rapturous release, males felt no sexual urges until they found their *Mharai*. If Brundor had had his Crossing as Drakor did, there would be no issue. But since he had not yet begun, his brother was an explosive combination of sexual pressure and stubborn immaturity.

Drakor's headache returned. Now he not only had Erin to subdue, but his own brother as well.

"Do not touch her or I will kill you."

Brundor managed a half-smile. "Then you will take me to that place, that dance club to find someone else."

"I'm not sure you can handle yourself there. The females there are far too tantalizing and you could lose control."

"You said some are willing."

"Some are, but not right there, you would have to wait. It is not a good idea."

His brother narrowed his eyes and pushed his arm away. "Either you take me there or I will find a way to go myself." Then, he opened the front door and stepped inside.

Drakor followed. If there was ever a time he wished he were still a boy scouring through hot and dark caves and searching for hidden jewels, this was it. How could he survive the next five minutes, much less the amount of time it took for Ankra to get pregnant? He didn't want to be in control of this mission, of his family. He never wanted to come here in the first place.

He looked in all of the downstairs rooms for Erin but didn't see her or his sisters. Then a shout and door slams at the top of the steps sent him running. He bounded up the grand staircase taking two steps at a time.

But at the top he saw no one. All doors were shut.

He opened his brother's door first, struggling against the frenzied rush in his veins. But Brundor was alone. He sat on the edge of his bed, his elbows on his knees and his head in his hands. Even from across the room, Drakor could see him trembling.

"Tell me." Drakor managed to hold his voice steady.

"I–I can't take this. You have to do something."

Drakor took another step closer. "Brundor…"

"Forget the dance club, take us home."

He crossed the room until he stood directly before his brother. "What just happened?"

"I–I saw the door to Mother and Father's room open." Brundor continued to shake and stare at the floor. "I went to look in and I saw Erin there. I mumbled something about her not going in there and she shrieked."

Drakor sucked in a deep breath, needing to protect Erin rather than be concerned over her prying. "Then what happened?"

"She started to explain but I must have scared her because she pushed me out of the way and ran out the door. I think she went to Ankra and Sitora's room."

"Did you touch her?"

"No. She touched me. I came straight in here." Brundor glanced up with frightened, red eyes. "This is killing me. I can't deal with the Crossing on Earth. We have to go home."

Drakor backed away and sat on his own bed. He wanted nothing more than to go home, to take them all and vanish from Earth forever. But he promised his parents, he owed it to them to complete the mission. He owed it to his brother and sisters to not let dishonor ruin their future.

If just a brush with a human female made Brundor this way he would have to keep him locked up for the remainder of their stay. And he was going to have to make sure that Erin did not come here again. She was far too dangerous. For everyone.

Drakor got up and went to his sisters' room. He knocked first, listening to the giggling and shuffling.

Ankra opened the door. Erin was lying on the floor and Sitora sat on top of her, straddling Erin's hips. For an instant he saw himself on the floor and Erin straddling him. A thread of desire snaked in his veins and he shoved his hands into fists trying to stave it off. No. He had to get her out of here.

He stood over the pair. "Erin, you need to go now."

Her eyes narrowed and she bit her lip, just like she did after Father died when she wanted to stay to comfort Sitora. Or did she want to comfort him?

"Erin's not leaving." Sitora crossed her arms.

"We're having a slumber party," Ankra explained. "Erin told us all about this custom where girls get together and spend the night. We thought it would be fun."

Drakor's pulse slammed at his temples. He could not allow Erin to spend the night here with Brundor ready to explode at any moment. And yet the thought of her sleeping nearby strangely pleased him.

"I am in charge." He crossed his arms, feeling more like little Sitora than like the leader of this family. And yet, how dare they make these decisions without consulting him? Ankra and Sitora knew nothing about the risky games Erin played. "I make the decisions here."

"Oh, but it was going to be a surprise," Sitora whined. "For your anni— birthday."

Drakor glared at Erin. "And was that *her* idea too?"

"No," Ankra said from behind him. "It was mine."

Chapter Seventeen

Once Erin heard deep and even breaths from Ankra and Sitora, she sat up. She never liked sleeping on the floor. Even as a girl in grade school, she hated slumber parties where she had to bring her sleeping bag. There was nothing like a nice, soft bed. But she could sacrifice one night's sleep for a chance at the object she saw still under the dresser.

The moon cast long shadows in the dim room. She couldn't reach the electronic thing from this side of the dresser, it was too far the other side. But Sitora's bed blocked the other side. The only way to reach it was to climb over Sitora and reach behind her head.

Erin crawled out of her blankets and over to the sleeping girl. An angelic face nestled close to the worn doll. There couldn't be a sweeter image anywhere.

Erin sighed. This would be easier if she had gone home to get her pajamas and other necessities, but a part of her feared Drakor wouldn't let her back in if she left. But he did let Ankra convince him to lend her one of his shirts. So here she was on her knees, wearing a green shirt smelling every bit like the man in the next room, ready to steal something she knew was important to him.

She scooted over Sitora and wedged herself between the girl and the large bed. Erin reached under the dresser but couldn't touch it. She pushed herself flat on her stomach, held her breath, and extended her fingertips toward the wall.

Contact. She crept forward another inch or so until her face was pressed against the mahogany drawer. With a small tip forward, the device fell against her palm. Erin snatched it and pulled away.

Finally, she held it safely within her grasp. This thing had to be something more than that light—or whatever it was. She clearly saw Brundor touch one of these and make the spaceship disappear.

Erin pushed herself up against the bed and stood. For a moment, she watched the two sisters sleeping. They looked so peaceful, so happy, so…unaware. Exposing Drakor for her article was one thing but it would also affect the rest of them. What would happen to these two once her story broke?

She stepped over Sitora and bit her lip. Her big bag sat near Ankra's bed and she tiptoed across the room to it. She didn't want to hurt them. In fact, despite the way Drakor treated her, she didn't want to hurt him either. But for once in her life she had to think of herself, of her professional life. Rita wouldn't let a friendship stand in her way. A reporter needed to be apart from emotional ties. She'd learned that lesson well enough. The shame from it all still burned her cheeks and twisted her stomach.

Erin opened the small zipper deep inside her purse and dropped the electronic PDA-thing in it. She took a quick check on the others and found them still sleeping, the moonlight spilling across Sitora's sweet face.

She bit her lip again and stole out the bedroom door. The hallway was nearly pitch black, save for a gray light coming up the steps from the window in the parlor room. Erin glanced at the next door and swallowed. Inside laid both Brundor and Drakor.

Something about Brundor worried her immensely. His hot eyes held desperation. And desperation drove people to do reckless acts. Even if Erin somehow knew Drakor would protect her, she didn't want to take that chance around his brother.

Erin wiped her palms on Drakor's shirt and tested the door at the end of the hall. The room she snuck in earlier. It was unlocked! She slipped inside and quickly closed the door behind her, locking it.

This room too was darkened by the shadows of the moon. If only she could have gone home and gotten her flashlight. Now, she'd have to poke around in the dark. There had to be something in this massive bookshelf to her left. She already knew that nothing was on the other side of the room other than a bed. This must have been his parents' bedroom. It seemed creepy to be in here when they only died two days ago. But still she had work to do and she couldn't let anything stand in her way.

She went closer to the screen on the desk. It looked similar to a computer monitor, but much flatter and shinier. Erin reached out to touch it when a sound startled her from behind.

Had someone come in? She locked the door, she was sure of it.

Erin tried to ignore the galloping of her heart and slowly turned to face the dark corner of the room. She could see nothing against that shadowed wall but then a figure stepped forward.

"So this is the real Erin."

Her breath stilled but her heart jumped for an entirely different reason. Drakor.

But how did he get in here? Or was he in here all along? There was no sense in lying like she tried to with Brundor. Drakor knew what she did for a living and why she was here.

She folded her arms under her breasts, suddenly very aware of her bare legs and his scent on her collar. "And? What of it?"

He took another step forward and Erin had to muffle the intake of breath in her dry throat. The glow from the window lit up his bare chest, narrowed waist, and arms, casting shadows along the hard lines of his muscles. He wore a pair of shorts, unbuttoned but zipped, and nothing else.

Drakor leaned one hand against the shelves near her. "I never imagined you would use my sisters to get what you want."

Erin tilted her head, trying to not be tempted by the allure of his body.

He moved closer still and Erin backed up until her butt hit the edge of the desk. Drakor put an arm on either side of her head, blocking an escape.

Erin stared up at him, wanting to run from him but knowing she could not. Not when he was this close. Not when shivers coursed through her body in the anticipation of his next move. She licked her lips but couldn't control the deep yearning crashing through her blood. He held her spellbound, intoxicated by his raw sexuality.

Drakor leaned toward her face, stopping just inches from her lips. "You and I are playing this game, but only one of us can win."

Why couldn't she respond to him with some witty comment? One glance into those mysterious eyes made her heart skip a beat. His heady, masculine presence enveloped her so completely that all logical thought emptied from her brain.

Erin muttered something unintelligible and lifted her chin a little. Damn it, why didn't he kiss her?

A hot hand clamped down on her thigh and Erin gasped. Her pulse rocketed. She could see one corner of his lips curl as he slid a knee between her legs. "What do you hope to find, Erin?"

She tried to answer but her mouth was too dry to even swallow. If only he would kiss her...

His other hand came down from the shelf and slowly lifted her shirt. "I like the way you look in my clothes."

With one hand on her thigh, the other resting on her bare hip, Drakor leaned forward to within a whisper of touching her lips. Shivers had long since been replaced by a spiraling heat inside of her. Her nipples reached forward, her legs weakened.

Still, he did not kiss her. The bastard was teasing her. He must know the effect he had on her, the way he could make her brain so fuzzy that she could concentrate only on him.

Erin had one thought only at that moment—to have the aching void deep inside her filled. And Drakor had to be the one to do it. But she'd be damned before she'd let him know that.

℘℧

If Erin only knew how much this tortured him. From the moment he saw those firm muscular legs poking out from beneath his shirt, Drakor knew he had to have her tonight. Of course, the fact that it would distract her from prying around was an added bonus.

In the hazy light he saw her lick her lips. She wanted him to kiss her and yet she would not make the first move. If she wanted it so badly, why didn't she reach her arms around his neck and pull her to him? Maybe she enjoyed this other game they played.

"Admit it," he said against her mouth. "You want me, despite everything."

She didn't answer so Drakor raised his hand and caressed her breast, his thumb massaging the pointed tip. This time a whimper was his response. His whole body tightened with need.

Drakor pressed against her. "You can feel how much I want you. Tell me that you want me inside you."

Erin arched her back, pushing herself against his palm and erection. Her actions gave him the answer he sought but she refused to say the words. Why could she not admit it? Because he wasn't human?

He moved his other hand around to cup her bottom. She lifted her leg and he slid a finger inside her underwear. Oh yes, she wanted him all right. Thank the Great Sun he'd learned much about his control within the last week. Clenching his teeth, Drakor held still while fire pumped through his blood, jerking his erection.

"I will have you answer me." He nibbled on her lip. Erin closed her eyes, apparently waiting for his kiss.

Instead of obliging her, Drakor slipped a finger within the very wet and waiting spot between her legs. She groaned and bucked up against him. He had to suck in a deep ragged breath to hold himself under restraint.

But he would break her, he would make her admit that she wanted him. Then he would know that he could sway her with his touch anytime. He could make her forget everything about revealing who they really were.

Drakor added another finger and she cried out against his lips. "Do you want me to kiss you?" The words came out more urgently than he intended.

Her hand found his zipper and yanked it down. Within seconds his shorts dropped to the floor and he stood against her completely bare.

He followed her lead and moved his hands to her waist, then pulled down her panties until they sank to her feet. In some strange way it aroused him even more to leave his shirt on her.

Erin pulled his hips toward her, moving her legs apart to greet him. Her eyes stared at him and he could see her face flush with desire. He rubbed himself against her, but refused to enter.

He would win this battle.

Drakor captured her head in his hands. "You have to tell me."

She whimpered and her eyelids fluttered. He moved his face close to hers until he could feel her hot breath on his mouth. "You will say you want me or I will put your clothes back on you and take you to your vehicle."

Erin reached down and touched him, the contact sending tremors skittering throughout his body. She tried to guide him inside of her, but he was stronger. He took both of her wrists with one hand and held them behind her back.

"You must do it my way."

She bit her lower lip and glanced up at him. Even in this low light, he could see the fury and need in her gaze. "Damn you!"

Drakor couldn't withhold his grin. "So you want me to kiss you."

"You've bewitched me somehow. It-it isn't fair."

"That's not an answer."

She struggled briefly against his hold on her wrists. The movement massaged him to a dangerous edge. "Tell me."

Erin stared at his lips. "Yes, damn it. I want you."

Drakor plunged his tongue between her lips at the same he thrust his erection deep inside of her.

Erin moaned, but then put her hands on his shoulders and pushed him back. "Stop."

"Now?"

"The desk, it hurts. Can we…can we go onto the bed?"

Drakor lifted her, never withdrawing from inside her and carried her to the bed. But this time he leaned back across the blanket and sat her on top of him. Just as he imagined in Ankra's room earlier.

The new vantage point gave him a vision he knew he would never forget. Despite her wearing his shirt, he could see her breasts bouncing. The soft glow from the windows gave him a shadowed picture of her face, with upturned lips and half-closed eyes.

Erin moved on top of him, guiding him to a release he could barely delay. But then a strange expression passed over her features and she suddenly lifted herself off of him, hovering just above the tip.

Drakor cried out and reached for her hips. He tried to yank her back down but those strong legs of hers held her aloft. What game was she playing now?

"What are you doing?" he managed to croak between the surges of ecstasy and frustration.

"I–I want to know what you need from–from us."

Erin seemed to be in just as much agony as he was and she also could barely speak.

He grabbed her waist and tried to pull her down again, but she wouldn't budge.

"What do you need from humans?"

Drakor lifted his hips to find his way back inside of her but it didn't work. She turned the tables on him and now she wielded the power.

He sighed. "Many from where I live can't process something…you call it Vitamin D, their bones are weak and deformed."

Jordanna Kay

Erin slid down over him again and he closed his eyes with relief and contentment. He could feel her hips moving above him, her sweet thighs rubbing against his sides.

Then the feeling was gone again. She had lifted herself off.

"What do you expect to–to find on Earth?"

She grunted out the words and the look of concentration on her face clearly told him her questions did not come to her easily.

Knowing he wouldn't feel the pleasure of her warmth around him until he answered, he didn't bother to force her down. "We hoped to find something humans developed to strengthen bones." It wasn't a total lie.

"Like medicines or supplements?"

He nodded, but somehow he knew that she would figure out the answer was too easy. If that were all he was after, he could have purchased them and be gone by now. Eventually, Erin would come back for more answers.

When she lowered herself onto him this time, Drakor reached behind her neck and pulled her down to his chest. "No more questions." Then he captured her lips with his own. He snaked both of his arms around her back, holding her tightly against him. She continued to move along his shaft, bringing them further along their quest for overwhelming relief.

When Erin started to whimper, Drakor let go of her mouth and dropped his head back onto the bed. He closed his eyes, relishing the sensations of her soft, urgent noises and wet, quivering body. She cried out, hips jerking.

Then he could hear nothing but the frantic rush of his pulse and the echoes of his own groans.

This time Erin collapsed on him. They lay unmoving, with no sounds other than their own labored breathing. After what felt like both an eternity and barely a second, she moved herself off of him and rolled to her back on the blankets.

He wanted to say something to her, to tell her that he didn't want to play this game. He wished there was a way so that they both could win, but somehow he had a sense that in the end, they would both lose.

176

Drakor turned to touch her but she slipped away from him and stood. He sat up and watched her as she glanced around the room for a moment, shrugged and then found her panties. Her face wrinkled in mild disgust as she pulled them on.

"You don't have to go," he said as she reached for the door.

She wouldn't look at him. "Oh, yes, I do." Erin unlocked the door and turned the handle. "Oh, and happy birthday. I hope you enjoyed your gift."

She vanished into the hallway and shut the door behind her. Drakor fell back on the bed. Giving him pleasure was her gift? She couldn't possibly know the irony that. Today marked the day he would never again know desire, love, or happiness when he returned to Elliac. Only Erin Price, a human, could now give him those.

Drakor rolled over and pulled the blanket over his legs. He squeezed his eyes closed but the images of Erin on top of him plagued his peace.

Only the one female determined to destroy him could give him what he would soon lose forever.

Chapter Eighteen

The ringing phone startled Erin awake. She scrambled around on her bed until she knocked the receiver off the hook. Blinking in the morning light, she found it on the floor.

"Hello?"

"Erin? Is everything okay?"

"Greg? What time is it?" She yawned.

"It's eleven o'clock. Don't you have to be at work? What happened to you last night? They said you left the office yesterday and never came back. I couldn't get a hold of you at home."

Erin stretched but she couldn't dislodge the tingle still skipping through her from last night. "I was over at Dra…Ankra's. I had a slumber party with her and Sitora."

"Slumber party? On a Monday night?"

"Look, Greg, I'm fine, okay. I'm getting up now I was just tired from being up late and I needed some extra sleep."

He sighed. "Sorry, I was just worried, you know. You sounded really freaked on the messages you left."

Erin rolled her eyes. She knew she should be flattered or feel loved that he worried about her but instead it made her feel like a helpless child. Like she was the baby sister he always had to keep an eye on. She was a grown woman, for God's sake.

"Well, what was it?"

She heard his other line beep. "Shouldn't you get that? My thing can wait."

He sighed again. "Okay, okay, hold on." Erin heard a click and he was gone.

She really shouldn't tell him at all. Yes, when she first saw that spaceship she was freaked and scared and excited. She wanted to warn him about Ankra. She wanted to gush about what a fabulous opportunity this was.

But now that she had seen Drakor again, now that she spent the night nestled between the oblivious sisters, she couldn't let Greg in on her secret. What if he in some way refused to let her go back there? What if he blabbed about it and told someone else? What if he went over there himself and ruined everything?

Telling Greg was not the right thing to do.

The line clicked again. "I'm back. Erin, tell me what had you so worked up."

She got up from the bed and started digging through her drawers. "Why don't you tell me what had you MIA the last few days first?" Stalling seemed like a good tactic.

"Oh, it's been a mess. First I couldn't find some files I needed on our new software, then one of my top engineers left an unintelligible message on my machine. I tried to call him over the weekend but there was no answer. Then, on Sunday after coming back from getting some stuff done, my neighbor tells me a woman was poking around outside the house."

"Could it have been Ankra?"

"No. The description didn't fit her. Anyway, after the crap you rambled on about at my house on Saturday morning, I started getting really worried. I think I should call an attorney."

Erin sank down on her bed. "Oh, damn, Greg, I'm sorry. You know, maybe you and I can sit down together and try to work it out. Figure out what's going on."

"Yeah, maybe." She'd never heard him sound so dejected. And afraid.

Jordanna Kay

"Listen, maybe if you spent some time with Ankra you'd feel better. She seems to do that for you."

"Yeah, I haven't seen her since that one crazy night last week. Maybe I should go over there."

Erin smiled with the new lift to his voice. For once *she* was taking care of *him.* "I should forewarn you, though, that both of her parents died on Saturday."

She heard him suck in a breath. "Both? I thought just their father was sick."

She didn't get it either. What did Drakor say? *She chose not to live without him.* It didn't make any sense, but maybe that too was something to do with their culture.

That and casting a dunce spell on their sex partner. She could barely hold a thought once the desire for him had invaded her neurons. Forcing herself to ask those questions, to move herself off of him, was harder than trying to speak in a complete sentence after she recovered from anesthesia when her wisdom teeth were removed.

But somehow, through a strength honed in her investigative instincts, she found a way to take advantage of his vulnerable position. And it had worked. So far she didn't have time to think it through, but he did answer her. And if that's what it took to get answers, she would just have to subject herself to it.

"Is she upset?"

Greg's question interrupted her memories of Drakor's warm hands on her waist. "Um, she seemed okay yesterday. But I'll bet she would still love to see you."

"So what are you going to do today? Are you going in to work?"

Erin glanced up at the window above her bed. The partially overcast sky promised another humid day of summer. One that would be best spent inside her office building, where she could be bringing her story together, figuring it out piece by piece. That's what she loved about this job, putting the puzzle together and making it something that would entertain, inform, or startle others.

And yet there was something else tugging at her heart, something else she felt compelled to do before she could commit herself to this story.

"I think I'll go to the cemetery today. I haven't visited Mom and Dad in months."

Greg cleared his throat. "Say hello to them for me, will you?"

"Of course." Erin stood again and headed for the bathroom. "Why don't you come over one day this week so we can figure out this mess at Invasion Shield?"

"I'll call you later toward the end of the week."

"Fine."

They hung up and Erin started the shower. Thank God her stalling tactic worked with Greg. He never even asked about her freak-out messages again.

Now she just needed to find a way to get information from Drakor without having him fog her brain. Though the way he made the rest of her feel wasn't such a bad thing.

The cemetery was an hour's drive away and Erin reviewed last night's event on the ride. She had that small electronic device in her purse but she knew there was so much more in that house. Next time she would come back with a flashlight and a camera, though somehow she knew Drakor would be far more careful about her being there. Hell, he might not even let her come back.

Plus, she'd made the assumption that her John Doe, with a mysterious marrow deformity, was the friend Drakor was looking for. And Drakor had come to Earth looking for help for deformed and weak bones. Perfect.

Erin swung by the flower shop first and then into the gates of the cemetery. Pristine, green fields reached toward the bordering trees. Having markers rather than headstones, this place sometimes seemed more like a quiet park than a place to bury the dead.

Erin parked the car and stepped out into the cloying summer heat, flowers in hand. She went down the row and stopped between two sites. Yes, it had been too long since she had come. Far too long.

Her little nothing life had consumed her and she had neglected her parents in the process. What would they think of her now? Would they be more impressed by fame and fortune at her amazing discovery or by the fact that she finally felt alive? Somehow in the last two weeks she felt she had lived two years, she had seen, felt, and touched enough for two lifetimes.

Erin sighed and went over to her father's marker. She placed the blue carnations in the vase next to it.

"Good morning, Daddy," she whispered. "I'm sorry I haven't been coming by to visit."

Then she turned to her mother's plot and dropped the rest of the flowers in that vase. "Look, Mom, I brought daisies, your favorite."

Erin brushed the dirt from the plaques and cleared away the stray grass. The sun burned the top of her head and sweat ran down her back, but Erin didn't mind. She owed this to them, at the very least.

"I wish we could chat." She sat back on her heels. "What would the two of you think of Drakor? Would you find him handsome and charming? Would you think him evil when you found out he was an alien?"

The taste of salt filled her mouth and Erin sniffled. How could she figure these things out on her own? Could she trust Drakor? She needed this story, she needed to prove herself again. It had been her goal for three years to overcome the bitter taste of her embarrassing lack of judgment.

But what would it all mean for Drakor's family? Were her dreams worth more than theirs?

80CB

Drakor heard the distinct sound of a vehicle engine and bounded down the staircase to the front door. Erin was back. Perhaps she was here to sneak another look around for more evidence. Or maybe to torture him again.

He grinned at the memories of last night, the images tightening his groin. He pulled the door open and stepped out onto the front porch, squinting in the bright sunshine.

But it wasn't Erin's small, faded blue vehicle parked out front. It was Greg's larger, boxy one. Disappointment coursed through him, dousing the heat stirring in his veins.

Erin's brother came forward, his light hair combed neatly away from his face. He wore sharp, pressed pants and stiff, blue shirt and carried a small telephone in one hand. Greg offered the other hand as he came forward.

Drakor accepted it and shook it as expected.

"Erin spoke of your parents' passing. I'm very sorry."

His gut tensed. What else did she tell Greg? He could be here now as a spy or a decoy. Drakor swallowed, forcing himself not to react. For all he knew, Erin might have told her brother nothing of what she saw.

Greg glanced at the dry dirt on the ground. "Hey, is your sister inside? Is it alright if I see her?"

Drakor tried to steel the intense jealousy roiling through him. Why could he and Erin have this type of relationship? Why could the two of them connect and yearn for each other without the distrust and animosity hovering between them?

"She's in the kitchen with Sitora," he answered and stepped aside.

Drakor listened to the door close behind him and then wandered out to the spot where Erin had hidden that day. What had she actually witnessed?

He placed palm against the rough bark of the tree and tried to get a view of what Erin might have seen. From this vantage point, she could have seen everything. Drakor sighed. There was little he could do about it now but to continue to distract her. Or, if necessary, to use everything at his disposal to plead to the chance she may reconsider. Even if that meant his little sister.

Even if that meant making her…what did the humans call it? Fall in love with him.

The sound of the front door closing redirected his attention. He watched as Greg and Ankra came down the steps together, his arm around her shoulders. His sister looked around, her face pinched in concern.

Drakor came forward. "You are going back with him?"

Her features relaxed with relief. "Y–yes. But Sitora is inside alone."

"Where is Brundor?"

Ankra shrugged. "I don't know. I haven't seen him all morning."

Drakor tried to shake off the unease building inside of him. Perhaps he was within the invisible shuttle again. Once Greg left, he'd have to get his brother out of there.

"I'll find him," he reassured her and she nodded.

He watched the two of them leave, half-praying that Ankra would finally get pregnant so they could be back on Elliac within days. The other half feared he wouldn't have any more time with Erin, that once they were gone from here he would never lose himself in a female's arms again. And the ever-present failure at finding his friend's body nagged at him.

Once the large vehicle was out of site, Drakor punched in the code on his crystal pad. The craft materialized and he headed down the hill for it. Hopefully, unsupervised Sitora wasn't causing any trouble inside the house.

He lowered the ramp and stormed up into the interior. The dim glow illuminated the hallway and Drakor headed for the cockpit area first.

"Brundor!"

His voice echoed off the walls. The cockpit was empty. He searched the rest of the craft, room by room, and found them all empty.

A cold weight of dread sank in his stomach. Great Sun, where had his brother gone? If he wasn't in the house and he wasn't in the shuttle, where was he?

Drakor bounded down the ramp and into the yard. He made the ship vanish again and headed toward the house. He had to find Brundor before Brundor found trouble. And he was forced to drag Sitora with him.

His little sister was still in the kitchen room when Drakor came inside. She seemed oblivious to everything but the food she held in her hand. A cookie, Erin had called it. Supposedly, it was sweet, like the frosting he tasted, but he couldn't bring himself to try it now.

"Sitora, we need to leave now."

She looked up, her eyes bright. "We're going somewhere? Can we go to see Erin?"

He wished they could. He wished he could leave Sitora with Erin so he could find Brundor alone. More than anything, he wished he knew how to pilot one of those Earth vehicles. But they would either need to walk or use the Elliacian method of Transfer.

"Maybe we'll see Erin later, but we need to find Brundor first. Have you seen him recently?"

She shoved the last bite of cookie between her lips. "He weft a wong time ago," she said, her mouth stuffed with crumbs. "Soon after Erin weft."

After Erin left? That was hours ago, just a short time after daybreak.

Drakor pulled Sitora to her feet and went out the front door. For now, they'd walk. Maybe Brundor would be on his way back. He wouldn't want to miss him.

"It's hot out here," Sitora whined the moment they started down the dirt road.

"Not as hot as it is at home." Drakor took her hand in his.

"I want to go home. I don't like it here."

"You like it when Erin comes to visit."

"But you don't like her."

Like her? Drakor sucked in a breath. How did he feel for Erin? Anger? Resentment? Frustration? Desire? All of those things at any given moment. But like her? What was that? If she was his *Mharai*, he would love her. There

185

would be no one but her. But she wasn't. And he had lost all chance to find the one the fates had chosen for him.

He clutched his sister's sweaty hand and continued down the dirt path. They had just about reached the paved road when a sleek, black vehicle slowed.

Drakor's lungs squeezed, dread burrowing into his gut.

A tinted window slid down with a motorized whirr. A female with vibrant yellow hair and dark eye coverings smiled at him. A strong, flowery smell tickled his nose and increased the ache in his head.

"Well, hello, Mr. Tall, Dark, and Extra Hot."

Drakor blinked at her. He recognized the voice from somewhere but couldn't quite place it. But what made him the most nervous wasn't only that his brother was not in the car, but that this female was headed toward the house.

She chewed something in her mouth and made a loud popping sound with it. "I didn't realize this worthless path would bring me something so worthwhile."

He wiped the sweat collecting on his forehead. "Have we met?"

Her red-painted lower lip thrust forward. "I'm hurt that you don't remember me. It's only been a little over a week."

His mind scrambled to remember the females he met the short time he had been on Earth, but no one remained firm in his memory but Erin.

"At Mickey's," she said, removing the eye coverings from her face. Eyes, a different shade of blue than Erin's, glanced up at him with obvious seduction. "My name is Rita. I work with Erin."

Sitora popped around to the front of his legs. "Erin? You know her? Can we go see her?"

Rita smiled, but it didn't reach her eyes. "And who is this little girl?"

"My sister."

"Can we go see Erin?" Sitora asked, her dark gaze imploring him.

"Not now, we have to look for Brundor, remember?"

"Brundor?" Rita reached forward and adjusted a knob on the vehicles interior. Cool air hissed out of small vents, blowing her hair. "Who is that?"

"My brother. We are looking for him."

"Oh, you have a brother? Is he anything like you?"

Drakor shrugged. He was wasting his time standing here talking to her and her silly questions annoyed him. "We look somewhat alike but he is much younger. I'm sorry we cannot stay but it is important that we find him soon."

She reached out the open window and grabbed his arm. "Wait. I could probably help you find him. Town is several miles away from here."

"Can we go see Erin?" Sitora repeated, tugging on his shirt.

Rita licked her colored lips. "Erin did not come in to the office today, perhaps she is at home. I could drop off the girl and take you to find your lost brother."

Sitora bounced up and down on her toes. "Can we? Can we? Please, Drakor!"

Rita glanced him over and he felt strangely embarrassed by her lingering stares. Her fingers stroked his forearm. "Drakor. You know, I never did learn your name. Interesting."

He wasn't stupid. He knew the signs. She wanted him. If he gave her the slightest gesture, she would open herself to his embrace. This was the type of female Brundor needed. But she held no appeal for Drakor. Even if he did find her attractive, he had no desire for her. His Crossing complete long ago, he would only crave his *Mharai*. And, for some odd reason, Erin Price.

Drakor took a step back and her hand fell away. "Do you know where Erin lives?"

"I do."

"It would be kind of you to take us there, but if she is not home we will need to bring Sitora with us."

The thing in Rita's mouth popped again. "Of course."

Drakor helped Sitora to the backseat and tightened the harness straps over her lap. Then he climbed in to the seat next to Rita. She eased the car forward and his stomach tensed. He didn't want her to see the house. If it had aroused suspicion in Erin, it would no doubt do the same for Rita.

"You should turn around now," he said, touching her hand briefly, hoping it would distract her. "It is a long way until there will again be enough room."

She smiled and turned the car. Once they were on the paved road, her fingers left the steering wheel and came to rest on his knee. Drakor sucked in a breath. It wasn't that he felt the powerful yearning Erin's similar touch had given him, it was Rita's intent. If only it were Brundor sitting in this space. If only Brundor had not disappeared, leaving him in this predicament.

"So, Erin tells me you two are close," she said, "but I don't believe her lies."

Drakor tilted his head back on the headrest and closed his eyes. He felt the rush that signaled a need to protect Erin, but kept himself in check. Defending her with words or actions would only make his present matters worse.

"Erin doesn't lie!" Sitora cried from behind him.

"Cute," Rita mumbled. "Erin has a fan club."

Drakor groaned as a nauseating taste filled his mouth. Somehow he knew that he was going to regret getting in the car with this female. One way or the other.

Chapter Nineteen

After the trip to the cemetery, there was no way she could go into work. Putting up with Rita's sneers and Rockford's questions was not on her list of priorities right now.

Erin took out the tub of Chocolate Chip Cookie Dough ice cream and scooped herself a huge chunk into a bowl. She was going to need complete silence to piece this story together and all the comfort food she could find.

She spread all of her notes on an old Formica table Greg had handed down to her. As usual, everything in her notebook was a jumble. She always amazed herself that she could piece together a story out of her scrawled, unorganized notes.

A knock at the door made her jump. She tried to swallow the ice cream but the bite she just took had been too large. Quickly swooshing it around in her mouth, Erin hurried to the door. Hopefully, it wasn't some solicitor trying to sell her a magazine subscription or a new vacuum cleaner. She just needed peace and quiet.

Erin opened the door and nearly choked on the cold blob sliding down her throat. Drakor stood at her door, his hair slick and tousled and his eyes worried.

"Erin!" squealed a high-pitched voice.

She looked down to see Sitora let go of Drakor's hand and grab a hold of her legs. "Hey, you, what a nice surprise."

Jordanna Kay

Surprise wasn't the word for it. How did they get here? She never did ask Drakor how he got to her office building the other day. But not only how, but why?

"Um, come in."

Sitora ran inside with glee and immediately started poking at the stereo, TV, and anything else her little five-year-old hands could touch.

Drakor stepped just inside the door as if he didn't intend to stay. His scent wafted toward her and she instantly reacted to it. An embarrassing flush rose to her cheeks while a low heat pooled between her legs. His dark eyes locked onto hers and her lips tingled, yearning for him to kiss them.

But then he glanced away. "I'm sorry to come unannounced like this but I have a favor to ask you."

She could think of a favor too, but not with Sitora around. "What is it?"

He sighed and raked his fingers through his hair. "Brundor is missing."

"Missing?"

"I didn't even realize he was gone, but when Greg came and got Ankra this afternoon we couldn't find him anywhere. I need to look for him."

Questions swirled through Erin's head. What if Brundor told someone who he was? What if Brundor was lost somewhere and Drakor couldn't find him? What if Brundor had found a release for that ever-present hunger in his gaze—and it wasn't welcome?

She shivered at the memory of her encounters with him. She didn't really want to run into Brundor again, but she knew it wasn't wise for him to be out alone. "You want me to help you find him?"

Drakor shook his head. "No, I want you to watch Sitora for me."

"Oh." Not that she minded playing with the sweet cherub, but a part of her wished she could spend more time with him. To get information, of course.

"I'll try not to be gone too long. It would just be so much easier not have her along."

Erin smiled. "I'd be happy to keep her here for you."

They heard a crash in another room and a small cry of "uh-oh!" Erin resisted the urge to investigate the disaster or to check on her notes in the kitchen.

Drakor grinned but the lines around his eyes barely moved. She couldn't tell if he was concerned about Brundor, Sitora, or something else. Either way, he certainly wasn't the same man from last night. What she would give to torture him for more information again.

"Thanks." He turned for the door.

"Drakor? How are you getting around? I mean, you can't drive a car."

He visibly tensed and glanced away from her. Did they have a method of transportation that she didn't know about, other than the large spaceship? Hmmm…she might just have to ask Sitora about that.

"I've taken care of it." The words were abrupt, giving Erin more proof that he had something to hide.

"Well, I hope you find him soon."

Drakor's anxious expression softened slightly. "I'll try not to be gone too long." Then he stepped out the door and pulled it closed behind him.

Erin found Sitora trying to pick up clods of dirt on the kitchen floor. One of her houseplants had toppled off the window ledge and now lay in ruins on the vinyl flooring.

The girl glanced up with dark, saucer eyes. "It was an accident…"

Erin smiled gently. "It's okay. Let's just get it cleaned up."

Once most of it was swept up and thrown out, Sitora pointed to the now melted ice cream. "What's that?"

"Ice cream. It's a dessert. Most kids love it."

Sitora climbed up on the chair in front of it. "Can I try it?"

"Sure. It's kind of melted now. Would you like me to get a fresh scoop?"

But it was too late, the girl had already spooned a dripping mound into her mouth. "This is better than the cookie," she declared, and slurped up more.

Erin sighed and sat in one of the other chairs. She gathered the notes she was supposed to be sorting through into one pile. Far away from the messy five-year-old.

She watched Sitora eat. What was it like for her at home? What did she do for fun? Did she go to school? Did she have friends? What would she do now that her parents were gone? What would happen to her if Erin published a story on their existence?

Erin's stomach pitched, throat tightened. She just couldn't let herself get involved with their lives. She couldn't let herself care about them. War correspondents and photojournalists had to remove themselves emotionally from the story they were after. How else could they do their jobs properly?

Sitora continued to slurp the ice cream like a kitten. If she wasn't going to let herself feel sorry for the girl, the least Erin could do was use her for information.

"Sitora, how did you and Drakor get to my apartment?"

"Drakor told me I can't tell you," she replied without looking up from the bowl.

Erin clenched her teeth. He either said that because they used some alien technology to get them here or was he just trying to be spiteful.

"But he's a meanie." Sitora held out the dish. "Can I have some more?"

Erin gave her more ice cream. "Does that mean you'll tell me anyway?"

The girl swallowed a large chunk. "Oh, that's cold!"

"That's why it's called 'ice cream' because it's cold like ice." She tried to hold onto her patience. "Did you come here in a machine of some sort? Did you walk?"

"What is that thing called that you have?"

"What? My car?"

Sitora nodded. "We came here in one of those."

Erin's mouth dropped open. But who would have taken them here but Greg? And if it were him, certainly Drakor would have just told her that.

"Why doesn't Drakor want me to know?"

"I don't know. He just said not to tell you."

So much for getting some information on a new technology.

"But the lady wanted me to tell you."

Erin's head snapped up and she stared at the messy-faced girl. "What lady?"

"The one driving the car. Her smell hurt my nose and she gave Drakor weird looks."

Hair rose on Erin's neck in anticipation of something she didn't want to know. Like waiting for a test score in Physics when she barely answered a question. "What–what else? Do you know her name?"

Sitora shrugged. "She said mean things about you. She's even meaner than Drakor."

It couldn't be, could it? Erin felt her throat closing in. She could barely breathe. "What did she look like? What color was the car?"

"The car was the color of Earth's night. The lady's hair was yellow like Earth's sun. Her lips were bright red."

"Rita."

"Yes, that's her name." Sitora finally looked up from the soupy mess in her bowl. "But don't tell Drakor I told you. Please!"

Erin collapsed on the table, her head buried in her arms. No, not again. She would not let Rita take away this story—or her man. Not only that, Drakor knew Rita was writing a story about Greg. His acceptance of that bitch's help was more than a slap in the face. It was clear betrayal.

ഈറ

They hadn't found Brundor and Drakor couldn't get Rita to leave him alone. The strong perfume scent from Rita increased the pounding inside his skull to such a level that he felt physically ill.

They sat in the parking lot of a small restaurant, where Rita insisted many young humans hung out. Whatever that meant.

"Drop me off at Erin's." Drakor leaned his head back against the headrest and his eyes closed.

"Damn," she trailed a long fingernail along his arm, "what muscles. Is the rest of you this…big?"

He clenched his jaw, refusing to answer. If only it were Erin next to him, seducing him. Like the first night, when her mouth licked its way down his stomach and over his—

"You and Erin, you don't have a thing together, do you?" Her fingers moved from his arm down his chest. He sucked in his stomach and held his breath. "You shouldn't waste your time on her," she continued. "Erin is nothing. Whatever she's done for you will pale beside what I could do."

A prick of adrenaline spurted into his veins. The unpreventable urge to protect Erin began its climb toward his heart. But he knew to defend Erin would only make matters worse.

"I–I need to get my sister and go back home." He opened his eyes but stared straight ahead. "Please drop me off at Erin's."

He could see Rita shrug from the corner of his eye. "Suit yourself. But come find me when you're bored with her."

Rita brought him back to Erin's home and drove off with a squeal of her tires. He sighed and then knocked on Erin's door. He hoped she'd be willing to take them back home. If not, he would be forced to Transfer both Sitora and himself. He'd hate to frighten his sister that way.

The door opened to Erin's cold stare. She glanced beside him. "Where's your brother?"

Drakor breathed in her essence. Just being near to Erin soothed the incessant throbbing in his head. "I didn't find him."

She raised her eyebrows. "He could be getting you into some real trouble." Her voice had changed, become more monotone and hard.

"I know. I hope he has returned home. I need to get myself and Sitora back there."

"Is that Drakor?" came his sister's voice from another room.

"We must go back," he called to her.

Sitora whined in response.

Drakor smiled at Erin. "She was good while I was gone?"

She took a step back from him and he saw her swallow. "She was an angel. I'll get her cleaned up and then you two can go."

He reached out and touched her arm, the contact spreading heat to his loins. "I would like for you to drive us back in your vehicle."

Erin stiffened and yanked her arm away. "Why don't you ask Rita to drive you back?"

Drakor sucked in a deep breath, his shoulders tensing. Great Sun, he should have known Sitora couldn't keep her mouth shut, especially considering how much she loved Erin.

He chose his words carefully. "I would prefer for *you* to do it."

She scowled and put her hands on her hips. Hips that he caressed only last night. Hips that tormented him in the most intimate of ways. Sliding up, sliding down, sliding up…

"Oh, is that so? Is that because you fear what she would do if she saw your house? And you're worried about me when Rita would have you guys as front page news without a second thought!"

Drakor grinned. He closed the distance between them, ran his fingers through her silky, short hair. "And so the difference is that you *do* have a second thought."

Erin's mouth dropped open, but as he lowered his face to hers, no sound came from her lips. He didn't care that Sitora was in the other room. He didn't care about anything but holding on to Erin's good graces. And holding her in his arms.

Drakor pressed his lips to hers and she yielded to him, ushering a small gasp. He tasted the shiny gloss on her lips and a sweet flavor on her tongue.

195

Kissing her was like savoring treats without having to assault his unsuspecting stomach.

But it was too hard to have this small part of her and not have the rest. Too hard to not take advantage of every moment he had with her. His erection throbbed, begging for her warmth.

"Erin…" he said against her mouth. "Come back with me. We can lock the door…"

She sighed but then suddenly pushed herself away from him. "Rita wasn't enough to satisfy you?"

He cocked his head. "Rita? What are you talking about?"

"Don't tell me she wasn't all over you. I know her. I know she'd jump your bones at the first chance she got."

"Jump my bones?"

Erin rolled her eyes and crossed her arms under her tempting breasts. "She wants you, Drakor, and I know she must have tried while you were alone. And now you expect me to be a sloppy second. No, thank you."

Sloppy second? "Erin, I did not touch her."

"I know how much she wants you."

He shrugged. "I don't want her, I want you."

Something flickered in her sky-colored eyes and her face softened, but then the hard façade was back. "Get your sister and go."

Heat still swirled under his skin but he pushed the desire aside. He worried about her anger more. "Erin, I did not touch her."

She waved her hand in the air, dismissing him. "It doesn't matter. You and I…we aren't. I mean, we don't have a relationship or anything."

He followed her to the other side of the room. "I don't want her, I want you."

Erin glanced in the kitchen and Drakor followed her gaze. Sitora sat at the table in the kitchen, scribbling on paper with a writing tool.

He pulled her back to the front door, away from his sister's ears. "You must believe me."

196

"Why did you go looking for Brundor with her instead of me?"

"Would you rather have had her watch Sitora?"

"No," she answered immediately. "But we all could have gone together."

Drakor brushed a stray hair from her eyes, steeling himself against her enticing scent. "She was out near the house and saw us walking. When she offered, I thought I was being polite to accept."

Erin tensed. "She was near your house."

"Yes. It concerns me, as well."

"But how did she find it? How would she know?"

"I do not know the answer, but come back with us. I am unsettled at not finding my brother."

Erin crossed her arms again and leaned against the front door. She seemed to have dropped her concern over his ride with Rita. "Things aren't going too well for you here, are they?"

Did she mean here in her home or on this miserable planet? He swallowed. The mission has been a disaster. But he would not tell her that.

"Drakor?" She touched his arm.

He smiled at the contact but when he looked into her eyes, his gut tightened. Something was wrong. "Tell me."

"You told me you were looking for a friend."

He nodded, not wanting to hear her next words.

"I believe your friend is my John Doe. He was the one in the cottage before you got here." She bit her lip and glanced away. "He's dead, Drakor. That's why I was at your house that day a few weeks ago. I was trying to figure out who he was—"

He suddenly felt as if he'd been kicked in the stomach. "Why-why were you investigating him?" Great Sun, he'd hoped Alaziri was in hiding. But not only was he dead, the local government knew of him.

"Well, for starters, no one knew his name or where he came from. But also…" she walked across the room and tapped her nails on that creature's cage, "the coroner said he had an unknown malformation in his bone marrow."

Helta! Alaziri's body was locked up somewhere, having been dissected by these humans. They were suspicious. He had to get his family off this planet as soon as possible.

"Erin." She looked back at him and he felt an odd tingle at the sadness reflecting in her gaze. "Where is he? I want to take the body back with me."

She stiffened. "You can't take the body. It's at the coroner's office, locked up."

Heat flushed his face, burned his ears. "He deserved honor, to be buried among his own kind."

"I realize you want to bring him back to his family, but you can't just go in there and take the body."

Frustration roared at his temples. Nothing had gone right on this planet. Nothing. His parents were dead. His sister couldn't get pregnant. His brother was missing. And now his best friend was locked up in some room, unable to return to Elliac.

No. He had to do something. "I'm going to get him back, Erin. He doesn't belong on Earth. This is wrong."

The compassion in her eyes vanished under a cold glare. "Again, you are insulting me and my planet, as if we aren't good enough."

"He deserves the honor of a *proper* burial."

"He's an alien, Drakor! Once someone realizes that, they'll never let him go."

Fury choked him, blinded him. Pain throbbed inside his skull. Disaster. Everything was spiraling into a disaster.

"Take me to him, Erin."

Her lips twitched, lips that only moments ago he ached to press against his own. Now helplessness and agony superseded any tender emotions.

"I-I can't, Drakor. You'd have to fill out all kinds of information. Show identification. It would be a huge mistake to take you there. You'd find yourself in deeper trouble."

Deeper?

Great Sun, he had to get out of here. Rage boiled up inside of him, threatening to destroy the tenuous relationship he had with Erin. If he blew up at her now, it could ruin everything. She could have the government at his door in the morning.

"Sitora! Let's go. Now."

His sister whined but came forward.

Erin tucked her hair behind her ear. "Drakor, you aren't going to do anything stupid, are you?"

He stared at her, jaw clenched, unable to speak.

She reached her hand out to him then pulled it away. "I'll see what I can do about getting the body released, okay? I'll try."

He nodded. Right now, it would have to be enough.

Chapter Twenty

Drakor held Sitora tightly as the air swirled around them. He tried to find the most secluded spot he could before taking out his Transmitter and tapping in the code.

Within seconds, they stumbled on the ground next to the house. Its brightly colored paint mocked his distress. His family's demise seemed to loom before him like the long shadows of the trees.

"My tummy hurts," Sitora said in their native language.

He scooped her up in his arms and headed for the front door. It didn't surprise him that the spinning upset his sister's stomach. It took years to get used to. But it was a useful mechanism when needed.

The low throbbing returned to torment the inside of his skull. Was it the Transfer or being away from Erin? He despised the thought that she was the only way to cure his pain. It meant choosing between suffering without her or drawing her in closer.

The only thing that made sense to him right now was to get off this planet as soon as possible.

Drakor pushed open his front door and set Sitora down. Immediately, she scampered upstairs to her room. No doubt she was mad it him for making her leave Erin's side also.

Wishing he had some illegal Rizitzi Root to blot out his headache and dull his senses, Drakor headed instead for the staircase. But a sudden shuffling sound of papers brought his attention to the parlor room.

There, on the flowery couch, sat Brundor, casually flipping through a soft, paper book.

Fury strangled Drakor, flaming the tips of his ears, tightening his lungs. He stormed into the room. "Where have you been?"

Brundor shrugged and didn't look up. "I couldn't stand sitting in this house anymore. So I took a trip around town."

"You must have my permission, you know that."

"And what would you have said?"

"You aren't ready to be out there, not in your condition."

Brundor laughed and pushed his long, messy hair from his face. "Precisely my point. Besides, you're too busy indulging yourself with Erin to pay attention to your family's needs."

Drakor recoiled as if stung. He paid attention to their needs. Brundor could not handle his impulses around females right now. He knew that. He'd been there once himself.

"Erin has nothing to do with this."

A sneer lifted Brundor's eyes. "She has everything to do with this. You use her for your needs but deny me mine. You first risked the family's honor by insisting on returning early and now you allow us languish here while you have your fill of her."

Drakor stood before the fireplace and crossed his arms. "All of you insisted on staying until the mission was complete. And so I took on the responsibility of my family and the duty, sacrificing my own future, to bring honor to us. We cannot go until Ankra is pregnant, did you know that?"

Brundor's shocked face said that he didn't.

"So they kept the secret from you, as well. She is to mate with a human and carry the offspring. That is our real assignment. We are forced to stay on Earth until Ankra is with child." Drakor swallowed the bitter taste filling his mouth. "My time with Erin is only that—time. I am ready to leave her when the time comes."

Brundor returned his attentions to the text and pictures on his lap. "Once you realize she is your *Mharai* you won't be so ready to go."

"She is not my *Mharai*."

His brother shrugged. "I still want to go that dance place, the one you went to before. You said I could find a willing female there."

"Brundor," Drakor swallowed the trepidation creeping up his throat, "tell me you did not touch anyone...satisfy any of your...desires while you were gone?"

"It wouldn't matter if I did."

Drakor sucked in a deep breath. "What do you mean it wouldn't matter? If you assaulted someone, it could mean our capture."

Brundor gave a cocky laugh. "I am not a fool. I managed to control myself to the best of my ability—"

"Your ability!"

"But you've no need to worry about it."

The pressure in Drakor's head increased to such a point he felt nausea rising in his gut. He staggered slightly then caught himself against the mantel. "How...how could I not worry?"

"I was invisible, of course."

෴

Erin drummed her fingers on the wooden table. Greg was late, as usual. Didn't he think she had better things to do with her time?

She stirred the ginger ale in her glass with her straw. Okay, well, maybe she was a little grumpy. It didn't help that in the several days she hadn't seen Drakor, she started feeling drained and unnerved. What was it about him? Whenever he stood within a few feet of her she turned into some promiscuous harlot with raging hormones. And now that she had gone the rest of the week without seeing, hearing, or speaking to him, she felt like total crap.

"Sorry I'm late." Greg dropped into the chair opposite hers. "Hey, you didn't order the Crunchy Rings. We always get that."

Erin took a sip of her soda. "They didn't sound very appetizing to me right now. What took you so long, anyway?"

"Had to drop off Ankra."

Something bloomed in Erin's chest, like a tulip opening to the sun. She knew why. Drakor. Why couldn't she forget him?

"So you guys are doing great, huh?"

Her brother's cheeks colored. "Yeah, she's really special." He grabbed her soda and swallowed a few gulps.

"Um, could you ask next time?"

He ignored her and looked around for the waiter.

"I told him to bring a beer when he saw you here, so don't worry it'll be coming."

"Thanks. I could use one."

"What's the latest? Anymore ideas about what's going on at Invasion Shield?"

Greg sighed and sank back in his chair. "I don't know what to do. I've done some research and it seems that the software that I've sent off for a patent is exactly the same as one developed by Securicon."

"Securicon? Who are they?"

He seemed to shrivel in his seat. "A competitor. A very important one."

Erin tucked a stray hair behind her ear. "So, did someone from Invasion Shield sell the technology to Securicon?"

The waiter came over and placed the beer in front of Greg. "Any dinner for the two of you?" he asked.

Erin didn't quite feel in the mood but she would eat if Greg ordered something. Fortunately, he shook his head. "Can you just bring out the Crunchy Rings with the special sauce? And I'll probably need another beer soon."

"Anything for you, madam?"

"No, thank you. Just some water with lemon."

The waiter left and Greg took a long pull on his beer. When he came up for fresh air, he wiped the bottle across his forehead.

"I could be in some deep shit, Erin."

"It's not your fault if someone sold information to another company."

"That isn't what happened."

"What do you mean?"

"Securicon had this technology first. They applied for their patent on it well before us."

Erin shifted in her seat. This wasn't sounding good. "Maybe they were just faster."

Greg leaned forward, elbows on the table, head in his hands. "No, Erin, somebody stole that information from them and we've claimed it's our own. That's called Patent Infringement."

Her churning stomach froze. "What are you saying exactly?"

"Someone from my company took Securicon's information and used it to build our software."

"Who would do that?"

"I don't know but I have a guess."

There had to be a way to figure this out. "Greg, did anyone in your company work for Securicon before Invasion Shield?"

"Not that I remember."

She would fix this for him. She had to. "Let's meet soon. Your house or mine, it doesn't matter. But bring your employee files and we'll go through them with a microscope."

His blue eyes pleaded with her. She had never seen him so distraught, not since their parents died. "I hope we can find something, 'cause Invasion Shield is in a whole lot of trouble and I'm the one responsible."

ఏ౧౪

"I have another one and they won't stop itching."

Drakor winced as Sitora's whine cut through his fog of pain. He'd not heard from Erin since leaving her apartment that day.

He and Sitora took nightly walks to ease their boredom, and now she complained of red bumps on her skin. He tried to look it up in a manual but all that was mentioned was hives, rashes, and the occasional insect bite.

"Last time you scratched so hard you made it bleed," he told her, pressing a damp cloth across his face.

"I can't help it."

"What did Ankra say about it? Did she ask Greg for you?"

"She keeps forgetting." He felt Sitora climb up on the bed next to him. "Please, can't you do something? Mother and Father would have done something for me."

He moved the cloth and propped up on one elbow. She would be underhanded enough to use their dead parents against him. "You have something you want me do."

She gave a shrug, her eyes wide with innocence. "You could ask Erin."

He dropped his head down again. "So that's what this is about. You want to see Erin again."

"I don't have to go." She lay next to him and reached her pudgy arm across his chest. She smelled like soap and cookies. "I'll stay here and you can just go over and ask her."

"Sitora…" What could he say to his sister? He didn't know why Erin stopped coming by to visit. But he did know that he couldn't stop thinking about her. The scent of her hair and softness of her skin haunted him each night. He could not forget her smooth shoulders and creamy white thighs. Especially since he now slept in his parents' room, upon this very bed.

"You'll go, won't you?" his sister asked, then pressed a kiss on his cheek. "Tell her I wanted you to."

The poor girl had enough disappointment already. "I'll go. Let me just make sure Brundor will stay here this time."

Drakor just reversed the coordinates on the Transmitter and landed behind a clump of trees near Erin's building. He would have preferred to Transfer directly into her home, but it would probably frighten her and give her more fuel for her story.

Drakor sucked in a deep breath and knocked on Erin's door.

A strong smell filtered out from one of the closed doors, making his mouth water. The odor was strong, pungent, but not necessarily unpleasant. Was he starting to yearn for the Earth food? Had he started to transform into a human?

Great Sun, he needed to get off this planet, even if it meant returning home as an *Unmhar*.

The door opened and his gaze fell upon Erin's surprised face. Her light hair was scattered in all directions, her skin paler than normal and eyes underlined with a lavender hue. She looked unwell, almost as if she somehow had contracted the illness that plagued his father.

He took a step inside the door and the heat from her body enveloped him, immediately easing his suffering. But seeing her distress, sensing her weakened state, Drakor felt a trickle of ice slither through his veins. Similar to the frenzied rush that overtook him when he wanted to protect Erin, this cold sensation connected him to her.

His *Mharai*.

No. These feelings, desires, sensations were nothing more than a trick of being on a strange planet. The pull he felt in meeting his first human female. No Elliacians ever found a *Mharai* anywhere but Elliac.

"What's going on?"

Drakor took a step toward her. "Sitora..." He wanted to tell her the reason he was here, why he came all this way. But the words wouldn't form in his mouth. He couldn't concentrate on anything but her, on having her nestled in his arms.

206

Her face softened and he watched her lips move as she spoke. "Is she ill? What's happened?"

"It's nothing really. Small bumps on her skin that itch."

She raised her eyebrows. "Rash?"

Drakor shrugged.

"Are they large or small? The bumps."

He hedged closer to her, desperately wanting to run his fingertips along her silky hair. His tongue burned to taste her. "They–they are large. On her arms and legs. Everywhere."

Erin smiled and the tension in his body eased a bit.

"Are they like this?" She lifted her leg and put her foot on the couch's armrest. She pointed to a swollen, red lump.

The sight of her firm calf and curved ankle made him swallow. But his throat was thick and dry. He nodded.

"What about this?" This time she slid the waistband down on her shorts slightly to reveal her hip. Another bump like Sitora's rested on her velvety skin. She scratched it.

Again, he nodded, unable to speak.

Erin pushed a few strands of hair behind her ear and leaned against the armrest. "It sounds like she has mosquito bites."

"Mosquito?" he croaked.

"Common in summer. They love the taste of blood."

"They are–are insects?"

Erin cocked her head. "Is something wrong? Why can't you talk?"

"I–I don't know. My mouth feels…strange." He tried to swallow but his throat closed up on him again.

"Maybe you need something to drink."

She brushed past him and disappeared into the kitchen. He heard the tinkle of glass and the rush of water. Then she emerged holding a white cup with a handle.

"Drink this. It should help."

He took the cup from her and stared into it. The liquid inside was clear, like the stream behind the house. Water. There was plenty of it on Elliac, it was just difficult to get to. Long ago, his ancestors built viaducts and pipelines to bring the water in. But most was used for sanitation and bathing. Once weaned onto the capsules, there wasn't a need for drinking liquid.

Erin came up to him and pushed his hand up to his face. Her contact on his skin warmed the ice still trickling in his veins. "Bring it to your lips and drink it."

She lifted up on her toes and helped to guide the cup to his mouth. He let the cold water wash over his tongue and slowly swallowed it down his closed throat. A cool tickling sensation swam into his stomach. Drakor took another sip, feeling the sides of his mouth and his tongue reawaken.

"Ah, that's it," she crooned, stirring his blood. "You must be feeling better."

Drakor finished the cup and handed it back to her. She put it away then leaned against the doorway. "Are the bumps the only reason you came over?"

"Are the mosquito bites a problem?" he asked, ignoring her question.

Her mouth twitched. "They can be in extreme cases. Mosquitoes can carry diseases, but most likely they'll just cause a lot of annoying itching."

He wanted to touch her but shoved his hands in his pockets instead. "Tell me how to stop the itching."

"How can I get you to tell me why you're really here?"

"I told you, to find out about Sitora's bumps."

Her sky-colored eyes narrowed. "You could have found that information out other ways. You didn't have to just show up at my door."

"Sitora asked me to come and see you."

"You want to know about your friend, don't you?"

Helta, yes, that was true. But he came mostly because he couldn't stand to be away from her anymore. The wave of sensations flooded his system. The cool taste of the water, the enticing scent of Erin, and the hot rush of blood to his groin.

Drakor pulled his hands from his pocket and leaned forward, trapping her against the wall. "I came because I couldn't stand being away from you anymore."

Chapter Twenty-One

Erin's breath caught. She wanted to think clearly, but she couldn't do it. "No. Don't. I have to tell you something."

But those predatory eyes never moved. Solid walls of muscle held her trapped against the wall. That raw, male power radiated from his stance, burned through her hesitation, flooded her body with instant warmth.

His lips moved closer.

"No, I have to tell you something…"

Oh God, she didn't want to. She didn't want to stop this sensual buzz inside her. And she didn't want to give him the news she had.

Erin ducked under his arms and dashed into the kitchen. Gripping the back of a kitchen chair, she inhaled deep breaths of Drakor-free air. She had to clear her mind. Damn it, she had to find a way to tell him this information without setting off the anger she'd witnessed a few days ago.

Sighing, Erin tried to calm her galloping heart, but then she heard him walk up behind her. She could more than hear him, she could sense him, she could smell him.

Erin stiffened to stave off the impending torrent of desire but Drakor pressed himself against her back.

"What do you think you're—?"

Her words died away as his lips found the curve of her neck. Willpower slipping, she closed her eyes and sank back toward him. His tongue traced a damp line along her shoulder and she felt his fingers move her shirt and bra strap out of his way.

"No..." Her weak protest served no purpose as his other hand reached under the front of her shirt and cupped her breast.

His erection pressed against her lower back. Quivers raced down to her toes. Awareness shivered over every nerve ending. Fire sparked in every blood cell.

The thoughts and emotions of a few minutes ago eluded her grasp. Now there was nothing but her and Drakor. There was nothing but lust surging into every pore.

Through the haze she felt her shorts and panties fall to her ankles. Then there was contact of his bare skin against her.

His large hands lifted her hips, pulling her up on her toes. She fell forward toward the table and caught herself with her hands, scrunching and scattering papers.

One hard plunge and he was inside. That familiar balloon expanded, reaching, widening for release. With each thrust, each groan, the balloon stretched, rising until it pressed tightly against her nipples.

Drakor gripped her hips, holding her steady while he continued to drive himself deeply inside. Her pulse matched his rapid breathing. Another deep lunge and he moaned near her ear. The taut balloon burst with a shower of sparkles, tickling her skin, leaving her gasping.

He withdrew and backed away. Without turning, she knew he leaned against the counter, waiting for his breathing to slow. But she didn't want to wait. Now that he was away from her, her head started to clear.

Erin yanked her clothes back on and hurried into the bathroom. What had she just done? She was like a horny rabbit when he was around. Is that why he came over to see her, because he knew she would give it up whenever he reached for her? No wonder he didn't need Rita's big breasts and overt seduction. All he had to do was come within a foot of Erin and she turned into his sex slave.

Erin cleaned herself up and splashed water on her face. She looked like hell warmed over. No make-up, pale face, messy hair.

She found him standing over the kitchen table trying to read her notes.

"What are you doing? Get out of my stuff."

"It's about me," he replied without looking up. "But don't worry, I can barely read what it says."

So she had messy handwriting, it caused her enough bad grades in school. She didn't need to be scolded for it now. Erin snatched the paper out of his hands. "Then don't bother trying."

He glanced over at her and his steamy dark eyes threatened to melt her again. "Why don't you read it to me, then? Weren't you looking for something earlier?"

She *was*. Before he came up behind her and took advantage of her weakness. Erin cleared her throat and flipped through a few loose sheets then sucked in a deep breath. "You know what, maybe you should just go."

Instead, Drakor dropped into the chair next to her. "Wait...what's wrong?"

She crossed her arms and glanced away. She'd better tell him now, just get it out of the way. "Your friend, you know, my John Doe, I looked into getting his body released. I said a relative had been found."

Drakor rose to his feet. "When can I get him?"

Erin closed her eyes for a moment. Shit. He wasn't going to like this. "You can't."

"Erin—"

"No, Drakor." She stared at him, at those mysterious eyes that haunted her dreams. "You can't get him because he's no longer there."

"I'll go to wherever he has gone."

Erin shook her head. "He's gone for good. His body has been taken away."

His faced bloomed scarlet. "He has been buried in the ground *here*?"

No, worse. She wouldn't tell him. If she told him the truth, he'd be gone from this planet tonight. And...and she didn't have all the information she needed for her article. He couldn't go yet.

A little lie at this moment wouldn't be such a bad thing. "All I know is that he's been moved from the facility to an undisclosed location."

Drakor slumped back into the chair and dropped his head into his hands.

Erin stood there, unmoving. She wanted to comfort him, to ease his sadness. So much had happened for him in these last few weeks, with the death of his parents and all. Now he bore the responsibility of his family and she was setting out to destroy them.

An ache rippled in her heart. She'd never felt so torn, so uncertain as to what to do. This was the break she'd been searching for, the very thing to blow away her mistakes of the past. And, yet, she'd never felt so alive since she'd met Drakor. She'd never embraced such passion.

Oh God, what if she was falling in love with him?

She had to make him leave. His constant presence agonized her, threatened everything she knew about herself. They had no future together. Why waste the biggest thing in her life over something that would only last a few more weeks, at most?

Erin had to end it. Once and for all.

She tapped him on the shoulder. Her heart twisted at the look of despondency in his eyes. "I'm sorry, Drakor, but you have to go."

"I don't understand."

A sob lodged in her throat but she gulped the salty taste. She could do this. She had to do this. No more sex. No more contentment in his arms.

"We can't see each other anymore." Erin walked to the front door, willing back surprising tears. "This has all gotten too tangled and I can't do it anymore."

Drakor followed her, his face paling. "You will not see me anymore?"

"I've had enough of the games we're playing. I'm ending it between us. Please don't come back."

Erin left him standing in the open doorway and hurried back to her bedroom where she could shut him out and lock herself in. She knew that all Drakor had to do was pull her into an embrace and she would forget everything.

She heard him growl and pound his fist on the door, but then it slammed shut.

Thank God he'd gone. Idiot that she was, she left her notes, the light casing, and the PDA thing all within his easy reach.

$\wp \mathcal{C} \mathcal{R}$

Drakor turned the key and set the lock. Now only he would be able to make the space shuttle invisible. Brundor's stunt petrified him and made him wonder if he would ever be ready to be a father. Of course, it didn't matter now. No, once they returned home he would be an *Unmhar* and only his family and coworkers would come near him.

He turned at the sound of footsteps, anticipating his brother but Ankra stepped into the light. "What are you doing?"

"Making sure Brundor doesn't make himself invisible again."

"Are you the only one programmed to vanish the craft, then?"

He nodded and sank into the pilot's chair. "He had me very concerned."

She came over and sat in the seat next to him. He noticed she had pulled her hair away from her face. It was held with some type of band. Something else influenced by the human culture. She even smelled like the human females with flower scented lotions and shampoos.

"Are you still anxious to return home?" He could hear the disappointment in her voice and her eyes wouldn't look at him directly.

If she had asked him that yesterday he wouldn't be able to answer her. Before Erin told him it was over, he thought he might want to stay on Earth a

214

while longer. In Erin's arms he had found contentment. With her touch he felt desire. Perhaps the Fates had brought her to him as a final gift, a memory to serve him for the next forty years.

But now Erin didn't want to see him again. With the threat of her story and the ever-present lure of her body, he couldn't tolerate Earth much longer.

He tried to catch Ankra's gaze but she stared at her hands in her lap. "I am ready to leave the moment the mission is complete."

"But I…I cannot seem to complete my duty."

Great Sun, not tears. Not from his sister. "Ankra, you are doing the best you can, yes?"

"He won't—he won't mate without the barrier."

"You can't convince him?"

She sniffled and shook her head. "He said that he once got a girlfriend with child many years ago and it nearly ruined him. He won't take chances again."

Archaic human anatomy again. If they were more like the Elliacians they would only be able to impregnate their *Mharai* and the females could control their fertility. Instead, as Erin had mentioned, many children were born as accidents.

"You could damage it. That's what I tried."

Ankra gave him a weak smile and a quick glance. "I tried that too. I found where he keeps them and poked needles through them."

"And it still hasn't worked?" Drakor's stomach fluttered. Why the *helta* couldn't she conceive?

"I–I don't know what else to do."

"When did you poke the holes?" Maybe it hadn't been enough time.

She gave a shaky sigh. "This week. Every one of them have been damaged and nothing is happening."

"You were examined by the Researchers before we left Elliac, weren't you?"

"Yes. I am very healthy and fertile." She wiped her eyes with her fingers. "But they said there was no guarantee. No one has tried to mate with a human before."

"And he couldn't be your *Mharai*."

She lifted her chin and glared at him. "Why not?"

"He's human. A *Mharai* must be from Elliac."

"Says who?"

He felt his muscles tense. "Says history. Have you ever heard of anyone finding their *Mharai* anywhere but Elliac?"

"Has anyone tried before?"

He shrugged. "If you ask me, you aren't with child because Greg is not your *Mharai*. It's as simple as that."

"I think you're wrong. I think it has something to do with the different atmosphere on Earth. Maybe that's the reason they can't control their fertility."

Drakor leaned forward and dropped his head into his hands. The memory of Erin's rejection increased the pain thudding inside his skull. He'd failed at retrieving Alaziri. And now his sister could not complete her mission.

"Whatever the reason, we have to find another way to bring back the genetic code." He lifted his gaze to hers. "I'll give one more week to resolve this issue and then we return. Even if we have failed."

Dishonor. Failure. Loneliness. They all awaited him on Elliac.

෨෬

"Is this everyone's files?"

Greg flipped through each manila tab. "Yep, that's everyone."

Erin sat on the floor across from him and picked up the first one. Cindy Anslo, the receptionist. "Do you think we need to look in hers?" She couldn't imagine the curly haired sweetheart doing anything this horrible.

216

Her brother finished gulping his Coke and sighed. "Better check everyone."

"We're looking to see if anyone has worked for Securicon, right?"

He nodded.

The smell of greasy pizza oozed from the kitchen, making her both hungry and queasy. Between her headaches and stomachaches, she must have picked up a summer cold or flu. The only time she felt really well recently was a few days ago when Drakor was over. That brief time they touched soothed her aching. But now she was back to feeling lousy again.

Greg reached out and pulled an armful of files toward him. "I'm going to start with Jay. He's my biggest suspect."

"Wouldn't you have known if he worked for Securicon? Wouldn't he have mentioned it in the interview or something?"

He scanned the application in front of him and then looked over the resume. "Nope. Not on here."

After draining his glass, he leaned back and propped himself up on one elbow. "If Jay was angry at his former company, he might set out to get revenge. He could have lied to me about where he was during that time."

"So you think he worked for them, then lied about it to you so that he could use that technology for your company? What kind of sense is that?"

Greg lifted his shoulder. "Who knows? If they pissed him off enough, he'd look for a way to get them back. And by letting Invasion Shield have the technology and patent it, it would be a rub in their face."

Erin shook her head. "But wouldn't he have signed a non-disclosure form or something when he left?"

"Yeah, I'm sure he did. That's probably why he seemed so nervous all the time. His revenge drove him to do it but he knew he could get in big trouble if he got caught."

None of this made any sense to her. Why go through all that trouble just for revenge? Or was it control? Or some wacky god-like feeling of knowing he could alter companies, alter people's lives? Hell, he was about to put Greg out of business.

She pushed a hair out of her eyes and behind her ear. "So he lied on his resume and application so that no one knew he worked for them? Didn't he think someone at Securicon would eventually track him down? That one day he'd get discovered?"

Greg sat up and leveled his gaze at her. "Erin, we both know that you once wanted something so badly that you didn't think everything through clearly."

Her stomach burned. "Must we make this about me?"

"I'm only proving the point. That one day you start to want something too much and you're not careful anymore. Your infatuation for Evan made you blind."

"Yeah and led to my disaster."

His mouth curled. "Hey, it also led to the discovery of who you really are and what's important, right?"

Erin pulled her knees up to her chest and rested her chin on them.

Discovery. Why did that word have such a double meaning? On one hand, discovery had once meant Drakor's tongue reaching into the intimate parts of her. It had meant her educating herself on what pleased him, on what made him pant with desire.

But what of discovering who Drakor really was, that he was an alien? What would it mean to her career? What would this discovery mean to the world?

"So," Greg said, interrupting her thoughts. "Does this mean I'm home free with Rita's article on the patent infringement?"

"I don't know, you'll have to call your lawyer on that one." She stood and stretched. "But I am going to call Rita and tell her that if she's trying to ruin you, it isn't going to work."

Nor would that bitch get the front page spread.

Chapter Twenty-Two

Drakor crossed his arms and stared at what remained of his family. His brother, who leaned against the doorway with a surly look and hot eyes, filled Drakor with dread. Like the vision of the rainbow, he knew that Brundor spelled trouble for them. When, not if, was his only question.

Sitora was quiet today, finally having realized that her days of crying and whining were not going to bring Erin to their door. She played with her doll, pretending to feed it cookies and ice cream—whatever that was.

And then there was Ankra. His sister spent much of her time these last several days with Greg. Each day the gloom and sadness in her eyes grew worse. Certainly it had to be more than her lack of completing her duty that brought such anguish to her.

Drakor knew that only Brundor would relish his announcement. And somehow that did not cheer him.

"I asked all of you to come in here," he motioned to the parlor room, "because I have made a decision. We will begin to dismantle and pack for our journey home."

"What?" Ankra's face paled. "We can't go yet…I haven't…we aren't…"

Drakor lifted his hand to halt her. "A decision must be made regarding our safety. To stay here indefinitely is unacceptable."

"But you told me we had another week."

He nodded. "And I will continue to grant that to you, but I want to begin the packing process. Now that Mother and Father are gone there is a lot more work for us to do." He looked at Sitora to see if she was paying attention. "And that includes everyone."

Ankra sniffled and came up close, near to his ear. "But I need to spend as much time as possible with Greg."

"It's okay." He cocked his head toward Brundor. "He knows about it."

His brother jammed his hands in his pockets. "I'm not going anywhere until you take me to that dance club like you promised."

Drakor's heart pounded, keeping rhythm with the pain in his head. "Brundor, you will be home shortly, you shouldn't feel the need to go there."

"Why not? You and Ankra got to experience humans, why should I? I've been stuck in this *house*," his nose wrinkled, "and I deserve a last shot before we go."

Drakor sighed and ran his fingers through his hair. Bringing Brundor there was bound to be a mistake, especially when there was so much else to do. "You should be able to wait."

His brother rushed toward him, his nostrils flaring. "You're only ready to leave *now* because Erin won't see you again."

Drakor stiffened. "Who told you that?"

"Greg told Ankra and she told me when I asked why you were stomping all over the house and never going anywhere."

"You're only concerned about me not going anywhere because then you can't find a way to escape."

"Hah!" Brundor threw his hands in the air. "Even you talk as if this house is a prison."

Drakor felt the fury invigorate him even as the pain of Erin's rejection drained him. "You have no idea what it has been—"

Ankra stepped between him and Brundor and pushed them apart. "That is enough from both of you."

She took a deep breath in and let it out slowly. "As much as my feelings differ from Drakor's, he is now the leader of the mission. It is his job to do what is best for us."

"You mean what's best for himself," Brundor grumbled.

"Any day the media and government could be knocking on this door," Drakor said, pointing to the front hallway.

"Enough!" his sister shouted. She turned to face him. "What do you want us to do first?"

Drakor unclenched his hands and sighed. "I want to take stock in our equipment. Bring me all of the Transmitters so I can make a count and calibrate them properly for the journey home."

An hour later, Drakor sat out on the top front porch step counting Transmitters. There should be seven. One for each member of the family, plus an extra. But no matter how many times he counted them, he kept coming up one short. Six.

Ankra went upstairs to search her room again. Certainly it was Sitora who lost hers. After all, what did a little girl need with one of them anyway? She didn't know any of the codes. She was too young to Transfer by herself. But policy stated there had to be one for each individual.

The door opened behind him. "I can't find it," Ankra said. "I even looked under the beds and the dresser."

Drakor mumbled a thanks and jumped down the stairs. The suffocating heat closed in on him but he felt the urge to get away from the house. He had to think. He had to think without being interrupted.

He paced along the dirt driveway. Where could it have gone? What would his little sister do with it? Could Erin have found it and stolen it from them?

Again the haunting image of the rainbow sent shivers up his spine. A tragedy prophesied to the viewer. Was the tragedy the death of his parents? Was it the loss of Erin's attention? Would it be their discovery and inevitable imprisonment?

Sweat trickled down the sides of his face, but Drakor couldn't stand to sit still another day. He had to get that Transmitter back. He had to face Erin one more time. He knew it would be the last and so perhaps he would tell her truth. Tell her why they were really here. What would it matter to him or Elliac once they were gone?

He looked up and saw Ankra on the porch, testing each Transmitter. He needed to get a message to Erin without having her slam the door in his face.

"Are you seeing Greg today?"

She nodded. "Later, why?"

"It is urgent that you get a message to Erin for me."

Her eyes widened in surprise. "Okay, what?"

"Tell her to meet me Saturday night at Mickey's. We have things to discuss."

She gave him one of those mysterious female grins and disappeared back inside the house.

Drakor gathered up the Transmitters and shoved them in his pockets. After tomorrow, he'd feel better. Once he saw Erin he'd have the last Transmitter in hand, and perhaps a few final moments of contentment before returning home in dishonor to face his life as an *Unmhar*.

Drakor swallowed against his tight throat and opened the front door but the sound of a vehicle stopped him short. It didn't grow louder but sat still, idling. He turned to look out onto the dirt drive in front of the house but saw nothing.

Then his eyes traveled down the dusty road until they reached the bend. There it was. He squinted, barely able to see a corner of it as it sat just before the curve. But he saw enough to make his hair stand on end and his stomach churn. Earth's sun glimmered off the sleek black paint of Rita's vehicle.

考考

Erin drained her glass of ginger ale. It was the only thing she could seem to drink these days. This icky feeling must have something to do with Drakor. She knew it had to. It must be related to the way he could turn her on with mere contact or empty her head of all thought while scorching hunger blazed through her. And now, when he was away from her, her body seemed to fall apart.

She sighed and tied her hair up in an old rubber band. Not the smartest move to keep her hair from breaking, but right now she didn't care about much but getting this story together.

Okay, she had all the stuff in front of her. Plastic light thingie. PDA looking thingie. Notes on everyone. How could she turn all of this into a story that would win her that spread, sell papers off the racks and rocket her career?

Erin tapped her pen on the table. There had to be more that Drakor and his family were after than just supplements. Couldn't they have just bought them at the store and be gone by now? There must be something else involved, something that required time.

But what else could they need to replenish their lack of Vitamin D? Did any of this have to do with his parents' deaths? Did they die from a lack of the vitamin? Could they have been saved if a remedy had been found on Earth?

Erin dropped her head into her hands. She needed answers. But how? She told Drakor she didn't want to see him anymore.

Damn, now her headache was worse. The deadline for her story was only three days away and she had nothing but her own chicken scratch on the paper, plus two items that she didn't know how to work.

Erin glanced up at the phone hanging on the wall. Maybe now would be a good time to call Rita. She promised Greg she'd do it yesterday and never got around to it. If Erin couldn't get her own story together, the least she could do was ruin Rita's.

She grabbed the receiver and called.

Rita answered on the first ring. "Rita here."

"It's Erin."

Gum popped in her ear and Erin clenched her teeth. She hated that sound.

"Erin...well, this is a surprise. What? No hot date on a Friday night?"

"I would say the same about you."

Rita gave a throaty laugh. "The night is young, my dear. Whatever are you bothering me for, anyway? Tired of your man and want to hand him over to someone who knows how to deal with him?"

Erin's heart jumped a few notches. The fight she had with Drakor over Rita still tormented her. Even if Drakor could explain it all away, the feelings of betrayal didn't fade.

"I called about the story you're doing on Greg and Invasion Shield."

"Oh that." Pop. Snap. "That story is finished. Handed it to Rockford this afternoon."

Erin couldn't stop her gasp. Not only was Erin still stuttering here without a story while Rita's was complete, Greg's future sat on her boss' desk.

"Was there something I needed to know?"

Erin sank back down into the chair and gathered her wits. She promised Greg she'd take care of it and she couldn't let him down now. "My brother had no knowledge of his employee's involvement with Securicon. He isn't at fault."

"Are you telling me that he didn't know that brilliant idea they had was already patented? That he didn't check the references on his candidates?"

Erin swallowed. "None of his employees listed Securicon on their resumes. How would he know?"

"I would think one of the references would have mentioned the dates of employment and from there he would have deduced a time span discrepancy."

Oh, shit. They hadn't thought of that. Erin took a deep breath and prayed she could bluff her way through. "Still, Greg had no real knowledge of a disclosure statement or the patent infringement. He is not to blame."

Rita chuckled and snapped her gum. "Well, it might not matter come Monday when you turn in your story. Rockford could find yours much more compelling. What is it about again?"

Erin wanted to crumble into a heap of ashes there on the chair. Now she really had to complete her story for Monday or Rita's could very well be published instead.

"You'll find out Monday," she managed to squeak.

"Could it be about that new beau of yours? He is mighty handsome and very mysterious."

Erin's palms started to sweat. Was Rita on to them? Did she suspect something? Had she seen the house that day?

A knock on the door made Erin jump. Saved by the bell. At least for a moment.

"Hold on," she told Rita, "someone is at my door."

The snapping gum was her answer.

Erin didn't know who to expect. Certainly Drakor had surprised her many times in the past but would he be so bold as to come again after she told him it was over? She hated to admit it to herself, but a sliver of excitement coursed through her at the idea of him standing there. Her body reacted by shifting from miserable to aroused.

Erin took the cordless away from her ear and went to the door. But it wasn't Drakor standing there; it was her brother and Ankra.

"Well, this is a surprise."

"We can't stay." Greg slid his arm across his girlfriend's shoulder. "Ankra has a message."

"A message?"

Ankra nodded. "From Drakor."

Erin's heart skipped a beat. So he did still think of her. "What did he say?"

"He wants you to meet him at Mickey's on Saturday night."

"Tomorrow?"

She nodded.

"But why?"

Ankra's eyes dropped to the floor momentarily but when they came back up there was a light in them. She reached out and took Erin's free hand, holding it gently within her own. Erin felt the veins in her arm expand and then contract. Startled, she pulled her hand away.

Ankra's face broadened into a wide grin, certainly the happiest Erin had seen the woman in a long time. "Drakor only told me that you and he had some things to discuss."

Fine. Whatever. Erin needed more answers for her story. She needed to know why he was really here and this could be the only way to find that out.

"Tell him I'll be there."

Ankra nodded, the mysterious smile still in place. Greg shrugged, then pulled them away from the door. Erin closed it after them and went back into the kitchen.

She stared down at her notes, at the question marks littering the page. Maybe now she could get some solutions.

"Hello? Hello?"

Rita. Erin forgot about her. She held the phone to her ear. "I'm back. Sorry that was my brother."

"Oh. Well, are we done here?"

What else could she say? Rita's article was already complete and turned in. Erin would just have to hope her story would top the one on *Invasion Shield*.

"Yeah, we're done," Erin said to the popping on the other end.

"Great," Rita answered and the line went dead.

Erin stared at the silent phone in her hand a moment and then punched in Greg's number. She knew he wasn't home yet but she'd just leave a message, letting him know it was taken care of. No need to worry him when there wasn't much she could do about it.

Besides, once she met with Drakor tomorrow, she'd have enough information to write this damn story. And the discovery of aliens had to be more impressive than some mistaken patent infringement. Didn't it?

₳)(₻

Drakor sucked in a deep breath and knocked on Brundor's bedroom door. This was probably one of the biggest mistakes of his life, but he did promise his brother he'd take him to Mickey's. And it was now or never.

"Come!" Brundor called in Elliac's language.

Drakor stepped inside the dark room, shadows greeting him as they usually did. "Get ready," he said with a sigh.

Brundor sat up instantly. "Why? Are we leaving now? We aren't packed completely."

"No, not yet. But I'm going to Mickey's tonight. Need to meet Erin."

His brother leapt up from the bed. "You mean, you'll take me with you?"

Drakor wiped the sheen of sweat on his forehead. Between the headaches and this summer heat, desperation prowled. He must get off this planet. "Can you be certain you can control your reactions? There are many, many females there."

"I can. I've proven that over and over. The other day I was so close that I could touch them and did nothing."

"You were invisible."

Brundor shrugged. "It doesn't matter. I could have grabbed them and they wouldn't have known. But I kept my distance." He reached for his shirt and pulled it on over his bare chest. "I will touch no one unless she asks me to."

Drakor nodded and turned from the room. His heart hammered inside his ribcage even as chills sprouted on his skin. Was it because he was seeing Erin again or was it the unspecific feeling of dread nagging within him?

Either way they'd be leaving Earth soon, without the gene needed to process Vitamin D.

Chapter Twenty-Three

Erin still felt lousy. In fact, she almost made an appointment with the doctor this morning, despite it being Saturday. But a trip to the drug store suited her patience better.

She smoothed out her silk shirt and adjusted her hair in the silver clip. Why did she go through the effort to look good for him? He didn't mean anything to her. Besides, after tonight she would be writing the story of her career. Possibly the story of her life.

Erin paid her fee at the door and entered Mickey's. She slipped over to the side, letting her senses become adjusted to the dim interior with flashing lights, overwhelming smell of cigarette smoke, and pulsating music.

Erin took a deep breath and started to wander the first room. Lots of tall men with dark hair, but no Drakor. She pushed her way through the crowd and headed down the steps to the black light room. She squinted at the sea of people dancing. Oh God, she'd never find him here. She should have told Ankra a specific meeting place. This was ridiculous.

Erin sighed and cruised the perimeter of the room, momentarily stopping if she saw someone remotely looking like Drakor. Several good looking guys out there and one or two asked her to dance, but she shook her head.

The blinking lights and loud music dampened her adrenaline and made her feel miserable again. She made it to the other side of the room before running into the bathroom.

The bright illumination made her wince as she headed straight to the row of sinks. So much for her carefully applied make-up. Already her face was sweating. Erin splashed some water on it and patted her cheeks dry.

Damn, she looked tired. Tired and worn. How did this happen? Before she met Drakor she appeared young and eager. Then, when the whole ordeal with him started she felt more alive than ever before.

Now that she had made love to him, felt a strong need to be near him, couldn't stop thinking about him…now she felt and looked like crap.

Erin headed to the door but it opened before she could reach the handle. A busty blonde walked in, snapped her gum, and Erin's stomach dropped to the floor.

"Rita…" she murmured.

"Oh, hello Erin."

"What are you doing here?"

Rita lifted a nicely arched eyebrow. "It's a free country. I can be at the same place you are."

Erin crossed her arms. "Do you come every Saturday night or just the nights you know I'm here?"

The gum snapped. "Did I know you were going to be here tonight?"

Erin's chest tightened. This was just great. All she needed after the way she was feeling. Once Rita spotted Drakor, she'd be all over him.

Erin brushed by her. "I have something to do."

The gum popped in her ear as she passed.

Feeling worse than ever, Erin left the relative quiet of the restroom and sunk back into the depths of the club. She started toward the stairs but a hand clamped down on her shoulder. Ready to push some drunk, obnoxious guy away, Erin turned in anger.

Drakor smiled down at her. "There you are," he shouted over the noise.

Without waiting for a reply, he took her hand and led her back into the room with the blinking lights. A river of calm coursed through her at the contact with his fingers. She wanted to pull away, to not give him any ideas, but she needed the feeling of wellness again.

He led them to the far end of the dance floor and pulled her into his arms. Instantly, her body reacted to his closeness and arousal skirted up between her legs. All traces of illness were gone. No. She couldn't let him do this. She couldn't let him distract her like this.

Erin struggled in his embrace, but he held her firm. He bent his head low and spoke directly into her ear. "I just want to dance. I want to hold you. Won't you let me do that for the last time?"

She ceased her fight. He was right. This would be the last time. Besides, she couldn't very well have sex with him on the dance floor anyway. And she'd much rather suffer through hot surges of desire than to feel achy and tired.

Giving in to her urge, Erin rested her head on his chest. They swayed like that through two songs, completely offbeat to the rhythmic sounds from the fast music, but it felt so good.

She closed her eyes, hoping to block out the future she knew would arrive too soon. The future that would make them enemies.

Suddenly, Drakor stopped. Erin looked up to find Brundor standing next to them. His long dark hair slicked back away from his shining face and his eyes were hot and dangerous.

Erin couldn't hear much of the conversation between Drakor and his brother but she could feel Drakor tense. Eventually, Brundor turned and left, heading straight for the bar. He stopped next to a blonde with a drink in her hand. Rita. Well, that would work fine. The two of them deserved each other.

She glanced back at Drakor, whose face looked just as worn as hers. A sadness dulled his eyes and she ached to bring him back to the sexy and mysterious man he was.

Erin reached her fingers up to his face and brushed his cheek. The action brought a smile from him and in the next instant his lips were on hers. For once, Erin didn't care that she was in public, didn't care who saw what went on, she only wanted his contact.

Drakor pulled her in close, one of his hands around her waist, the other behind her head. She could feel desperation in his touch. Erin let herself be caught up in his intensity until the thumping of the music no longer echoed in her head.

The taste of his tongue and the feel of his hard body cracked her motivation. If only he wasn't an alien, if only he could stay here with her forever, if only she didn't have save her brother's future and re-establish her own.

Feeling a sob rising in her throat, Erin pulled away. She couldn't handle his kiss and his good-bye. She couldn't mix her job responsibility with her basic desires.

The look on Drakor's face told her that he didn't want to move away from their kiss to the real reason they met here. But Erin knew she had to do it.

She took a hold of Drakor's hand and led him toward the stairs. They pushed their way through the crowds, past the tinkle of glasses and heavy air of smoke and out the front door. The warm night air felt surprisingly cool compared to the stifling heat of the club. She continued down the sidewalk, his hand still in hers, until they reached a bench on the next block.

With the sun gone, only the glowing streetlights lit the way, but they were enough to cast long shadows down the street and along the sides of buildings.

Erin sat down and pulled her hand away. Enough contact. She had already seen where it could lead them.

Drakor sat next to her and ran his fingers through his hair. He wore the same shirt she had slept in the night she was over and the memories from then flashed before her. A tingling sensation raced to her toes, pebbled her nipples. Erin gulped. The shirt looked much better on him, emphasizing his broad shoulders and hard chest.

She had to look away and so she watched couples giggle and kiss down an alleyway, their bodies only silhouettes against the bricks. "So," she squeaked, then cleared her throat. "Why did you ask me here tonight?"

"You have something I want."

Erin bit her lip and held her breath. That could mean a hundred things. Did he want her? Her body? Or what she took from him?

"I am missing a Transmitter and I believe you have it."

She let out her breath. So he knew she took it. Didn't matter how, but he knew she had it and he wanted it back. But if she returned it to him what proof would she have of their existence? Especially if they left Earth.

"Why do you need it?"

Drakor sighed. "I need it for when we return home."

"Oh? And when are you going?"

He shrugged and watched someone walk past them. "Soon. There is no longer a reason to stay."

Well, in that case, she had a story to write and she needed all the info she could get. Erin swallowed against the tightness in her throat and sat up taller. She knew he wouldn't stay forever, but she wasn't ready for him to go either.

"Drakor, why do you hate humans so much?"

His features hardened. "My friend Alaziri came earlier to seek out the resources on Earth. To prepare others that would follow with knowledge of the culture and the language."

"And now he's dead. But you didn't know that before."

"No, but I knew he'd experienced trouble when he first arrived. His house attracted too much attention."

"His house?"

Drakor gave a weak smile. "He saw a picture once and recreated what he'd seen."

She raised her eyebrows. "The cottage?"

"Yes, I suppose it was too odd in that location."

"Is that why you live in a Victorian house? You didn't want to make the same mistake?"

Jordanna Kay

He nodded. "When Alaziri finally returned with books and documents, we saw pictures of houses like that and so we had an idea of what to do."

Erin stifled her giggle. No wonder the house was like a museum, they took all of it straight from a book. Too bad their information was a hundred and fifty years old.

A couple passed by them and headed down the shadowed alley. Erin saw Drakor tense and she leaned over to get a closer look at who it was. Brundor and Rita. They seemed like the perfect match so she didn't understand why Drakor looked so concerned. Rita wanted hot guys, of which Brundor fit the bill, and Brundor wanted willing women, of which Rita fit the bill. What was wrong with that?

Erin tapped Drakor's arm. "Leave them alone."

He pulled his gaze back to hers. "Tell me what else you want to know."

Well, since he asked. "Why are you here? Why did your family come to Earth?"

"To find help for our lack of processing Vitamin D. I told you that already."

She lifted her chin. "You told me something about supplements and vitamins. You could have gotten those and gotten out long ago, before your parents died."

He glanced down. "I had thought that too when I first came."

"What do you mean?"

"When we arrived here I thought it was only to find supplements, but I was wrong."

Anxiety prickled under skin. The way he spoke, something in his words, told her that she might not like his next statement. She could imagine all sorts of reasons why that had come—everything from murder to kidnapping to colonization.

She swallowed and pressed her purse against her stomach. "What was the real reason?"

234

"We don't just need supplements to help us process the Vitamin D, as you call it." He took a deep breath and glanced away from her to the alley of entwined couples.

"Well, what is it. What do you need? Why did you come?"

"We need the gene."

She must not have heard him right. "The what? Did you say 'the gene'?"

He nodded. "In order to fix the disfigurement and suffering on my planet, we need the working gene back into the population."

"But *you* don't have any issues. Your bones look healthy."

"Yes, my mother still had a working gene but my father didn't. He was an experiment to the Researchers. They gave him medicines and doses of an imitation Vitamin D, but they eventually killed him."

Oh God, what a tragedy. "He-he died from an overdose of it, you think?"

Drakor looked at her again, his eyes raw with emotion. "I'm positive that's what killed him."

"So how were you going to get this working gene from a human? Take blood?"

He stood up from the bench and walked to the empty building in front of them. His tense shoulders fueled the fire in her stomach. Then he pounded a fist on the brick wall.

"Are you going to tell me?" Erin said to his back.

"Ankra had a secret duty." She could hear the despair, the edge in his voice. Whatever he was going to say, he did not approve of it. "She was…she can't…"

He sighed and leaned both palms against the wall, his back still facing her. "Blood wasn't enough to guarantee the gene. We needed more but we are not permitted to kidnap a living human."

"You're taking a dead one?"

"No. We need the gene alive. But we couldn't impose ourselves to disrupt another creature's life. We couldn't just kidnap someone and take them from Earth."

Erin watched his back move, the shadows from the street lamp moving along his muscled arms as he resumed pounding his fist on the wall. For the life of her, she still couldn't figure out what he was talking about. She stood up and went next to him.

"So what about Ankra, Drakor?"

When he turned to look at her there was fury and disapproval in his eyes. "A baby, Erin. Ankra was supposed to get pregnant and bring back a baby with a working human gene."

Erin took a step back, bile bubbling up from her stomach and burning her throat. Her lungs tightened until she could barely breathe. "A baby? Greg's baby? She...she would take Greg's baby back and...and not tell him?"

"Look, I didn't like the idea either. Human genes should not be mixing with ours, there is too much distance in history."

This was all happening too fast. She couldn't comprehend it. "History? What history?"

"Many thousands of years ago a race of beings came to Earth and took away many, many humans in their ships. They were brought to our planet, Elliac, and taught how to care for themselves. Eventually, the beings left them there alone. As a people, our ancestors were too primitive to understand how to fly machines or find our way home, so they stayed. Now, we have developed in a different path than humans. We are not the same species."

Did mutations occur in that short of a time? Wouldn't they still be humans, but with different adaptations?

Erin's knees wobbled and her bowels cramped.

Drakor reached out for her, but she flinched away from him. "It doesn't matter. Ankra can't get pregnant. It isn't working. That's why we no longer have a reason to stay. And since I'm unable to get Alaziri, I've failed at everything."

236

"Isn't...what isn't working?" She tried to take in a deep breath, but found it impossible.

"It's been three Earth weeks, Ankra would know by now. It's part of our culture. Females can plan their conception and know when they are with child and she is not."

Erin hiccupped. "You-you came to steal-steal a baby..."

His midnight eyes narrowed, nose flared. "We weren't going to steal it. The child would be Ankra's too and Greg would have never known. Erin, are you feeling alright?"

She couldn't...couldn't catch her breath and tears stung her eyes. She had to get out of there. This was too much for her to handle, too much for her to grasp. A baby? They were going to take Greg's baby?

Drakor reached for her hand again but she yanked away in horror. Who was this man in front of her anyway? She didn't really know him, she didn't have any idea who he was or what he was or where he came from.

Erin took a step back and looked at him once last time. His jet hair curled gently over the shirt collar, framing a gorgeous face. Black, sexy eyes surrounded by thick eyelashes stared at her with uncertainty and worry. His tall, muscular body held a power that could steal her breath and make her writhe in ecstasy.

This was the man she once sought out, the man who made her feel alive, the man she gave her body to.

The man—the alien—who may have gotten *her* pregnant.

Chapter Twenty-Four

Drakor watched her go, fighting the overpowering urge to chase after her. The look of fright, of shock, of disappointment that plagued her face still haunted him. He knew she would have a strong reaction. He knew she would feel concern for her brother and his child, but something else must have made her face that shade of green.

Great Sun, this was all falling apart and fast. Obviously, he did a terrible job of being in charge of this mission.

Drakor waited until Erin was completely out of sight and then went to find Brundor. There was no use staying here any longer, nothing else for him to do. He wasn't ever going to get that Transmitter back, but what did it matter? No one could put it to any use without the codes and all the information stored on it was in his native language.

Sighing, he headed down the darkened alleyway, wrinkling his nose at the repulsive smells. It was so hard for him to see he had to get almost to the couple's faces before determining they weren't who he wanted. Finally, at the other end of the alley, he heard voices and recognized Rita.

The two of them were in a doorway. They had not spotted him yet but he heard Rita say, "Get the hell off me now!"

His brother murmured something Drakor couldn't catch but he knew what Brundor went through. He remembered the agony of his Crossing, the desire that left him feeling like a voracious animal ready to snap up his next meal with each blow of the wind. Drakor knew that once Brundor allowed himself to feel the urge, he would not release his prey easily.

"I'm warning you," Rita said, her voice surprisingly calm. "Take your hands off of me."

"But you brought me out here," Drakor heard his brother reply. "You wanted me to kiss you."

There was some shuffling noise and groans. "I wanted to kiss you, yes, but I also wanted to talk and you aren't doing that."

Brundor pulled her closer. "Who needs to talk when there is so much else to do?"

Though his brother outweighed her easily, Rita gave him a good shove and a hard kick. "I'm not going to ask you again. Either take your paws off of me or you will find every cop in the city ready to tear you apart."

She did another impressive maneuver and his brother tumbled backwards and landed on the ground. Drakor rushed over to him and yanked him to his feet.

"Oh, so big brother has come to save the day." Rita crossed her arms. "I guess your girlfriend must be gone."

Drakor ignored her and pushed Brundor down to the open parking lot. "Go," he whispered. "Now."

A series of clicks on the sidewalk and she stood next to them. "Where are you going now?"

"You wanted him gone so I'm taking him home."

She raised an eyebrow and shook her head. "Oh, no, he's not going that quickly. I'm calling someone on an assault."

Drakor could hear Brundor's labored breathing next to him, could feel the heat from his skin. On his other side, Rita stared at him with a raised eyebrow and a no-nonsense grin. Suddenly, the aching in his skull increased to a nauseating pitch. Any minute now the situation would explode right along with his head.

There was no way Drakor was going to wait around here with Brundor while the local law enforcement came. Nor was there any way he could stay on this planet another day. Rita knew where they lived, she could come by at any time, bringing others who could destroy them as they did Alaziri.

Rita traced her fingernail down his arm and the goose bumps it sprouted weren't from desire. "I thought he could be like you," she purred, "but he's no substitute for the real thing."

Drakor clenched his jaw, using all of his willpower to prevent himself from pushing her away. "Must you call someone?"

She reached into her purse and pulled something out, unwrapped it and stuck it between her lips. "I'd rather have your tongue there instead of this gum."

He'd rather be kissing Erin right now, just as he did inside. He would never forget the way she tasted, the way her body fit so well against him. A surge of raw need poured into his veins.

"I must bring Brundor home."

"Suit yourself." Rita opened her bag again and then cursed. "Damn, I don't have my phone. I'd go inside and make the call but I'm sure you guys will be gone by then."

"I apologize if he hurt you, but none of this is necessary."

Drakor stepped away from Rita and put his hand on Brundor's shoulder, guiding him toward the parking lot. Thankfully, there was no sound of Rita's shoes or her snapping noises behind them.

"Hey, don't think you've seen the last of me," she called as they slipped into the trees bordering the pavement.

Drakor pulled out the Transmitter in his pocket and lead his silent brother to a secluded spot. Without another word, he entered the code and they swirled into the hazy light and away from Mickey's forever.

They landed next to the house and Drakor didn't even wait for Brundor to get up before racing inside. He didn't care to hear his brother's excuses. And, honestly, Brundor probably didn't do anything wrong and just got suckered by the wrong female.

None of it mattered now. What was most important was packing up as much as they could, as soon as possible. Drakor had to forget about Erin, he had to take care of his family, before he'd completely failed that too.

The house was quiet and dark, indicating that his sisters were sleeping. Well, he'd have to wake them up, they couldn't waste any more time.

Drakor knocked on their door and then opened it.

Ankra sat up startled and then yawned. "You home already?"

"Yes, we need to get moving immediately."

"Why? What's happened?"

"Erin knows the truth and Brundor went too far with a female at the club. It's too dangerous to stay here any longer. We leave as soon as possible."

"But Greg—"

Drakor shook his head and went over to Sitora's bed. "I hope you said your good-byes to him already." He reached out to shake his little sister awake but the bed was empty. He turned to face Ankra. "Where's Sitora?"

She leapt from the bed and ran over to him. "What do you mean? She was sleeping here. We went to bed at the same time, early in the night."

Drakor went from room to room calling for her while Ankra and Brundor searched outside. But Sitora hated the dark alone, none of them could imagine her leaving here on her own.

Finally, when their search turned up nothing, they collapsed on the front porch. Ankra was crying and Brundor curled in a ball at the far end.

Where could she have gone? Who would have taken her?

Drakor had to find her. They couldn't leave Earth without her. And he wouldn't want to. Sitora was family and it was his job to look after them. A job he failed at just like he did with the mission.

He stood up and slowly went down the stairs. "You two continue packing, but be aware of any approaching vehicles. If you don't recognize it, Transfer out of the house."

Ankra nodded and Brundor mumbled an agreement.

"I'm going to find Sitora."

∞∞∞

Pink. The damned line was pink.

Erin blinked, shook the stick, then chanced another peek at it. Nope, still pink.

Her throat closed in, choking her. Oh, shit. How could this have happened? How could she have been so stupid?

Erin sank down to the bathroom floor. She knew how this happened. That mind control Drakor used, the one that rendered her common sense and thought process completely useless when he touched her. That's how she let herself be this stupid. That's how she ended up pregnant.

She dropped her head into her hands and pressed her palms against her eyes, hoping it would stop the surge of tears.

Had Drakor planned this? Was she a backup plan in case something went wrong with Ankra? Was that why he resisted using the condom so much?

But that didn't make sense. He told her that they didn't want to bring a human back with them and unless they were going to wait for her baby to be born, they'd have to bring her along.

Her baby...

Oh God, this couldn't be happening. Not now. Not with Drakor as the father.

She sniffled.

Now what? Rita suspected something about Drakor and his family. Erin really believed that. Plus, if Erin printed her story of them, told the world that aliens lived in Virginia, what would they think when she gave birth? Rita would tell the world that her child was an alien baby. They'd be fodder for those weekly newsrags.

And the worst thing was that she did know what happened to Drakor's friend. Her connection told her that several people in black suits, with FBI badges, had come to take him away.

No way could she do this story now. She'd be virtually slitting her own throat, not to mention that of her child.

She couldn't find something compelling enough in two days. Hell, she could barely think past right now. Erin would have nothing to turn in on Monday. Not only would she not get the front page spread she deserved, she'd lose her chance at redemption. She'd also be allowing the story on Greg to go forward. She'd screwed up everywhere.

The dam broke loose and a sob tore from her throat.

A hard knock startled her.

"Hey, Erin, you in there?"

Greg. She forgot that she had called him in a panic on the way home from Mickey's.

Erin scrambled to her feet and tore toilet paper from the roll, wiping at her nose and eyes. She tried to splash cold water on her face to even out the mottled skin tone, but it wasn't working. He'd know she was crying. Greg would know something was very, very wrong.

"Erin, you're worrying me," he called. "Open the door."

She cleared her throat. "Com–coming."

She sucked in a deep breath and opened the door. Greg stormed in and looked around, as if to find a burglar hiding behind her couch.

"It's alright. Nobody's here."

He went into the kitchen. "You were really freaked out on the phone. You could barely talk."

Erin had called him because she couldn't handle the anxiety and inconceivable information. She wanted to tell him everything. That Drakor and Ankra were aliens, that they were here on a mission to get a human gene, that Greg's child was to provide that gene.

But now that she was pregnant, now that she couldn't write the story anymore, everything had changed.

Greg came up before her, arms folded across his chest. "So, what's going on? And why do you look like you've been crying?"

Damn, she knew she couldn't hide it from him. "I-I wanted to tell you that Ankra is leaving."

"What? That made you cry?"

"No." She hurried over to the couch and curled up in a ball on the far end. "That's not why I'm crying, but she is leaving. Forever."

His eyes widened. "How do you know this?"

"I saw Drakor tonight at *Mickey's*. He told me that all of them are going home."

Greg's face paled. "When? Where are they from anyway? Ankra wouldn't tell me."

Erin squirmed. She knew where they were from but she didn't want to tell him. Not anymore. Not when she would be raising a child by herself. No one could know that Drakor and his family were aliens. Not even Greg.

"I don't know where they're from," she lied. "But I know they're going soon. Real soon."

Her brother thrust his hand through his hair. "Oh, man, I've got to get over there. I've got to see her."

Erin felt her throat tighten. "She really means something to you, doesn't she?"

"More than I ever realized." He sat down on the loveseat but then bounced back up again. "I can't just let her go, Erin. Not after these weeks we've had."

So there it was. Greg had finally fallen in love again. Not since Sarah in college had he allowed himself to really feel again. And out of all the women in the world, he chooses one from another planet.

"So why were you crying? Drakor?"

Yes and no. She was crying because she lost everything. Her story. Her future. Her freedom. And Drakor. She was losing him too.

Erin dropped her head on her knees. "Just go, Greg."

"Why don't you come with me? Maybe together we can convince them to stay."

She didn't want them to stay. Even without her story, someone would eventually notice their oddities. And since the FBI had taken Alaziri...no, they had to go. They had to go soon.

"No." She pulled her legs tighter against her chest. "I'm not going."

Erin heard the door open. "Suit yourself. I'll tell Drakor you send your love."

Before she could stop him, the door slammed shut.

℘)Ↄ℘

Drakor pounded on Erin's door, his heart slamming inside his chest to the same hard beat. He couldn't find Sitora. She disappeared, just as Brundor had done. But Drakor knew that Sitora didn't turn herself invisible and venture in to town on purpose. Still, there was always the chance that she somehow ended up here.

"Go away, Greg!" Erin shouted from inside. "I'm not going."

Drakor swallowed and knocked again, this time softer. "It's not Greg. It's me. I need to talk to you."

"Go...go away. I don't want to see you either."

This discord between he and Erin made him feel as if he had spent a week under the Elliacian sun. And yet, the sound of her voice eased the pain in his head.

Drakor leaned against the door. "Erin, I'm looking for Sitora. She's missing."

There was a shuffling noise and then the door swung open.

"She's missing?"

If she looked bad the last time he had come here, Erin looked far worse now. Besides untidy hair, her unusually pale face had blotches of pink all over it. The make-up she put on her eyes had smeared and her nose looked bright red.

And still he wanted to hold her against him. But he didn't.

"We can't find her." He jammed his hands in his pockets. "And we need to leave here immediately."

Erin shoved some hair behind her ear and moved away from him until she reached the couch. "Why-why do you have to go right away?"

Drakor sighed and leaned against the wall. "Brundor got a little too friendly with Rita and she is threatening to call your law enforcement. I'm sure they will be at my house very soon."

A flicker of panic rose in her eyes. "And you can't find Sitora?"

"No. I was hoping that she was here."

She shook her head. "I haven't seen her for a long time. Not since that day you asked me to watch her for you."

The burn, which threatened at the back of his eyes earlier, returned in full force. He couldn't leave without his little sister, but how he could stay? Rita would come with the law and all of them would pay the price.

Erin slipped on her shoes. "We have to find her."

Drakor swallowed the lump in his throat. "You'll help me look for her?"

She grabbed her big bag from the floor and dug out her keys. "I don't know how you got here but we're leaving in my car. Hopefully, we'll get lucky and find her either on the way to your house or back there safe and sound."

Drakor steeled himself for the ride in her vehicle. He hoped he could stop himself from touching her, from healing her ills, from easing his own pain.

And she'd better be right about Sitora.

Chapter Twenty-Five

If Drakor's presence hadn't unexpectedly calmed her, Erin might have lost both her dinner and lunch.

Little Sitora was missing!

Erin bit her lip. Tears filled her eyes and ran down her cheeks but she kept the sob in check. If she let that go she might not be able to stop. Not after realizing the shamble her life had become. How could it possibly get any worse?

She drove up to Drakor's house and pulled in behind Greg's SUV. The three of them came running out of the house before she and Drakor could get out of the car.

Ankra looked a mess. She had probably been crying for hours. Obviously, Sitora was not back at home.

"Did you find her?" Greg asked, the only one of them able to speak apparently.

Erin shook her head. They had driven many of the streets in the city and several of the back roads, but she could be anywhere. The only option was to call the police and report her missing, but Drakor refused. He was trying to escape from the law, not ask their help.

Drakor got out of her car and walked past all of them. His hands balled and shoulders tense, he went to the front of the house, near the bay window and pounded on it.

Erin fought the compulsion to run over and comfort him. She knew he bore the brunt of the blame. Or that he felt responsible. It was his job to look after the family. But from what she had learned everything had failed. Ankra wasn't pregnant, Brundor couldn't control his urges, and Sitora was missing. He'd even lost the chance to retrieve his friend's body to take home.

Oh God, it would really send him over the edge to learn his genes had mixed with a human, spawning a half-breed child. There was no way she could tell him, no way she could add that burden to everything else.

She felt a tug on her arm and looked up to see her brother standing by her side. He looked pale and his eyes glittered wildly.

Erin followed him to the front porch.

"Why didn't you ever tell me?" he asked, leaning on the top rails.

"Tell you?"

His arm swept outward, motioning to the house. "About them. About who they are and where they came from."

Erin locked her arm around one of the poles. "For all sorts of reasons. You knew I suspected it from the beginning. Hell, you were the one that saw the spaceship first."

His eyes widened. "First? You've seen it?"

She sighed. "I came here one day unexpected and saw it in their backyard. I saw them put the bodies of their parents inside. After that, I knew for certain."

"Why didn't you tell me then?"

She sucked in a deep breath and turned to watch Ankra bury her head in her hands on the roof of her car. "I had a story to write and I didn't want you in the way. I didn't want you forbidding me to come see them or ruining it for me somehow."

"What are you talking about?"

"I didn't want you looking out for me. I needed to do this on my own."

Greg took a step closer. "But I've always looked out for you. Ever since we were kids. It's been my job. I beat up all those kids that made fun of you in school, I—"

Erin felt her throat closing in. "That's just it. I'm grown up now. I don't need you to do that anymore."

"Are you sure? You came back here, to me, after the fallout with Evan."

She glanced up at him. "Yes, that's true. But I needed to prove I could turn myself around, that I could use better judgment. Though I'm in a worse mess now than I was before."

Before he could respond the sound of a car sent all of them scurrying to the front drive. Drakor gasped behind her.

Erin tried to see if she recognized it the way he did, but in the eerie summer darkness she could not determine the color. But once it pulled up behind Erin's car, there was no doubt as to who it was.

Rita emerged and before saying a word, she went around to the other side and pulled Sitora out from the front seat. They walked around to face everyone, but Rita was holding her with a hard grip. Alarm gripped Erin's stomach at the look of fear on Sitora's face.

Something was wrong. Rita didn't just find her on the street and lovingly bring her back. Something was up.

Before Drakor or Ankra could take a hold of their sister, Rita pulled a gun from her bag.

"Stay back," she warned.

"What–what are you doing?" Erin cried, seeing Sitora's eyes fill with tears.

"I'm not letting her go unless I get someone else in her place."

Drakor took a step forward. "Give her to me."

Rita waved her gun at him and then seeing no reaction, she pointed it at Sitora. That stopped Drakor cold.

"Ah," Rita snarled. "So bullets can still harm you, huh?"

Drakor stiffened and a trickle of sweat rolled down the side of his face. "What do you want?"

"I've told you already. I want an alien. Oh, I'd love the whole lot of you, but unless my cohorts show up in time, I'll take just one."

Silence descended on them.

Erin's mind raced, her stomach in knots. How did Rita know? Did she find Sitora on the road and the little girl told her? Had Rita somehow read Erin's notes or overheard a conversation?

Finally, Drakor took a step back and leaned on a car. "There is no need to do this because of what happened with Brundor."

Rita laughed. "This isn't about that. That scene with Brundor was a set up. I was hoping to snatch him, but I had to get this little one when that fell through."

Drakor appeared calm, but Erin could see the vein pulsating on his forehead and the balling of his fists. "I don't understand."

"I'd show you my badge but my hands are a little tied up at the moment."

"What badge?" Erin asked. They didn't need any badge at the newspaper office.

"FBI—Special Extraterrestrial Investigations Unit. We've been looking for aliens ever since the other disappeared several months ago." They must have known about Alaziri. Oh God, had they killed him?

Erin's knees weakened, but she steadied herself.

Rita grinned and winked at her. "And lucky for us, Erin led us right to you."

ഇറ

A knife of shock sliced through Drakor's chest. He stumbled back from the blow. "Erin led you to us?"

Rita nodded. "We figured that someone from your planet would be coming back after your friend disappeared."

It didn't make sense that Erin would lead the officials to them, not on purpose anyway. He couldn't look at her. He couldn't control his trembling, especially when looking at his frightened sister.

"Alaziri. That was my friend's name."

"Huh? Oh, yeah, that was his name. Anyway, once we lost contact with him, we set up satellites to check the skies, looking for a return visit. And there you were…just about a month ago."

"But I knew where he was all the time." Erin's face was pale, her mouth pinched. "And now you've taken Alaziri, haven't you?"

Rita grinned. "Thanks to you again. We located the John Doe you were investigating and have removed him to a secret FBI location."

Fury bubbled up with Drakor, ready to burst if he let control slip. Confusion, fear, failure all swirled in his aching gut.

Erin cocked her head. "But I thought you were a reporter."

"Nope. Was all undercover, my dear."

"You weren't really investigating me?" Greg asked.

"Well, I did have to write something to keep my cover. My sister was dating some guy named Jay in your office so it was the perfect story for me. You will have to do some management on that patent infringement issue."

Erin moved closer. Drakor could feel the heat from her, different than the thick air of the night.

"What about Rockford? There never was a competition for the front page spread?"

"Rockford has no knowledge of who I really am. He thought I was a reporter just like you. So the spread was real, but your story on Drakor would have never made it to his desk."

Drakor snapped his head up and stared at Rita. "So Erin's investigations were for nothing?"

Sitora whimpered and Rita loosened her hold on her arm but didn't release her. "Oh, it wasn't for nothing. In fact, Erin did all the hard work and had the brains to keep the information as quiet as possible."

"You used me?"

"Why not? You found them before I did and set up a friendly relationship. Once I realized that these guys truly were who we were looking for, we set up a plan to retain them. Because I really like you guys, especially Erin, I'm going to risk my job and just hold on to one. Who's it going to be?"

Drakor knew time was closing in on them. How long would it be before Rita's associates arrived? He must get them all off Earth, assuming he could overtake Rita and do away with her firearm.

Sweat ran down his face, his stomach burned. How could he have gone from kissing Erin on the dance floor just a short time ago to facing a capture? None of it seemed real. But one thing was certain, little Sitora would not be the one left behind.

Drakor took a step forward. "Let her go and take me."

He heard Erin gasp behind him but Rita grinned. "Ah, now there's an idea I like much better."

She let go of Sitora, who rushed into Erin's arms, and pointed her firearm at his head. He walked to her slowly, not wanting to surprise her with any quick moves. But then Ankra suddenly jumped between them.

Startled, Rita fired a shot that zoomed over his head. Nearly weak with the near miss and this ultimate failure, Drakor felt his legs buckle. He sagged against the car. Ankra rushed over to help him but Rita pulled her away.

Then another set of hands were around his waist. Erin. He knew from her scent, the warmth of her body, the resurgence of energy in his veins.

Drakor turned to face Rita and his sister, but Erin did not leave his side. Sitora now clung to Brundor's legs, crying against his waist.

"Ankra, I'm ordering you away from there. It is my responsibility to keep all of you well—"

Greg rushed forward to grab her but Rita waved the gun at him.

"She will do just fine, thank you," Rita said, pulling his sister further away from the enclosing crowd. "You don't need to fear for her. She will be well taken care of."

"But Alaziri…" Drakor said, his mouth dry.

"Your friend did not die at our hands. We might have been able to save his life had he not escaped our detection. We lost tabs on him and then he was gone."

"What will you do with Ankra?" Greg asked, his eyes wet and his skin colorless under the full moon.

Rita squeezed Ankra's shoulder. "She'll be treated like a celebrity. Of course, the FBI and others will have questions and will do blood work and such but she won't be a prisoner."

Greg reached his hand out tentatively, but Rita allowed Ankra to take it. "Can I come see her sometimes?"

"Of course. You may even be able to live with her."

Drakor had to look away from their faces. So his sister found love on this strange planet, even without a *Mharai*. And the humans said they would not harm her, but could he trust them? Did he ever trust Erin the way Ankra trusted Greg?

"Erin." Ankra's voice was surprisingly calm. "You must go back with Drakor in my place."

Erin slipped from his side and backed away. "What? Me? No, that's not possible."

"A life for a life." His sister smiled that mysterious smile, a unique light in her eyes again.

As much as he might want to entertain the idea of bringing Erin back home with him, Drakor knew it wasn't possible. They couldn't bring back a human, only a developing fetus.

He glanced at Erin, whose eyes shone with tears. She hugged her arms as if she were cold and shook her head. "I can't go…he wouldn't want me to go…you don't understand…"

"Tell him, Erin."

Drakor swung around to see his sister again. She appeared happy, elated even, as if everything had suddenly gone from very wrong to very right.

"Tell me what?"

Rita glanced at the timepiece on her wrist. "You'd better make up your minds and do something soon, because my guys will be here any minute and they'll insist that everyone stay."

Drakor sighed and turned his attention back to Erin, but she was gone.

Chapter Twenty-Six

The full moon cast long shadows but provided ample light to find her way. Erin headed around to the back of the house, not really knowing where she would stop, but knowing she had to get away from that scene.

She saw the hanging tire and slipped inside of it, sitting on the warm rubber.

This whole night was insane. Maybe she'd wake tomorrow to find it all a bad dream. First Drakor tells her of their plans to take back Greg's child, then she confirms that she's pregnant with Drakor's baby, then Sitora is missing, finally to be brought back by a gun-toting Rita, claiming she was a special FBI agent who'd been tricking and following Erin all along.

No, this night could not possibly be real. Neither could the fact that she *wanted* to go back with Drakor to his planet. She wanted the kind of love that Greg and Ankra had found. She wanted a husband and a father for her child. Not the unimaginable mess she was in now.

But maybe if Rita was telling the truth and Ankra would be given a royal treatment then so might the baby inside of her. She may not have to run off and hide as she first envisioned. Staying here, finding a way to keep her job, she could just make it work after all.

Erin kicked the ground and the tire swung in a twisting circle. She felt free and relieved and…and wholly unsatisfied.

Because she loved him. It was as simple as that. She would do anything to make him happy, to make his world right.

If she could go back with Drakor, if he wanted her, her child could provide his people with a saving gene. This child could heal a planet. Even if Drakor didn't want her, he might like the fact that his whole mission to Earth was not in vain. In fact, he may return as a success. She may still not have a husband or father, but she would finally be doing something worthwhile with her life.

The crunching of grass brought her swinging to a stop. He came toward her, his large body a silhouette in the dark. Her heart leaped, her blood sizzled.

"Erin." He shattered her solitude. "I was concerned."

She took a deep breath. She had to tell him about the baby. Erin had to convince him that her child could help them just as Ankra's could have. She was willing to sacrifice her future on Earth to help him. To help his people. There was nothing save for Greg and Ankra to keep her here.

"I have to tell you what Ankra meant back there."

Erin saw him shove his hands in his pockets. "Go on."

"I'm pregnant, Drakor."

He cocked his head. "Pregnant? What do you mean?"

She got up from the swing and reached for his hand, the contact instantly soothing the torment in her soul. His palm on her belly, she dug for her courage and smiled. "I have your child growing inside of me."

ഇൽ

Drakor's heart galloped until he thought it might explode from his chest. Disbelief stormed his hope and blocked anything else from entering his brain.

"That-that's impossible."

"But why?" Erin's soft fingers still held his hand to her stomach.

He snatched his arm away. "Because you would have to be my *Mharai* and that just isn't possible."

She hugged her arms over her chest again, as if protecting her body from the cold. But it wasn't cold out here. It was hot, thick, and suffocating.

"What's a *Mharai*? And why must I be one to be pregnant?"

Drakor slashed his hand through his hair. "On my planet our mates are chosen for us by the Fates. After we complete our Crossing, we are destined to be with one person only and no other."

A low hum echoed from the front of the house and he was tempted to investigate, but he couldn't leave right now. Not until he discovered if Erin was telling the truth.

"I don't have a *Mharai*," he continued, seeing her perplexed look. "I never found her before we came here and now that the anniversary of my birth has come and gone I won't ever find her."

Erin cocked her head. "But what does that have to do with me expecting?"

"We only have desire for our chosen lifemates, we can only impregnate *them*. It isn't the same for us as it is for humans, who can choose their own mates and have children with whomever."

"But you desired me, didn't you? I remember those times together, at my apartment and in your house. Were you faking that?"

Drakor swallowed, his body automatically stirring at the memories. He still felt the urge to pull her against him, to taste the sweetness of her mouth. "No. That was all real, but…"

"But what? Either I am your *Mharai* or whatever…or your body follows Earth's rules when it's here."

The words from his conversation with Ankra tumbled inside of his head.

"If you ask me, you aren't with child because Greg is not your Mharai. It's as simple as that."

"I think you're wrong. I think it has something to do with the different atmosphere on Earth. Maybe that's the reason they can't control their fertility."

So was it Earth's atmosphere that lured him to Erin or could it be that she actually was his *Mharai*? Hadn't he had just about every sign that pointed to her as lifemate? But she was a human, just like Rita, just like all the others who regarded him with fear, repulsion, or annoying curiosity.

Erin sighed. "You know what, Drakor, just forget it. I thought maybe I could help you. Maybe I could help your planet or something, but I'll just stick around here with my own family."

He said nothing, his gut in turmoil, and watched her walk back up the hill and disappear around the front of the house.

Was she really pregnant? He never believed he would have the chance for a child.

Vehicle doors slammed and then a series of shouts snapped Drakor from his thoughts. Before he could react, Brundor came running down the hill, Sitora tight in his arms.

"Activate the shuttle!" he yelled. "The others have arrived."

Drakor's blood turned to ice. No. They couldn't be here yet. He hadn't tried to get his sister from Rita's grasp yet, he hadn't settled the issue with Erin yet.

But he had to save his family.

Drakor hastily punched in the code and their lifeline home appeared next to him. Brundor entered the code on the side and the gangplank lowered to the grass.

"Go on and get in," Drakor called. "I'm going back for Ankra."

His heart frantic and his throat tight, Drakor sprinted up the hill. Around the front of the house, he found several men wearing dark suits arguing with Rita. These must be the other FBI agents she sent for.

His sister leaned against the black vehicle, her face calm and Greg's arm around her shoulder. They looked peaceful, happy, and in love. But how could she feel that way with a human? Greg couldn't be her *Mharai*, could he?

A sudden "No!" caught his attention and found Erin in the middle of the melee. Drakor moved closer but hung back near the house in the shadows.

"You don't need the rest of them," Erin cried. "You have Ankra, let the others go."

"Our orders were to retain all of them," one man answered.

"They must return home. Why isn't one enough?" She turned to Rita. "Can't you do anything? You can't let them keep everyone."

But when Rita shook her head, Erin ran from the group and headed toward the backyard, not seeing him nearby.

"Hurry!" she shouted as she ran. "Go, before they stop you!"

The same agent from earlier ran after her and the rush of adrenaline fired in Drakor's veins. Save Erin. He had to save Erin.

But the man reached her first. A quick jab of his gun to the back of her head knocked her to the ground.

Drakor collapsed to his knees beside her, a frenzy of explosions echoing inside his skull.

The sounds of voices muted as he leaned over Erin's body. He could not see her sky-colored eyes or hear the sounds of her voice. All vision beyond her still form transformed into a haze as he focused on her.

Something or someone touched his shoulder and he roared. Primitive. Powerful. The contact ended and he hunkered down over her, shielding her, cradling her in his lap.

Amid the surge of protection, desire ebbed away...desire for passion, desire for home, desire for life. He wanted nothing if he did not have Erin.

His father's death plagued his troubled mind. Along with his mother insisting she join her mate in another life. She would rather be dead than be without him.

The truest test of finding one's *Mharai*. The willingness to die to remain together forever.

In an instant, his vision and hearing cleared. He leaned close and heard Erin's small breaths in his ear. She would live. And so would he.

Drakor stood, lifting her in his arms. He carried her to the waiting shuttle, expecting resistance from the agents, even expecting a bullet in his back.

But behind him he heard Rita's voice. "Let them go, that's an order. One is enough."

Drakor yearned to say good-bye to his sister but he didn't want to turn around and chance his luck. They could return here in a few months or so. He could check on Ankra's welfare and Erin could visit with Greg. But right now he had to get everyone out of here before Rita and her agents changed their mind.

He headed up the gangplank and Sitora squealed. "Erin! You're bringing Erin!"

Brundor eyed him suspiciously. "Why do you bring her?"

Drakor kissed Erin's forehead then smiled when her eyes fluttered open. "Because she's my *Mharai* and I can't live without her."

About the Author

Ever since she made up stories in her head as a child, Jordanna has dreamed of writing books for others to read. Romances entered her life as a teenager and she's never looked back. An active imagination, combined with vivid nightly dreams, Jordanna always has new ideas for stories. She's written everything from historical to futuristic to erotica; full-length novels to novellas to short stories.

Her "other life" finds her at a day job and married with a teenager, school-aged twins, and a spoiled cat.

Jordanna welcomes comments from her readers. Please contact her at jordanna@jordannakay.com

Jordanna's website: www.jordannakay.com

Jordanna's MySpace: http://www.myspace.com/jordannakay

Droid Wars: What do you get when you have an IQ that is off the charts, the inability to let go of someone you love and a lot of spare parts? The man of your dreams, of course.

Performance Criteria
© 2006 Mandy M. Roth

Dr. Aeron Braxton is on the verge of unveiling her newest creation—a droid who can pass as either human or Vanos.

An alien race took the man she loved away from her, but her revenge is at hand. Aeron has rebuilt Brad into a living, breathing killing machine she hopes will save the outer quadrants from a mass Vanos invasion.

Too bad the brilliant scientist didn't calculate the probabilities of love getting in the way.

WARNING: This book contains hot, explicit sex and violence explained with contemporary, graphic language.

Available now in ebook and print from Samhain Publishing.

Enjoy the following excerpt from Performance Criteria...

Planet Athena in the Epimetheus Quadrant of the A-QET73 System...

Brad pried the bay doors open, his heart feeling as if it were lodged in his throat as thoughts of something happening to Aeron filled him. He should have never agreed to leave her side. The idea of sending pact members to opposite corners of the galaxy to avoid capture hadn't sat well with him but he'd listened, to a point, respecting the others' wishes. Instead of completely leaving the planet, Brad declined a promotion and stayed on as a captain to assure he would be in the vicinity of Aeron's lab. He'd not told her his decision yet and had little doubt word would have reached her even if he wasn't showing up to face her.

It wasn't until he intercepted a transmission leaking Aeron's whereabouts that Brad knew he should have trusted his gut and never left her side. He'd wanted to take her with him and confess all he felt about her. Only one thing had prevented him from doing just that—Conell, her on-again, off-again boyfriend.

None of it mattered now. Aeron's safety was his only concern.

"Aeron," he called, rushing down the corridor towards her lab. The sound of his voice echoed off the walls and was the only response he received. Adrenaline coursed through his veins as Brad continued full force into Aeron's lab.

"Aeron!"

A quick look around the area showed no sign of her. Brad grabbed the end of a work station and fought for air not wanting to come. "Aeron, honey!"

"Ouch. Brad, is that you?" Her soft voice never sounded so sweet. She peeked up from behind a tall table, rubbing her head gingerly. "What are you doing here? I thought we agreed to—"

He was on her in an instant, dragging her petite frame against his body and holding her close. She smelled of mint and Brad knew Aeron had been playing with her hydroponics garden again.

"Brad?"

"You're safe? Not hurt? Unharmed? All right?" He visually scanned her, searching for any indication she was injured but finding none.

A tiny laugh came from her and tugged at his heartstrings. "I'm fine but aren't you Captain Redundant. Could you think of any more ways to ask if I'm okay? Want to tell me why you're here?" She pressed her cheek to his chest and he felt the tension in her ebb away. "Not that I'm complaining or anything."

"I need to get you somewhere safe, Aeron," he said, not wanting to let go. Holding her felt right. "*They* know where you are."

She tensed. "How?"

He'd wondered the same thing when he'd intercepted the transmission leaking her location. Brad would have assumed a pact member turned on Aeron if he didn't already know better. Each member was loyal to the cause— protecting humans from an all-out Vanos invasion. Aeron had also been one of the few pact members who remained on the planet Athena. She'd been adamant about not leaving her work behind and Brad had been equally as stern on her going. In the end, Conell stepped in, trumping Brad's decision. "I don't know, honey."

Aeron leaned back and lifted her sandy blonde brows to form a question on her face. "Brad, you're acting strange. You just called me honey."

"Is Conell here?" He didn't have time to worry about slips of the tongue. He needed to get her somewhere safe.

She shook her head. "No. He left, like almost everyone else did."

Anger coursed through Brad's body. As much as he hated knowing Conell held Aeron's heart, he hated the knowledge the man had left her alone more. The pact agreement didn't mean a thing. Not when it came to Aeron's safety. Brad would move the heavens to assure she was well. "Come on, we need to get you back to your father's ship. Is it still docked in the south bay?"

"Yes but it's not been serviced in the last six months." She closed her eyes and drew in a deep breath. "I couldn't do it, Brad. Not after they killed him. Being around the ship reminded me of my father too much. It's not ready to fly. Not yet." Aeron's bottom lip trembled as fear crept into her voice. "Brad?"

"Shhh, it's fine, Aeron. Every time you and the others got going on a new theory, I got the hell out of here and hung out on your father's ship. I've kept up on it. In fact, I think it's one of the best vessels out there." Unable to stand the sight of her frightened, Brad leaned his head down and pressed his lips to hers. He waited, stuck in the moment, sure she'd push him away. She didn't. Instead, Aeron parted her lips for him, allowing Brad to ease his tongue in. The kiss was intoxicating, stealing Brad's ability to do anything other than lose himself in the taste of her sweet lips.

The second Aeron went to her tiptoes and slid her hands into the back of his hair, Brad pulled her towards the ground, too many years worth of wanting but never having built up behind him to stop. It felt so good to finally have her with him. He wouldn't think about tomorrow, about how she'd no doubt push him away. No. He'd concentrate on the here and now.

Something whizzed past his head and his military training kicked in. Brad shielded her body with his as shots from a Vanos weapon flew by. He knew the ammunition they packed was often filled with a substance that ate human flesh. Having Vanos blood in him would retard the destruction, to a point, if he was hit. If Aeron was hit, she wouldn't heal.

A beaker exploded, raining glass down on them. Brad kept Aeron tucked safely beneath him. When he realized she hadn't made a sound, his worst fear hit him head on.

She's dead.

"Aeron?" He leaned back enough to look down at her. Her blue eyes were wide as she clung to him.

She peeked out. "Are they gone?"

"No," he said, relief breaking in his voice. "Are you hurt?"

Shaking her head, she whimpered before grabbing his neck and coming away with blood. "You're bleeding!"

"Just a scratch, baby." He planted a chaste kiss on her forehead and then rolled off her. "Stay put."

"Brad." She grabbed his hand. "They'll kill you."

He drew his sidearm and winked. "Not if I kill them first. Promise you'll stay here."

She nodded and he took one last chance to stare at her. Telling her how he really felt for her was on the tip of his tongue but he held back. He'd get her to safety and then tell her once they were airborne. Brad tugged his hand free of Aeron's and forced a smile to his face. "We'll get through this, Aeron."

* * * * *

Aeron watched in horror as Brad bolted upright and began firing off shots. The enemy returned fire—a multitude of bullets, breaking glass and fumes from lab experiments now destroyed filled the room. Each time something popped, Aeron yelped. She rolled to her side and onto broken glass. It bit at her exposed skin but she ignored the pain, too worried about Brad's welfare to mind.

She peeked around the side of the table and came face to face with a dead Vanos. Shocked, she lurched back, raking her legs through more broken glass. A portable microbiology system crashed to the floor next to her, a piece of its glass front flying wide and lodging into her upper leg, as sparks popped out of the back end of it. The cut, while superficial, resulted in a large quantity of blood. She pulled the shard free of her leg, careful to avoid cutting herself further.

Brad seized hold of her arm and yanked her to her feet. Aeron knew better than to question his judgment when it came to matters such as these. Brad was a soldier and a damn fine one at that. If he wanted to move, she'd follow blindly.

She touched her swollen lips with her free hand, still in awe he'd kissed her. For years she'd wanted him. When it finally happened, their kiss had literally been explosive.

He led her towards the double bay doors and stalled, just a second, as he raked his gaze over her. "Aeron, you're bleeding."

"It's just a—"

Something loud sounded and she watched in what felt like slow motion as Brad's body lifted off the ground. He fired his weapon towards the doors a nanosecond before he released his hold on it and continued his decent.

It took Aeron's brain a moment to catch up with what she saw—Brad, lying on his back. An array of wounds littered his once unmarred body. The only part still recognizable was his face. Bile rose and she steeled her nerves for the time being as she glanced towards the door and spotted a dead Vanos there.

"B-brad?" She reached out tentatively, already knowing the worst had come true. "No."

Instinct kicked in and Aeron shut off her emotions, focusing on Brad instead. She launched into the steps necessary to save him, if it were possible, all the while blocking out the sounds of station police heading her way. Help was coming, but for Brad, help was already too late. As his blood coated her hands, she knew she would do everything in her power to make this right.

Bending down, Aeron pressed her lips to his cheek and released a secret she'd held dear. "I love you"

Brad's hand jerked and Aeron dismissed it as nerves but silently prayed the action meant some part of him could still hear her.

Time might march on but hidden in each human are the embers of evolution that flicker to life when nature insists.

Evolution's Embers
© *2006 Mary Wine*

Earth is in trouble, flooded with pollution and uninhabitable for females, who are instead sent into space to live. As the birth rate becomes predominately male, the human race must find a way to stabilize the population. No chances will be taken on relationships doomed to failure because of personality conflicts. Males that desire a female to mate submit to intense testing and wait for a female whose results match. They will also agree to share-one female can provide children for two males and stabilizing the population must take precedence over personal choice.

Jala is an Estroko, a female gladiator who trains and competes in martial arts. Only females can be Estroko and winning freedom from matching is an Estroko's ultimate reward, but a dishonorable knee sweep ends that dream for Jala-sending her to be matched for reproduction.

She comes face to face with a pair of males who consider her their match-and their possession. Jala won't abandon her dreams because science says Cassian and Sion were meant for her. Cassian and Sion can't fathom why Jala ignores the passion igniting between them.

In an era when science controls attraction, what happens to the tender emotions that can bind more than just the body? Love doesn't show up on test pages, it flows through the blood and takes root in the heart.

Available now in ebook and print from Samhain Publishing.

Sion moved across the floor too confidently. Jala shifted back as she came face to face with just how much larger the man was than her. His lighter hair and eyes let him slip under her initial notice but now she tipped her head back to stare at shoulders that were twice the span of her own and packed with thick muscle. Her eyes were even with the man's collarbones and there was an insane little flutter of excitement in her belly which Jala frankly detested. A smaller male would be much easier to keep at arm's length. Sion wasn't going to be intimidated easily.

He considered her face a moment before he reached for her arm. Jala slipped back smoothly across the tile floor as his lips pressed together in a tight line. "Just because I'm a male doesn't mean we can't be friends."

His eyes didn't look friendly. Jala caught his attention moving down her length once again before he came back to her face. Sure, he wanted to get to know her which meant getting exactly what he wanted...her body.

Maybe she shouldn't let it bother her so much. It was just sex. If a child was in her future it was time to think about letting a male close enough to father one. But she couldn't divorce herself from her flesh. As her focus shifted from dealing with the pain of her injury, she suddenly began to notice her body's other needs. Her stomach growled and Sion smiled. He extended his arm towards the door.

"Maybe you'll reconsider over a meal. Cassian will be waiting for us to join him."

That flutter hit her belly once again as Jala turned to hide her annoyance. The darker-haired commander was every inch as large as Sion. There was one stark difference. Sion was willing to let her avoid him and she got the distinct impression Cassian was the type of opponent who charged in at the front of a battle.

Not that it mattered all too much. An opponent who took the time to set you up could be just as deadly. Letting her guard down with Sion could be an even bigger mistake than facing off with Cassian. Looking for a bright side took a lot of digging.

"Will there be clothing involved?" More importantly, clothing for her to wear that didn't leave her tender parts exposed? She didn't point that out because there was no reason to light a fire under Sion if she didn't need to. The man would be cranky enough when he took his erection to bed without her.

She had noticed the bulge in his pants and Jala really wished she hadn't. So what? The man had all the normal male genitalia. Just because he was prone to looking at her breasts didn't mean she needed to develop a mental idea of what he kept in his pants.

That sort of information led a girl right into trouble. Big trouble. There were fellow Estrokos who had enjoyed their military escort completely and loudly. They were the same females who tended to end up losers because they lacked concentration on the mat.

She might be matched for a solid five years but that didn't mean she had to fling every principle she had ever lived by into the forces of nature. Mother Nature was a controlling bitch who would land Jala on her back in one hour straight if she let her. The bulge in Sion's pants told her the male was interested in trying out their "natural" chemistry together.

Sion considered her for a moment before moving towards the doorway. "Yes, everything you need is waiting at our quarters."

Jala didn't snort at his words and Sion smiled at her back as she quickened her pace to get her face out of his sight. Too bad. He was sort of enjoying her stubborn streak. What an interesting turn of fate and one he laid at technology's door step. Jala wasn't boring. Sure, he had expected to want to have sex with his match but enjoying the time spent outside the sheets was a surprise.

No male really thought about their matches when they were separated. Once there were children involved, that tended to change a bit due to the care needed from both parents for growing offspring. Good teamwork skills would be essential to raising successful children. But the interaction would revolve around their children. Males and females just lived different lives. It was a fact which people in the past had deluded themselves into thinking wasn't so. It was. Everyone knew it.

But actually getting to know Jala was certainly a whole hell of a lot more interesting than his required lectures had hinted it would be.

Samhain Publishing, Ltd.

It's all about the story…

Action/Adventure
Fantasy
Historical
Horror
Mainstream
Mystery/Suspense
Non-Fiction
Paranormal
Red Hots!
Romance
Science Fiction
Western
Young Adult

http://www.samhainpublishing.com

Printed in the United States
61887LVS00001B/28-51

9 781599 982885